GREY DAWN

A Selection of Recent Titles by Clea Simon

MEW IS FOR MURDER
CATTERY ROW
CRIES AND WHISKERS
PROBABLE CLAWS
SHADES OF GREY *
GREY MATTERS *
GREY ZONE *
GREY EXPECTATIONS *
TRUE GREY *
GREY DAWN *

*available from Severn House

GREY DAWN

A Dulcie Schwartz feline mystery

Clea Simon

severn
House

This first world edition published 2013
in Great Britain and in the USA by
SEVERN HOUSE PUBLISHERS LTD of
19 Cedar Road, Sutton, Surrey, England, SM2 5DA.

British Library Cataloguing in Publication Data

Simon, Clea.
Grey dawn.
1. Schwartz, Dulcie (Fictitious character)–Fiction.
2. Graduate students–Fiction. 3. Detective and mystery
stories.
I. Title
813.6-dc23

ISBN-13: 978-0-7278-8261-5 (cased)

All Severn House titles are printed on acid-free paper.

Severn House Publishers support the Forest Stewardship Council [FSC], the
leading international forest certification organisation. All our titles that are printed
on Greenpeace-approved FSC-certified paper carry the FSC logo.

MIX
Paper from
responsible sources
FSC
www.fsc.org   FSC® C018575

Typeset by Palimpsest Book Production Ltd.,
Falkirk, Stirlingshire, Scotland.
Printed and bound in Great Britain by
MPG Books Ltd., Bodmin, Cornwall.

For Jon

ACKNOWLEDGEMENTS

Willing readers are a gift, and I have the best. Karen Schlosberg, Chris Mesarch, Lisa Susser, Brett Milano, and, of course, Jon S. Garelick all caught errors, inconsistencies, and general mistakes, and all made this book better. So, too, did my editor Rachel Simpson Hutchens and agent Colleen Mohyde of the Doe Coover Agency, who carefully ushered Dulcie's latest outing through to completion. Moral support came as well from Sophie Garelick, Frank Garelick, Lisa Jones, Vicki Croke, Caroline Leavitt, and Naomi Yang. I couldn't do it without you folks. Purrs out!

ONE

Wolves.

The word sprang unbidden into Dulcie's mind. *Wolf*, she amended it, as the unearthly howl once more split the night. But what would a wolf be doing in Cambridge, in Harvard Square of all places? Much more likely that she was hearing a dog, Dulcie told herself, even as she picked up her pace. It was late, and there weren't any other pedestrians on the little side street by the English Department offices. But she'd never felt unsafe here before. Certainly not afraid of an animal.

Another howl, wild and chilling. Dulcie took a deep breath. She hadn't told Chris she was going out. Her boyfriend worked the overnight shift in the computer lab, so Dulcie had been home alone when she'd realized that she'd left the English 10 papers in her cubby at the departmental office. He would've encouraged her to leave them till tomorrow, if she'd called him. Or told her to splurge and take a cab. But Chris wouldn't be working nights if they had any money to spare, and their apartment was really only twenty minutes away, if she walked quickly. Besides, grades were due by ten a.m. tomorrow. She'd already missed several of her teaching deadlines this semester, and this time she wouldn't have had her own thesis as an excuse. Carelessness seemed like a silly reason to push her luck. Martin Thorpe, her adviser and the acting department head, was prickly at the best of times. No, walking into the Square to retrieve them had been the sensible move.

It wasn't like it was an inherently frightening night. Between the street lights and a bright autumn moon, Dulcie could see all the way to the end of the block. Even the brick sidewalk, treacherous when icy, appeared to be in high relief. True, the shadows looked particularly menacing right now. But that, Dulcie told herself, was because she'd worked herself up into a good snit. And so, really, a little scare served her right.

In truth, it wasn't just the student papers that had sent Dulcie out into the cold November night. She'd been caught up rereading a section of a newly discovered novel. For weeks now, she'd worked in the library, painstakingly transcribing the stained, handwritten manuscript into her computer. The previously unclaimed pages, which she'd found among the unfiled documents in the Mildon rare book collection, made up a ghost story, full of all sorts of supernatural high-jinks and at least one particularly gruesome murder. It was also, most likely, written by the author of *The Ravages of Umbria*, the subject of Dulcie's doctoral thesis. If Dulcie could definitively place it in her author's canon, she'd have a significant academic credit. But all the time she'd spent squinting at the faded ink, trying to make out an archaic crossed 'S' from a half-smudged 'F' had distracted her from the story itself.

Tonight, for the first time, she had settled in to actually read what she had. And while that was a very welcome break from student compositions, it might not have been the best choice for a lonely moonlit night. Even Esmé, her tuxedo cat, had made herself scarce, as if spooked by the tale of ghouls and evil. And so, after one striking confrontation, Dulcie had been almost grateful to remember her real-life duties. Grading seemed so ordinary after an encounter with a werewolf.

Another howl, closer now. Dulcie paused, bending to peek underneath a hedge. The ink-black shadow made the glossy green bush look like it was floating in a void, but surely the space beneath was too small for any serious predator. Besides, it had to be a dog. Perhaps a hurt or injured dog. Maybe she should call animal control. At worst, it was a coyote. Dulcie had read that they'd moved into the suburbs. She'd never heard of one in Harvard Square, but she could imagine an adolescent male, lost, or on a quest for his own space. In that way, he'd be like so many of the young creatures that made their way to the city.

With that thought, she smiled. Cambridge was a city, and as such, it had its dangers. Wolves, however, were not likely to be one of them.

Part of the problem, she admitted as she turned toward Mass. Ave., was the departmental offices. Although, like all the senior grad students, she had both the key and the alarm code to the little clapboard building, she'd never been there late at night. Never been in the little house at all except when Nancy, the motherly departmental secretary, had been on duty, making coffee and fussing over the students like a hen with her chicks. Once the beep-beep-beep of the alarm had been shut off, Dulcie had found the old building creepy. Not silent, exactly, a three-hundred-year-old wooden building would never be totally silent. But the creaks and sighs of the old wood (and almost equally old plumbing) had seemed mindful, somehow, as if the house knew she was there. As if it didn't want her there, not at night, alone. Dulcie had gotten the distinct feeling of being watched and of being unwelcome, as if she were trespassing. She'd grabbed the folder she'd left hours earlier, and taken off so fast she'd almost forgotten to turn the alarm back on. As it was, she'd had to punch it in three times. Each time, she'd felt a little more flustered, sure that if she hesitated, someone – or something – would descend the uneven wooden steps from the top floor and catch her there. When she finally got the flashing green to go on, she'd bolted, slamming the door behind her.

That feeling of being watched had followed her out onto the street, and even the brightness of the night could not dispel it. Instead, she realized as she turned the corner, the light made it worse. It felt cold somehow, as if the moon were in league with the wind. Well, it was November. Dulcie pulled up the collar of her bulky sweater, a present from her mother. Soon she'd be off these side streets and in the Square proper. There would be people out, even at this hour, and she'd be able to shed these silly fears. And, if she still felt squeamish, she would take a cab – and eat ramen for lunch for the rest of the week.

A movement, across the street, made her jump and turn – and then laugh out loud. She'd been hoping for some company, and she'd gotten her wish. A thin figure, somewhat stooped, had appeared. Ultimately unthreatening, even with her overactive imagination. She nodded, despite knowing that here in New England nobody ever acknowledged strangers. Then, as the figure stepped into the light, she did more than nod. 'Hello!' she called. It was Thorpe, Martin Thorpe, her adviser, his bald pate reflecting the bright moonlight.

He turned at her voice, and any other words of greeting died in her throat. It was Thorpe, all right, but not as she had ever seen him. She had recognized the shiny spot on top of his head, but now she could see how wild his remaining hair had become, standing on end as if electrified. And even in the oddly cool light, how drawn his face was. Eyes wide and dark rimmed, as if – could it be? – outlined in red. Watching her, Thorpe ran one long, white hand over his head, as if to tame his disordered locks. He opened his mouth, bobbing slightly as if panting, and Dulcie found herself staring. There was something about his mouth. About his teeth.

'Mr Thorpe?' She heard the tremor in her voice. 'Are you all right?'

Silently, he shook his head, slowly and, Dulcie thought, with a look of profound sadness. Then he turned away and took off, rounding the corner into the dark.

Dulcie hesitated, wondering if she should follow. He was heading toward the Square, in the opposite direction from her home. Still, he seemed so troubled. She took a step, then another toward the corner. That's when she heard it. Off in the dark, where her adviser had disappeared, the wolf howled again.

Dulcie broke into a run.

TWO

D ulcie arrived home, breathless but safe, to find Esmé waiting at the front door.

'What is it, kitty?' Grateful for the sight of the little cat, for the off-center white star on her fuzzy face. For the pure normalcy of the scene, Dulcie had dropped the student papers on the floor and scooped up her pet. 'Were you worried about me?'

'*No!*' The answer came quickly, as Esmé pushed her white paws against Dulcie's chest. '*Put me down.*'

Dulcie obliged, a little saddened. 'No, you weren't worried about me? Or, no, you don't want to be held?'

'*So silly.*' The cat stalked away, tail held high, leaving Dulcie to wonder. Did Esmé mean she had gotten scared about nothing? Or had she done something else to merit her pet's scorn?

'Mr Grey?' Dulcie picked up the papers and took them into the kitchen. 'Are you there? Do you have any thoughts?' It wasn't that she didn't trust Esmé. Still, Mr Grey, the late grey longhair who often returned to advise and comfort her, was older and presumably had access to information that might not be available on the physical plane.

'*Why are you asking* him?' The answer came not in the calm voice of her older pet, but in the slightly peevish tone of an adolescent, as Esmé barreled back – and into Dulcie's shins. '*Why don't you play with me?*'

And so she did, tossing a catnip mouse until the young cat was exhausted. By then, Dulcie had calmed down enough to grade the papers she'd gone through so much trouble to reclaim. It was after two by the time she finished, and by rights she should have gone to sleep. After her various labors, however, she couldn't help but feel that she deserved a treat. Calling Chris was always an option – he'd be awake and at his terminal till seven. But Dulcie didn't want to confess that she had gone out alone so late, and unless she did that she certainly couldn't explain what had frightened – no, alarmed – her so. Agitated, that was more like it. The empty office had just been so quiet. And the howls, well, nobody likes to think of a dog in pain, and that was what it must have been. None of it any reason for her to disturb her boyfriend at work. Not when it might worry him. And so she got into bed – with her laptop – planning on reading just a little more of the recovered text.

'Esmé, want to read with me?' She called for the cat, who was batting at something – Dulcie really hoped it wasn't a bug – in the corner. 'It'll be fun.'

The cat simply twitched an ear, letting Dulcie know she'd had her fill of her, and so Dulcie started to read.

Fierce as the wind were the cries that rent the night. Foul and fearsome Voices rang from unearthly throats, wailing like the very hounds of Hell, they called to her, hailing her and keeping pace e'en as the coach raced forward, tossed like a Ship in a Storm, the horses white-eyed and screaming as the coachman whipped them on, breathless with panic, as were they all.

Daring a glimpse, she had pushed back the curtain and seen them, the foul demonic Beasts. Undaunted by the storm, as the flash of lightning rent the night, the glare of light revealed the sable tossl'd pelts, the glowing eyes. One damned Beast pursuing caught her glance with an eye o'er shot with Blood, and turning toward her visage e'en as she closed the curtain with hands that trembled, howled anew.

No wonder she'd been spooked. At least the woman had made it into the carriage. In the last passage, the heroine had been fleeing an evil stranger, leaving behind the relative safety of an inn for the crossroad where she faced the stormy night alone. Until the strange carriage had picked her up, anyway, just as the wolves had started howling.

What would merit such a danger? What prize was worth such risk? Such Questions she clasped to her bosom, held close within the very breath that warmed her. For her Soul's sake, they could not know. Yet, closer they came, fiendish voices whipped by the night's wind, jagged Fangs snapping at the air.

It was all so vivid – *jagged Fangs, the tossl'd pelts, glowing eyes . . . o'er shot with blood* – and strangely familiar. It sounded like . . . No, she was imagining things. Seeing a resemblance where there was none. She needed to focus, to think as a scholar, not a scared girl caught up in a ghost story too late at night.

Part of the problem was that it was hard to read this as a straight-forward narrative. Too much was unclear or missing. She had to focus on what was actually there, in the text. To start with, there was that curious question – what risk was the heroine talking about? And then the strange description.

After that, there seemed to be a gap, and she'd made a note to herself to look for a missing page. She scrolled down to the next bit: suddenly, it seemed, the woman was no longer alone. She was talking to someone who hadn't been mentioned when the carriage had pulled up, offering her refuge from the storm. Was there another traveler in the carriage? Or could it be the coachman? She shook her head. It wouldn't make sense that the character in the next scene would be the coachman. How would a passenger be able to converse with the driver, especially as they raced through a stormy night? But if the stranger – if that's what the word was, Dulcie still thought it might be 'Frenchman' – was there from the start, why had he not been mentioned before? A manuscript this old, and in this poor shape, could easily be missing pages, but everything else had followed pretty normally. Still, it wasn't like a character could just appear out of nowhere. Could he?

Of course he could, Dulcie reminded herself. Especially in an early, handwritten draft of a book. Because however it came to be, by the next scene, her heroine was conversing with the stranger – or the Frenchman. What he said, though, would have to wait, because after all the excitement of the night, Dulcie realized her eyes were growing heavy. She closed the laptop and pushed it aside, and felt, near her feet, the telltale thump of a feline landing beside her. Too tired to look, to see if her young pet had jumped up or if a spectral presence had joined her, Dulcie let her eyes close. She heard purring, she felt paws kneading, and that was all.

THREE

She couldn't help it. She couldn't stop staring at him. As Martin Thorpe called the departmental meeting to order, Dulcie found herself gaping at the balding scholar. At his pale face and his deeply shadowed eyes, still rimmed in red like the hellhounds in her story. At his teeth.

Partly, it was lack of sleep. Not only had she retired late, but despite the comforting presence of a cat on the bed, she'd slept badly, her night broken up by strange and disturbing dreams. At one point, she'd woken to the howls again, and she'd thought about getting up, about checking the doors and windows, only to be dragged back down by fatigue. At another, she was sure that an intruder had come in and turned on the lights, the moon was shining so brightly.

When she finally did slip into unconsciousness, it was with a sense of eyes watching her. Yellow, feral eyes that radiated menace. She had tossed and turned then, almost waking, when they had changed. It wasn't that they had dimmed, exactly, though they had softened from that poison yellow to green. It was more that their intent seemed to shift. When, near dawn, Dulcie finally fell into a deeper sleep, she had the sense of someone watching over her. *The stranger,* she remembered thinking, briefly, in a half-awake moment. *The man in grey.*

She had woken late to find Esmé gone and Chris beside her, snoring gently. His clothes had been left in a pile by the bed, and Dulcie could only imagine how tired he must have been when he'd come in. Maybe, she told herself, she had been subconsciously waiting for him and that was why she had had such troubling dreams.

Maybe he had been the comforting stranger, the new presence who had allowed her to slip into a calmer sleep. Except that Chris's eyes were brown.

Whatever. By the time Dulcie finished her shower, she was already late. Nancy always had a fresh pot on for the departmental meeting, so grabbing her empty travel mug, Dulcie ran out the door. It was funny, she thought as she trotted up the familiar brick sidewalks. By daylight, her city looked innocuous. More like a big town than some urban wilderness. It must have been the moonlight – the cool, blue light – interacting with the vivid scene she had read before heading out. Well, that and that poor dog. If she heard it again, she would call animal control. That howl had sounded like an animal in pain.

As luck would have it, she wasn't the last one into the meeting. Thorpe himself was late, which meant that Dulcie had a chance to file the student papers, slurp down half her mug, and refill it before tromping back to the meeting room. There, she found a seat between Lloyd, her office mate, and Trista. Although she'd successfully defended her thesis the spring before, Trista had swung a one-year post-doc at the university that let her add to her credits before leaving the nest to seek a tenure-track teaching position. It also let her stay around her boyfriend, Jerry, who, like Chris, was still a grad student in the applied math department.

'Hey.' Trista leaned forward as Dulcie sat down. But whatever she was about to confide was interrupted as the door opened once more behind Dulcie and Trista slid back into her seat. Martin Thorpe had entered the room.

'Good morning, good morning.' The acting head seemed more distracted than usual, and Dulcie and Trista exchanged glances. Only when Lloyd, seated to her left, nudged her, however, did Dulcie realize just how much of a mess their departmental boss was. Not only was his remaining hair standing up, but the shoulder bag he had dumped on the conference table in front of him was spilling forth folders. For the usually tightly wound acting head, it was an unimaginable display of disarray, and Dulcie couldn't stop staring.

'Obviously, we're running a bit late here. Mr Derwin, would you tell us the progress with the new grading procedures?' Whatever had happened, Thorpe wasn't going to explain it. If anything, he sounded more businesslike than ever, moving over the meeting agenda like clockwork, until he got up to Dulcie.

'Ms Schwartz, I'm glad to see you made the midterm grading deadline.' Dulcie looked down, blushing. She had – barely. 'Even if you had to resort to a midnight visit to our offices to do so.'

'I'm sorry.' She looked up, taken aback. 'Did I do something wrong?' The alarm – no, she was sure she had set it.

'Nothing *wrong*, Ms Schwartz.' He was staring at her now, and she saw how tired he looked. How pale. As if aware of the scrutiny, he ran a thin hand over the remnants of his wiry black hair. 'Only if you are going to set the alarm for a building as you leave, you might have the courtesy to make sure nobody else is still within that building.'

A general chuckle broke out around the table, and Dulcie felt herself blushing. So that was why she had felt another presence in the little clapboard. Because there had been someone there – Martin Thorpe, presumably.

'I'm sorry, sir.' She shook her head. 'At that hour, I just didn't think.' She paused. 'But, sir, when I came in, the alarm had been on. I had to turn it off.'

'Did you?' The dark eyes that held her were frankly skeptical.

'I thought I did.' Dulcie ran her hand over her own unruly curls. Had she? She'd kept going over the numbers in her head on her way there, wanting to be certain she had the correct sequence, so afraid of setting the alarm off. 'I was sure I did.'

'Well, if you're *sure* . . .' Another giggle leaked out of the crowd, and Dulcie felt her cheeks growing redder.

'I'm sorry. I must have been mistaken.' She shook her head. Part of her embarrassment was her unconsidered use of the word 'sure.' Wasn't it only the week before that the department had hosted a debate on the role of context in determining supposed absolutes, like certainty? It had been the latest in a series on dueling literary theories, pitting a more traditional style of study against a kind of post-structuralism that questioned everything. Very hip, but also increasingly abstract. The whole series was Thorpe's baby, and so Dulcie couldn't complain – even though she had begun to feel like in all the discussion of what was real and what was merely 'real' for some literary purpose, the actual reading of books was getting lost. For now, however, she tried to turn it into a joke. 'Clearly, I misinterpreted the context of the setting,' she said.

Another chuckle rippled through the room, and Dulcie realized that maybe, in this case, 'context' did have genuine meaning. After all, Thorpe was clearly upset because he'd been the one locked in. That also would explain why he had looked so distraught when she had seen him on the street. 'When I saw you on the corner after I left,' she added, 'I didn't think that you'd been behind me.'

'The corner?' Thorpe was shaking his head as he looked at her. 'I don't know what you're talking about, Ms Schwartz. The moonlight must have been playing tricks on you. A question of *context* confusing *content*.'

Dulcie smiled, accepting the gentle ribbing. Thorpe was showing off, but if she had locked him in, she could understand why. The rest of the meeting went by in a blur. Partly, that was because Thorpe seemed so intent on rushing through the usual agenda items, as if his theoretical points made the day-to-day basics of the department – teaching assignments, deadlines, and whatnot – passé. Partly, it was Dulcie's confusion. Context or no context, some things were simply facts. She *had* turned off the alarm when she'd entered the building; she was sure – or was it certain? – of it. And she had seen her adviser on the sidewalk about a block away. If she'd locked him in and his exit had unwittingly sounded the alarm, wouldn't she have heard it? Or wouldn't he have said something? Unless he hadn't left till after she was gone – and that had been some other thin, balding man in the moonlight. Perhaps that was why the man she had seen had looked so strange to her – because he was.

'Wow, you really did that?' After Thorpe dismissed them, the assembled scholars filed back downstairs for more coffee and to catch up on gossip. Lloyd, always skilled at getting to the coffee-maker when a fresh pot had finished brewing, topped off her mug. 'Locked Thorpe in the office?'

'I guess.' Dulcie shook her head. 'I had a sense someone was here, but I swear, Lloyd, the alarm was on when I came in.'

'I believe you.' Lloyd refilled his own mug before passing the carafe along to a colleague. 'I bet he turned it on himself out of habit. Maybe he fell asleep in his office, then was too out of it to realize what he'd done until he opened the door. I wouldn't be surprised, the amount of time he spends here.'

Dulcie nodded. Everybody knew that Thorpe was working overtime, hoping that the new dean would name him as permanent head of the department. His current emphasis on literary theory was only part of what was becoming an extended campaign. If Thorpe had been dozing and been caught unawares by the alarm, that would also explain why he had looked so disordered when Dulcie had seen him on the street – if, in fact, that had been him. And why he hadn't – or hadn't wanted to – remember it.

'Still, for him to call you out like that.' Lloyd shook his head, sadly. 'It's just not fair.'

'Thanks.' Dulcie kept her voice low. 'But we know why.'

'Both reasons,' her friend agreed, just as softly. 'Though which one is the 'signified' and which the 'signifier' is beyond me.'

Dulcie smiled at that. Although she was on the brink of an academic breakthrough, she was, she knew, out of favor with her adviser. Some of it was her adherence to a decidedly unhip approach: she read the writing; she found out what she could about the author. That was all. Beyond that, though, she deeply suspected that Thorpe still resented her part in an academic scandal that had rocked the university earlier that fall. Only a very few people knew the whole truth – that Dulcie had helped uncover the corruption that had led to the murder of a visiting scholar and a dean's abrupt resignation. Thorpe, as well as Dulcie's close friends, was among them. But since that dean had seemed to favor Thorpe's candidacy for the position of department head, and his departure had thrown Thorpe's future into doubt, Thorpe had persisted in viewing Dulcie as a troublemaker. 'If he gets the gig, my future here is doomed,' she summed it up.

'Well, it might not be that bad.' Lloyd began to protest as Trista came over.

'Dulcie, you were here last night?' She leaned in, her voice a stage whisper.

'Yeah, but I swear—' Dulcie began to repeat her protest, but Trista cut her off.

'Girl, you are one lucky fifth-year.'

Dulcie shook her head. 'What are you talking about? Thorpe obviously thinks—'

'You don't know?' Trista's voice rose in pitch. Then, as she took in the confusion on both Dulcie's and Lloyd's faces, she dropped it again. 'Really? You didn't hear?'

'Trista, I'm not in the mood . . .' Literary theory was bad enough. Dulcie had no stomach for the usual romantic gossip.

'Dulcie, this is serious. And, well, real.' Dulcie shut up and looked at her friend. 'A woman was attacked last night, like, two blocks from here. Her throat was torn out. They're saying it looked like she'd been ravaged by a wild animal.'

FOUR

T rista didn't have any more information than that, but what she'd said was enough. The Memorial Church bell tolled the hour soon after, sending them all off to their eleven o'clock sections, Dulcie among them. But Trista's bombshell echoed through her head for the next hour.

'Ms Schwartz?' She looked out over the class. A bespectacled freshman was tentatively raising his hand.

'Sorry,' she smiled her apology. 'Scott?'

'Are we supposed to feel sorry for Lily Bart because she's beautiful? And, like, what does that mean, anyway?'

'No, Scott.' Dulcie shook her head, sadly. She really must have been ignoring the turn of the discussion. 'First of all, you're not "supposed" to feel anything. But you should try to be aware of context, to be aware of the perspective of the world Wharton was writing about . . .'

She rattled on, and even found herself repeating some of the debate of the previous week. It wouldn't hurt them, she figured, to get an introduction to what was increasingly the vocabulary of literature. What did beauty mean, anyway? But her heart wasn't in it. How could she concentrate on a lesson plan when she might have information about a murder? No, she corrected herself as another of her students joined in the discussion. She could think about a book – just not *this* book. The text she'd been reading last night – now that seemed eerily relevant. One passage in particular kept coming into her mind.

Fierce as the wind were the cries that rent the night. That was how it had started, as those wolves – or whatever they were – had chased the carriage, driving the horses nearly mad with terror. There was nothing theoretical about that scene, nor the earlier bit, in which the heroine had been fleeing her pursuer and had run outdoors, into the storm.

On her first reading of that passage, Dulcie had been taken by a reference to the heroine's hair. Specifically to *her raven locks, ripp'd lose, tangled in the gale that swept the mountainous terrain.* The word 'raven' had been crossed out, and the scribble above it had not been improved by age or wear. Dulcie was pretty sure that the author had written 'flame-haired,' as if she were going to make the heroine a redhead as opposed to a brunette. To Thorpe, she knew, that would be a sign of something – the most basic kind of symbolism, with red hair as a mark of temper or some kind of witchery.

Dulcie knew that authors made such choices, using standard devices like shorthand to clue the readers in. She wasn't totally naive. But in truth it had interested her, at least in part, because of her own red – well, reddish – hair. Now that autumn was here, she was losing her copper highlights, but she'd grown up with her mother's stories of all the redheads in the family, and she liked to think of herself as simply a more subtle auburn. Of course, the indecision about hair color continued later in the book, too. In the first excerpt that Dulcie had found, a young man had been found murdered. His hair, too, seemed to change from red to black in subsequent versions. Maybe it was a signifier, as Thorpe would say. Or maybe the author was simply trying out different images, looking for the most dramatic. Or maybe, Dulcie couldn't help but wonder, something else was involved: a more personal choice, based on the real models for the fictional creation.

It wasn't a theory Dulcie could bring up with her adviser. Thorpe would tell her she was being unsophisticated. He'd already warned her against 'falling into the common hermeneutic trap of the implied author,' that is, confusing the writer with her fictional creation, and he'd dismissed Dulcie's uncanny sense that in this case the anonymous author really was writing about an aspect of her life.

This morning, the question of how close the author and her mysterious heroine were was moot. All that Dulcie could think about, to the detriment of her teaching, was what had happened next. The heroine, whatever her hair color or 'symbolic presence,' had been standing out in the rain, on a windswept mountain road. The wolves, or whatever they were, had been getting closer. And then a carriage had driven up and a stranger – or was it a Frenchman? – had opened the door and beckoned her in. The man in grey. If he hadn't, well . . . Trista's bombshell seemed a bit too real.

'Ms Schwartz?'

Dulcie blinked.

'Are you okay?'

'Yes, yes.' She shook her head to clear it, and saw that her students were standing. 'Um, see you next week.'

She saw a few of them exchange looks, but that was the least of her problems. The text – well, that was odd, and she was dying to get back to it. No matter what her quibbles with her adviser or her discipline were, however, she was first and foremost a member of the university community. And that meant telling the authorities what she knew. What she had seen and heard the night before.

Luckily, her noon section had been cancelled; the head tutor for English 241 had decided to give the students an extra week to work on their papers. Strictly speaking, she should have gone to the section room anyway; students always had questions. But she had posted office hours, and, really, murder took precedence over the Romantic poets. And so, with a determined toss of her almost-red curls, Dulcie set out for the university police headquarters.

She was in luck. As she entered the modern brick building off Garden Street, she recognized a particularly bulky detective.

'Detective Rogovoy!' She waved across the open lobby. 'It's Dulcie. Dulcie Schwartz!'

She tried not to read anything into the look he gave his colleague. He was probably finishing up something; that was all. And he did take a few steps in her direction before beckoning her over with a big, paw-like hand.

'Ms Schwartz.' His voice, always low, sounded particularly grumbly today. 'Like I wouldn't remember you. To what do I owe this pleasure?'

'I may have information.' She looked around the room. Cops in uniform were bustling about, and a few students seemed to be waiting at the front desk. 'About the murder. May we speak in private?'

The look on the big detective's face was answer enough, and Dulcie let herself be guided past the desk into a small, windowless room.

'You have news about a murder?' Rogovoy faced her, his hands on the table between them.

'Yes, about the woman who was killed last night.' She waited; he didn't move. 'Don't you want to take some notes?'

'First of all, I'd like to hear what you heard.' The detective leaned forward, and Dulcie had to remind herself that despite his size and ogre-like appearance, Rogovoy was one of the good guys.

'People were talking about it at our departmental meeting this morning.' She was proud of herself for not bringing Trista into it. 'That a woman was killed. Her throat torn open.' She swallowed. This was harder than she'd anticipated. 'I heard it looked like an animal attack.'

Rogovoy sighed and put one of those big hands up to his face. It must be hard for him, too.

'Man, this place is like a fishbowl.' He emerged from behind the hand, looking even more tired. 'Or something. Look, Ms Schwartz, I want to hear what you have to say, but let me set you straight. One, this is a police matter. Not some scandal to be gossiped about at your departmental meeting.' The way he pronounced the last two words sounded like he didn't have the greatest respect for the academic process of the university he served. 'And, two, don't believe everything you hear. 'Cause odds are, it's wrong. Like now.'

'A woman wasn't murdered?' Suddenly the day looked brighter. Maybe Trista had been being metaphorical. But, no, Rogovoy was holding up his hand to stop her.

'Please, let me finish.' He paused, and Dulcie did her best to not say anything while she waited. 'There was an attack last night. The victim is in the hospital, seriously wounded but alive. And, no, it was not some kind of "animal attack." We think it was a domestic. So, unless you have intimate knowledge of a friend's relationship gone bad, I'm not really sure what you can share with me.'

'Oh.' That took the wind out of Dulcie's sails. But, she realized, maybe that was for the better. For all their ongoing discussions of reading – and hearing – correctly, Trista had gotten this one wrong. And Dulcie had stayed up too late, absorbed in that scary passage. And Martin Thorpe? Lloyd must have it right: her adviser had probably fallen asleep in his office, then set off the alarm, scaring himself silly. He'd been too flustered to recognize her on

the street afterward, and this morning he'd vented. Except that she
hadn't heard the alarm . . .

'. . . witnessed something . . .'

Dulcie looked up, unaware that Rogovoy was still speaking.
'Excuse me? Detective?'

'I said, if you had witnessed something – a dispute, or anything
– that would be useful.'

'Oh, well, I don't know.' Suddenly, Dulcie felt rather silly.

'Or heard something.'

'Well, I did hear *something*.' She really wasn't the type who
could lie. Only now Detective Rogovoy was looking at her. Waiting.
And so, she started to explain. 'Only I don't know exactly what,
well, as we would say in Literature and Language, what exactly it
signified.'

Rogovoy cleared his throat. Dulcie had the feeling he wasn't into
literary theory and tried again. 'I know I shouldn't be walking into
the Square around midnight on a week night.'

'No, you shouldn't,' he interrupted.

'Chris always tells me to take a cab. But I'd left these papers I
had to grade . . .' He was being very patient, but Dulcie realized
she was going into much more detail than necessary. And so she
tried to sum everything up. 'And then when I was out on the street,
everything seemed very quiet and I heard something howl. I mean,
it must have been a dog, but I swear it sounded like a wolf.'

Rogovoy raised his eyebrows.

'I grew up in the forest, Detective.' Dulcie was beginning to feel
defensive. Her accidental use of synecdoche didn't help. 'I mean,
in a small arts colony located in a forest. I know what wolves sound
like.' He motioned for her to continue.

'I know it doesn't make sense, but that's what it sounded like to
me. And then I saw a man, and I thought it was my thesis adviser
– Martin Thorpe – but he looked all strange and wild. His hair was
messed up. And, well, today he basically denied seeing me on the
street. It was dark and all. But not that dark. I mean, the moon was
out—'

'Martin Thorpe? He works at the university?'

Dulcie nodded. 'He's the head of English and American Literature
and Language. The acting head. The director, I mean.'

Rogovoy opened a drawer Dulcie hadn't seen and pulled out a
pad. 'And you saw him on the street around when? Midnight?'

She nodded. 'But I thought you said it was a domestic?'

He shrugged, the big shoulders threatening to start an avalanche as he wrote down Thorpe's name and title. 'Sometimes in a domestic, there's a third-party involved. Another man.'

'Oh, no, I don't think . . .' Dulcie stopped herself. She really didn't know anything about Martin Thorpe's private life. If he'd been seeing a married woman or even a woman in a serious relationship, he could be involved in whatever had happened to her. He could also find out that she had informed the police.

'Are you going to talk to him?' This would not endear her to her thesis adviser. 'Maybe you can talk to the woman first? Maybe she doesn't even know him, and it was a totally unrelated attack.'

Rogovoy looked down at his pad. 'I wasn't completely honest with you, Ms. Schwartz, and I should be.'

She waited.

'The victim? She was taken to emergency services this morning, when she was found, and last I heard, she's in critical condition. But the doctors aren't what you'd call optimistic about her recovery. And even if she makes it, the blood loss and the extent of her injuries . . . She was stabbed, repeatedly, in the throat. It takes a lot of anger to do something like that.'

So that's why Trista had heard it looked like an animal attack. Still, something wasn't right here. 'Detective?' Dulcie heard how soft her voice had gotten. She cleared her throat and tried again, louder. 'Detective Rogovoy? Is there a reason you're telling me this?'

'Ms Schwartz, when your boyfriend tells you you shouldn't go out walking alone at night, he's right. Cambridge is a city, and like all cities, it can be unsafe at times. Especially for a young woman, alone.'

'Detective?' He looked up at her, his big eyes so sad, she didn't want to continue. 'There's something else, isn't there?'

'Mina Love, the young woman who was attacked?' He reached forward as if he were going to take her hand, then stopped himself. 'Ms Schwartz, she was young, a little, well, full-figured, and she had curly hair. Dulcie, she looked like you.'

FIVE

'**D**ulcie, please,' the voice on the phone pleaded. 'I'm worried about you.'

'Chris, I'm sorry I even called.' Dulcie was. After leaving Rogovoy's office, she'd dialed her boyfriend automatically. That had been a mistake. Not only had she woken her nocturnal boyfriend, she'd alarmed him with the news that she'd been near the scene of the attack. Along the way, she had managed to confess her own possible foolishness of the night before. 'I didn't even want to tell you.'

'I'm glad you did, Dulcie.' He sounded fully awake now. 'I don't want you to ever feel you have to hide things from me. But tonight, Dulcie? Won't you please stay in?'

Dulcie paused before answering. 'I can't, Chris. This is important.' She hesitated, before honesty prompted her to add, 'even if I don't like the guy.'

'Because it's the future of your department.' Chris repeated what she'd told him a few moments before. 'It's the Newman lecture.'

'The *first* Newman lecture.' Dulcie corrected him. 'And, yeah, this guy – Lukos – is possibly the future of the department. I mean, I hope not. He's one of those super post-structuralists who thinks that nothing matters but the text, except that the text isn't really a text because the author is only reacting to societal pressure. And the author may not even be "the author" of her own narrative . . .'

She stopped at the realization that she'd been making air quotes with her fingers, which, of course, Chris couldn't see. Bad enough she had just woken Chris; she didn't want him to fall back asleep before she made her point. 'But, yeah, it's important. The new dean has finally gotten around to inviting the top candidates to address the department, and they'll all be speaking over the next few weeks – all giving open lectures in their area of expertise. Whatever I think of their theoretical disciplines, they are some of the top scholars in my field, Chris. And one of them may be my new boss.'

'Well, Thorpe will still be your thesis adviser, right?' Chris knew about the balding scholar's temporary standing as head of the department, but the details of the academic hierarchy sometimes confused him.

'Yes . . .' Dulcie drew out the words. 'If he stays.'

'*If*? Isn't he tenured?'

Dulcie hesitated before responding. Somehow she hadn't managed to tell Chris about her strange interaction with her adviser. Or of her suspicions.

'Yes, but it will be a blow.' She said finally. 'He really wants the job.'

'Maybe he'll get it then.'

Dulcie hesitated. 'I don't know, Chris. He's spent his entire career here, and the university, well, they've done a national search. International – Renée Showalter is coming in from McGill.'

'And the journeyman teacher isn't going to be able to compete with the stars.' Chris finished her thought.

'Exactly.' Dulcie didn't go into what else she was thinking. 'Besides, I actually like Showalter, what I've read of her work, anyway. But Chris, I promise, I'll be careful. If I can't find someone to walk with me, I'll take a cab.'

'Okay.' He sounded resigned, rather than happy. 'And don't forget, you can always come over to the Science Center.'

'I love you, Chris Sorenson.'

'Good.' He was fully awake now. 'So have some pity on me, and stay safe, okay?'

It might not have been Chris's intention to make Dulcie feel better, but his concern warmed her – and took the edge off Rogovoy's warning. To think things out further, Dulcie decided, she really needed sustenance. She was halfway to Lala's, her favorite lunch spot, when her phone rang again. Hoping it might be Chris, she answered without looking.

'Dulcie! I'm so glad I caught you.' Lucy, Dulcie's mother, was often on the edge of a crisis. 'You're in danger! Terrible danger!'

'Hi, Lucy.' Dulcie kept walking. Her mother's excitable state was part and parcel of their, at times, strained relationship, and she didn't want to escalate things by telling her what had happened. 'How are you?'

'How did you—?' Her mother caught herself, sputtering, and Dulcie smothered a chuckle. In some ways, her mother was reassuringly predictable. 'Never mind, you didn't call me to talk about the ergot crisis.'

'I didn't call you at all,' Dulcie looked both ways before crossing Mass. Ave. Just because her mother was loopy didn't mean she should be foolhardy. Sometimes warnings made sense.

'Oh, you're right.' Lucy sounded sad. 'Sometimes I feel like I have a twin – or, no, maybe it's that *you* have a twin. A sister, who could help keep us in touch.'

'Yeah, well . . .' Dulcie let her words trail off. Her mother meant well, but her constant attempts to build a substitute family had never really worked for her only child. Lucy might get some sense of sisterhood from the commune – or, as she called it, the arts colony – where the two had finally settled. Dulcie found that sense of connection in books. Besides, right now she had other things on her mind. 'That's not happening.'

'Not on this plane, anyway.'

Point to Lucy, the eternal optimist. However, Dulcie was getting near the little café. 'So what's up, Mom? Besides – ah – the ergot incident?'

'Oh, that was horrible. How did I know that cooking would alter the effects so?'

'Is everyone okay?' This sounded serious. 'Are you?'

'Well, yes. More or less. Moonflower still thinks she's going to change again the next time the moon comes around, but she's always been very hormonal. But that's what I wanted to talk to you about, Dulcie. To warn you.'

'To stay away from iffy rye bread?' Dulcie loved her mother, and she knew Lucy loved her. Still, at times it was hard to take her seriously.

'No, Dulcinea. I'm being serious here. The ergot was only part of the message. Part of the warning.' Dulcie was at Lala's now and waited for her mother to tie things up. 'You see, ergot has many functions in the spiritual quest. I mean, in addition to helping us fly.'

'Uh huh.' Dulcie joined the queue for a seat and was hoping to speed things along.

'Dulcie, you're not listening and you should be. You see, you're just like your grandmother and her grandmother before her. I saw them, Dulcie. They came to me clear as, well, clear as moonlight. In fact, that was their message. They said, "'Ware the moon."'

'Where the moon?' Dulcie pondered how to respond. 'You mean, like, in the sky?'

'No.' Lucy sounded exasperated. 'Not "where," "*'ware*." Like, beware. At least, that's what I think they meant.'

'Well, at least it wasn't "were," like werewolf.' Dulcie tried to make light of her own recent scare. 'Did you know that "were" in that context derives from "man" . . .?'

'Dulcie, that's it!' Her mother broke in. 'I wasn't sure before, but, of course, the warning was twofold, which is why both of them showed up. Now it's clear as daylight. They were telling me to warn you on two fronts. Be careful, Dulcie. Please, be wary. You've got to beware the moon, Dulcie. And beware the *were*. Because the wolf is on the prowl.'

SIX

Great. Just when she had finally been motioned to a seat, Dulcie realized her appetite had gone. It wasn't just her mother's usual craziness. She suspected that empty-nest syndrome played a large role in her mother's constant stream of psychic warnings and dire predictions. It was the mention of that one word – *wolf* – on top of what had happened last night and Rogovoy's warning less than an hour before.

She picked up the menu out of habit, only to have it whisked out of her hands. 'I get you lunch.' Lala, the hefty proprietor, was standing in front of her, frowning.

'Thanks, Lala.' Dulcie wasn't sure how to explain. 'I don't know if I can handle the three-bean burger today.'

'Huh.' With a raised eyebrow, the chef-owner turned and walked away, and Dulcie reconciled herself to the inevitable. Maybe she could claim a previous appointment, and get the burger to go. That would be better than facing Lala's disappointment as she watched a regular customer pushing the spicy creation around the plate.

She was saved, though, by the rapid appearance of a wide bowl of lentil soup, steaming and savory enough to tempt Dulcie's appetite back. 'Thanks, Lala.' Dulcie looked up, but the chef was already walking away.

'There you are.' Trista squeezed into the seat next to Dulcie. 'I was looking for you. Wow, that looks good.'

'I had to go talk to someone.' Dulcie ignored the non sequitur, but gave her friend the spoon for a taste. 'I thought I knew something.'

'About the murdered woman?' Trista leaned in, her eyes bright. Clearly, this was more exciting than scary for her.

'She wasn't murdered,' Dulcie corrected her. 'Her name is Mina Love and she's in the hospital, but she's still alive. But, Tris, I heard something. When I was out last night.'

'You heard – the attack?'

Dulcie shook her head no, but Trista was waving down the counter guy and pointing toward Dulcie's soup. 'No, I didn't,' Dulcie said, once she had placed her order.

'Did Thorpe?' Trista turned back to her friend. He didn't say anything.'

Dulcie shook her head again. It was a lot to explain. 'No, but Tris? He wasn't in the building. I'm sure of it. And I *did* see him on the street. He looked wild, his hair all messed up.'

'He is kind of a mess these days.' Trista reached up to take her own bowl from the server. 'Poor guy, having to host the competition. I sort of feel bad for him.'

'Trista, it's more than that. At least, I think it is.'

Her friend looked up, spoon in mouth, and Dulcie waited for her to swallow.

'You know, when you said that it looked like the woman had been attacked by an animal?' Trista nodded. 'What did you hear – exactly – and from whom?'

Trista took another spoonful and sucked on the utensil thoughtfully. 'It wasn't Jerry, and it wasn't the news.'

Dulcie ate more soup while she waited. With that first sip, her appetite had returned. Lala really did have magical powers.

'I know! It was on the T.' Trista reached for a slice of the bread that had appeared between them, dunking it into her bowl. 'I was running late, so I jumped on at Central. It was still rush-hour crazy, and I barely wedged in. There was one guy who must have been talking to someone else farther back. A friend or something. He was saying, 'Tell her to be careful. A woman was attacked last night, right by DeWolfe Street – hey, maybe that's why I thought "attacked by an animal." I mean, I don't think he *said* "animal," though now that I think about it, what caught my ear was him saying something about "it can eat you up." But he definitely said, "Tell her to be careful." Then something like, "Watch out for the wolf." But he must just been repeating "DeWolfe," right?'

Dulcie had stopped eating, a chill running down her back despite the warmth of the crowded restaurant. 'This man, Tris, what did he look like?'

She shook her head and reached for another piece of bread. 'I didn't get a chance to see him. It was so crowded, I couldn't even really turn around and, you know, I didn't want him to know I was eavesdropping. I mean, I could tell he wasn't anyone I knew or anything. All I can tell you is that he had a really soft coat on. Like, really nice wool. Cashmere, maybe. Just some stranger in grey.'

SEVEN

A stranger in grey: Dulcie didn't believe in coincidence, not when soft-coated heroes were involved. But she also didn't want her friend to think she was as nutty as her mother, so when Trista had finished her story, Dulcie skimmed over the rest. She'd been out late. She'd heard – *something*. And then she'd seen Martin Thorpe, looking frantic about something.

'Martin Thorpe couldn't hurt a fly.' Trista had said, mopping up the last bit of her soup. 'The worst he can do is make your life miserable.'

'Easy for you to say. You're done with your thesis.' Dulcie didn't dare tell her friend her real fears.

'You will be soon, hon. And then we'll both be out job hunting. Just like Thorpe!' She hopped off her stool. 'See you at the Newman tonight?'

Dulcie nodded, watching her friend queue up at the cash register. She hadn't told her about visiting Rogovoy – but then, Trista hadn't asked where she'd gotten her own information about the attack. Besides, she decided, the victim wasn't blonde and multiply pierced. Trista didn't have to worry. At any rate, not until the next full moon.

With a wave to Lala, Dulcie paid her own bill and stepped outside. She should call Suze, she knew. Her former room-mate and long-time friend was a lawyer now, or at least a law school graduate. Suze had given Dulcie good advice every time she had found herself talking to the cops. Never mind that Dulcie wasn't in trouble this time, Suze would be a source of comfort – and information. Besides, she realized, they hadn't chatted in a while. Partly, that was because Suze was studying for the bar. Partly, Dulcie acknowledged with a sinking feeling, that was because they were both in relationships. Their lives were changing. But couldn't they still be friends?

Walking across the Yard, Dulcie dialed her friend.

'Please leave a message . . .' Well, it was the middle of the workday.

'Hey, Suze.' Dulcie thought fast. She didn't want to worry her friend. Not when she had an upcoming exam. 'Just calling to say hi.'

Feeling just a bit more alone than before, she kept walking. Ostensibly, she had office hours. Any students who had felt cheated by her absence this morning should be able to find her in the basement office she shared with Lloyd. In reality, she hoped they wouldn't. Maybe, she admitted, she just didn't want to deal with the very real and very scary thought that someone – a woman who looked like her – had been brutally attacked. But if she couldn't talk to a friend, then what she wanted to do, more than anything, was return to her research. Specifically, to that text. Outweighing her scholarly intent, she acknowledged, was plain old curiosity. She wanted to see what would happen next.

Besides, it seemed she had other friends looking out for her.

'Mr Grey?' She asked the trees as she made her way across the Yard. 'Was that you, this morning, telling Trista to warn me?' Even as she said it, she realized how far-fetched it sounded. Mr Grey – the ghost of her late, great cat – had never had any trouble contacting her directly. 'Or am I being silly?' A stray commuter who happened to favor mohair – that might have been all it was.

'If it was you, why did you contact me through Trista?' She paused in front of the Memorial Hall steps, another larger question forming in her mind. 'And why did you contact her this morning, not last night when I was out with the –' she didn't want to say 'wolf' – 'the attacker?'

'*Trust . . . friend.*' The word whispered by her; the 'r's trilling
into a purr. '*Look to a friend.*'

'Mr Grey!' Dulcie's heart leaped. 'That *is* you, isn't it?'

The brush of whiskers against her palm almost had her looking
down. But Dulcie had been through this before and knew better.
Instead, she kept her face averted and cupped her hand in what had
seemed, moments before, like empty air. She was rewarded with
another purr, rich and full – and then the smooth soft pressure of
a feline headbutt against her palm.

'Are you saying I should look to my friends more?' The damp
wet of a nose. 'I should trust them more?' Her next question brought
a lump to her throat, but she asked it anyway. 'But aren't you my
friend? And Suze?'

If there was an answer, it was drowned out by the sudden
rush of freshmen, tromping by and laughing. As Dulcie moved
out of their way, she lost contact with the feel of fur. With a
sigh, she turned her thoughts to her students and started down
the stairs.

'Hey there.' Lloyd looked like he was finishing up his own
lunch. As Dulcie crossed over to her desk, he was wiping crumbs
off an open book into a crumpled paper bag. 'You've got a
message.'

'Already?' Dulcie looked at the clock. Her office hours officially
started at one. By university time, she was hardly late at all.

'Oh, not a student. Sorry.' Lloyd balled up the bag and shoved
it into his backpack. 'Thorpe, I'm afraid. He came by about a half
hour ago, looking for you.'

'Great.' Dulcie sat heavily in her chair.

'What's the matter? I thought you were making great progress
with that new text? He should be proud of you.'

'Should be.' She looked over at Lloyd. 'Maybe he'll be better
when this is all over.'

'Really.' Lloyd nodded in understanding. 'Put the poor guy out
of his misery already.'

'You don't think he has a chance?' Talking to Chris, Dulcie
had been certain. Now, sitting with her colleague, she began to
wonder.

'I don't know, Dulcie. They've got Showalter coming in, and
Hanson next month, and he's a double doctorate – Anglo Saxon
and semiotics.' Lloyd shoved another book into his bag. 'And the

guy who's giving tonight's Newman, James Lukos? Everyone says
he's a real brute.'

'Sounds wonderful.' As much as she didn't like him, Dulcie at
least knew Thorpe. 'In what way?'

'Well, he's published in every major journal. I was reading his
article in *Victorian Embellishments*. He came up with a whole new
way to classify late-period character studies based on perceived
gender. I wanted to ask him about it last night, but I couldn't get
near him.'

'Wait, the talk is tonight, right?' Something Lloyd had said was
tickling the edges of her mind.

'Yeah, it is. Lukos flew in last night though. I don't know. He
wanted to get a good night's sleep, I guess. Anyway, Teitelbaum let
it slip that he was staying at the Commodore, and so I just happened
to wander over to the bar.'

Dulcie raised her eyebrows. The idea of Lloyd wandering into
an upscale lounge wasn't something she could easily picture.
Then again, she could easily see him wanting first crack at the
scholar. Lloyd always did have post-structuralist leanings. 'And
you thought he'd be up drinking?'

Lloyd shrugged as he stood to leave. 'It was worth a shot. And
he was there all right. I recognized him from the pictures. He was
like a movie star. Really, Dulcie, it's the kind of thing that probably
only happens in a college town, but they were all over him. Like,
a dozen women. But I'll tell you, he only had eyes for one – a
redhead. She had curly hair, kind of like yours.'

EIGHT

'**Y**ou don't think it was the same woman, do you?' Dulcie
knew what it was now – Lloyd's use of the word 'brute.'
'The one who was attacked?'

'Huh?' From the confusion on Lloyd's face, Dulcie realized he
was lost. She explained, then, about meeting Rogovoy – and about
his warning that the victim of last night's attack had resembled her.

'Oh, lord, I hope not.' Lloyd had sat back down at his desk. 'That
would be awful. Guest scholar turned slasher?'

Dulcie mulled it over. In a way, it was better than what she had
been thinking – that Martin Thorpe had been involved.

'Oh, no, it couldn't have been.' Lloyd started breathing again. 'I
distinctly heard her saying that she had to get going. And he went
up to his room after that. I know because I hung around, hoping to
get a chance to talk to him.'

'You're sure?'

'Yeah, it was wild. Two blondes walked him to the elevator, or
I'd have gone up to him. He was laughing and he kissed them both
goodnight, but he was pretty clear about wanting to go to sleep
– alone.'

'Huh.' Dulcie trusted Lloyd, but she also knew that people could
be devious when they chose. Perhaps the blondes had been camouflage, and the retreat just a ruse. Or perhaps her initial suspicion
– about her adviser – had been correct. 'Hey, did Thorpe say what
he wanted?'

'No.' Lloyd shook his head and went back to packing his bag.
'Just that he wanted to speak with you. He knew you had office
hours this afternoon.'

She nodded, letting her dread give way to relief. It wasn't great
that her adviser had come by – and she wasn't here yet. But at
least he knew she had the afternoon scheduled. Cell phone reception down here in the basement was awful, and her adviser
wouldn't expect her to leave while students might come by. She
watched as Lloyd reopened his bag, cramming more books in
than it should rightfully hold. So much for everything being
digital. With any luck, she'd have the next two hours to dive back
into the text and try to make sense of what was going on – then
and now.

*'Come.' The voice, deep and soft, and yet audible despite the wailing
of the winds, was accompanied by an arm. Reaching out from the
Shadow of the carriage, a gloved Hand, reached for Hers. Hesitating
but a moment, she took it, the Warmth and Strength emanating through
the soft leather a strange Comfort in that time. 'We must away,' the
Stranger said—*

'Ms Schwartz?' Dulcie looked up. A student. She tried not to
let her disappointment show as she motioned the student – a
junior named Beth, she recalled – into the chair in front of her
desk.

'Beth, how may I help you?' As she spoke, Dulcie folded her laptop closed, but left her hand on its top. It was probably her imagination that made its faint vibration feel like a purr. The warmth was encouraging, however: a promise that she could soon return.

'It's about the final paper.' Dulcie kept her smile in place. Of course it was. This was the time in the semester when she started to hear excuses, weeks in advance, for why the final assignments simply could not be done.

'I do have a letter from my doctor.' The student started rummaging in her bag, and Dulcie realized that she'd missed what the young woman had said. Something with cramps – the full moon, and all that. Lucy would have had an answer, Dulcie thought, her smile becoming real. She'd have encouraged this young woman to harness her lunar cycles for some kind of celestial boost.

'Okay,' Dulcie didn't dare try that kind of response, and instead took the note handed to her. 'Well, just try your best.'

With that, Beth left. 'So much for wanting to work on the material,' Dulcie muttered, as a gust of air – as soft as the brush of fur – smoothed past her face. It could have been a breeze whisked up by the student's departure, but Dulcie didn't think so. 'It's all about the grades, Mr Grey. I don't think they care about the reading at all.'

Only silence greeted her, and so Dulcie reopened her laptop. 'I know,' she said, as she waited for the system to awaken. 'I'm trying not to get discouraged.'

I have been summoned to assist you on your journey,' said the Stranger, his face shrouded in the shadow of the coach's deep recess. *'For dangers abound on this Road, as the bilious Moon rides to her turbulent zenith, and I would be your Friend.'*

'What?' Dulcie sat back. She had no recollection of transcribing this. True, deciphering those torn and stained pages had taken all her concentration; she hadn't been able to read while figuring out words, letter by letter. Something this evocative, however, she was sure she would have remembered.

'I did not summon you.' Breathless, still from the cold, which had whipped her flaming midnight locks – there was a question mark here, and Dulcie had added in brackets: [redhead? Brunette?] – and brought stinging tears to her eyes. *'And if I*

did not, then what Spirit demanded your Presence at this spot,
on such a night with a Moon—'

'Excuse me?' Another interruption. Dulcie couldn't help herself.
Her sigh was loud, audible for sure to the slim young woman in
the doorway.

'Yes?' Dulcie heard the peevishness in her voice. 'I'm sorry,' she
tried to soften it. 'I just got caught up in my own reading. Please
come in.'

'Thanks.' The young woman collapsed into the chair, her dark hair
falling over a pale face. Up close, Dulcie could see that she looked
frail rather than simply slim. She seemed exhausted, as well, her
large, dark eyes heavily shadowed. 'This has been a nightmare.'

Strange words, but she undoubtedly was referring to the assignments. 'Is it the class work? Is it too much for you?' Dulcie didn't
usually offer such fill-in-the-blank answers, but right now she didn't
want to hear more excuses. Besides, this student really did look to
be at her wit's end.

'It's not the class.' The girl surprised her as she pulled herself
upright, pushing her hair back as she did. 'It's my room-mate.'

'Ah.' Dulcie waited. She'd had a little experience with room-mate
issues – at any rate, until she and Suze got a double sophomore
year. But they'd never stopped her from finishing her work. That's
what libraries were for.

'She was, well . . .' The girl paused. Working on her story, Dulcie
figured. 'She – she was hurt last night. You probably heard.'

'That was your room-mate?' Dulcie knew what the student before
her had said, but the shock was talking. 'The girl – the young woman
– who was attacked in the Square?'

A nod of the head, and the student looked away, blinking. Dulcie
fumbled in her desk for a box of tissues. 'Here.' She pushed them
toward her visitor. 'I'm so sorry.'

'Thanks.' The girl took a bunch and wiped at her eyes, and then
blew her nose with a surprisingly loud honk. 'It's just been crazy.
We were close – we *are* close, I mean. Best friends since Freshman
Week, and we were supposed to study together last night. When
she didn't come back, I had, well, I had a feeling, you know? So I
stayed up, and then I called the police and then – then they found
her, and it's just been non-stop since. The detective, and her mother.'
Another loud honk. 'So I don't think I'll be able to lead the discussion tomorrow.'

Of course! This was Emily, Emily Trainor, and she was going to present on Wilkie Collins in the English 70 section.

'Oh, don't worry about it.' Dulcie's response was automatic. 'I can do it. We just have you present as practice. But next week, or whenever . . .' She was stumbling, unsure of what to say. Then it hit her. 'You said you were supposed to study together last night?'

'Uh huh.' Another nod. 'Mina isn't in the department. She's in History and Lit, but that kind of works for us. We're both basically reading the same books, you know? But we get two perspectives this way. We had – we *have* a lot in common.' She reached for more tissues, and Dulcie gave her a moment to collect herself.

'That's smart. Going at the material from two different disciplines. But . . .' She hesitated, unsure how to phrase her question without it sounding like an accusation. All she had were some vaguely matching descriptions . . . 'You said she didn't come home. Was it possible that she, oh, maybe forgot? And that she went to the Tap Room, over at the Commodore Hotel, last night? I heard there was a reception for the first Newman speaker.'

Dulcie hated herself for even asking. It sounded like she was blaming the victim. She blows off a study date for a party, and ends up in the hospital. But Emily didn't seem to see it that way.

'Oh, no.' She was shaking her head. 'Mina wouldn't forget, and I was working. I work at the Dudley Grill till ten. Mina was going over to that reception first. She's really interested in some of the theoretical stuff that he was into, and she was going to tell me all about it.'

This didn't make it easier for Dulcie. 'Is it possible . . .' She bit her lip. 'I've heard that Professor Lukos is a very attractive man. Could she have stayed later than she meant?' There, she wasn't blaming the girl. Nor was she actually pointing a finger at the visiting scholar. Just opening up the possibility that she had stayed later than intended.

To her surprise, the student in front of her laughed. 'You mean could the professor have picked her up?' She wiped her eyes again, but this time the tears had been squeezed out by her broad smile. 'No, not a chance. Mina was used to being hit on. She had that kind of look – the kind that men are drawn to. You know, the wild red hair, the body.' She squinted across the desk. 'You two kind of look alike, you know? But, no. She has a serious boyfriend, and he's really possessive.'

Dulcie was so flustered by the implied compliment that at first she didn't hear what her visitor had said. The kind of looks that drew men? Granted, she and Chris had their moments of passion – at least when their work and study schedules allowed. And she'd had a suitor or two before. But Dulcie had never considered herself a mankiller. The idea was rather pleasant.

And off the point. 'Her boyfriend.' She homed in. 'I heard the cops are talking to him?'

Another shake of the head. 'I didn't hear that. But, I mean, he adores her. And they have so much in common. A lot of history, you know? If anything, he's more into her . . .' She let the sentence trail off, aware, Dulcie thought, of how double-edged her last words might sound. Finally, she started over. 'He'd have no reason to hurt her.'

Emily started tearing up again, and Dulcie realized that she hadn't asked the most important question of all.

'How is she?' She leaned forward. All of this speculation, and she'd nearly forgotten that a young woman had been hurt. 'Will she be okay?'

Another shrug as Emily reached for more tissues. 'I don't know. They found her before dawn. She was bleeding – stabbed – I'm just glad I called—' Tears cut her off, and she buried her face in a handful of Kleenex. 'I just feel so awful. I'm sorry.'

'Please, don't be. It sounds horrible.' Dulcie knew from her own experience how violent crime could shake up everything. 'If there's anything I can do. Really.'

A brief flash of smile. 'Thanks, Ms Schwartz.' She stood up, shoving the wad of tissue into her pocket. 'I'm sorry. It's just such a shock.' She ignored Dulcie's protestations and seemed to gather herself together. 'I didn't mean to monopolize your time, just to, you know, let you know about the presentation.'

'My door is always open.' Dulcie paused, the inaccuracy of the statement poking at her. 'Metaphorically. I mean you can always call me. Or email.'

'You're the best.' With another smile, one that lasted a little longer this time, the student turned and headed down the hall, leaving Dulcie warmed by two compliments, the second even sweeter than the first.

NINE

Lloyd's return a short while later alerted Dulcie to the time. Her office hours were up, and as much as she would like to stay and read more of the mysterious manuscript, she knew she had a much less pleasant duty. Especially after this morning's reprimand, if Martin Thorpe wanted to see her, she shouldn't put it off.

With palpable regret, she powered down her laptop and shoved it in her bag. She hadn't thought she'd made any noise, but she must have, because Lloyd looked up as she pushed her chair back.

'You okay, Dulcie?' His pale face showed friendly concern.

'Yeah, I'm fine.' She tried to rustle a grin. 'I'd just rather be reading than running off to Thorpe.'

'Maybe he wants to apologize for this morning.' Lloyd had an optimistic streak a mile wide.

'Maybe.' Dulcie couldn't bear to disappoint him. 'Only one way to find out.'

'Hey, think of it this way,' her friend said. 'Maybe by next semester, he'll be as dead as a Lake poet.'

With that cheering thought, she left the office. November, and it was as light out as it would get – if cloudy, grey, and damp counted as light. Still, Dulcie felt strangely ill at ease as she made her way toward the departmental headquarters. This was silly, she knew that. Even if her worst fears were true, she'd be fine during daylight. Wouldn't she?

'Excuse me!' With her head down, deep in thought, she'd nearly walked into him. Tall, and rather wide, the man before her was staring at her as if she had suddenly turned into a fish. He was also blocking the sidewalk. 'Do you mind?' Dulcie didn't want to be rude. She did, however, want to get this meeting over with.

'Oh, sure.' The broad man, made broader by his black wool overcoat, stepped aside. But as soon as Dulcie had passed him, she heard him sputter. 'Uh, miss? Miss?'

She turned, but her annoyance faded as she saw his round white cheeks turn pink, as if from embarrassment. Despite a mop of glossy dark hair that matched the coat, he had the kind of face that made one think of antique dolls.

'Yes?' She looked up at him. He turned a deeper red.

'Oh, no.' He shook his head, the blue-black hair falling over his face. 'I'm – It's nothing.'

'Fine.' Dulcie turned away, determined to make up time.

'It's only . . .' He kept talking. 'You look so much like her.'

'What?' Dulcie spun around again to take in the big man. 'Who? And who *are* you?'

'Oh, I'm sorry.' The hand that pushed the hair back was white and looked soft. 'I'm Josh, Josh Blakely. And I – you look like my girlfriend, Mina Love.'

Mina. Emily's room-mate. 'The woman who was attacked last night?' As she said it, Dulcie remembered what Rogovoy had said – that the crime was probably 'domestic.' She stepped back.

'Yes, but – but no.' If his stammer was any indication, the pale stranger had correctly interpreted her slight retreat. 'I know – I know what the cops think. I've been with them all morning. But they're wrong.'

Dulcie shook her head. She knew Rogovoy. She didn't know this man.

'It wasn't like that.' He was still talking. 'I mean, we've known each other forever. They just – they don't know who did it yet, and they think, they think . . .'

'Look, I'm sorry for your troubles. Really, I am.' Dulcie knew what it felt like to be falsely accused. But this was not her problem. 'I wish you the best.'

She turned. As she walked away, however, she heard his voice. 'The resemblance is striking. You should talk to her. Maybe you're related. Distant cousins.'

'Great,' Dulcie commented to herself. 'Cousins.' This day was getting weirder and weirder, and Dulcie pulled the collar of her big sweater up as she turned the corner. All these years without any family besides Lucy, and now this.

TEN

Martin Thorpe was not behind his desk when Dulcie arrived. He was, she saw as she pushed open the unlatched door and peeked inside, pacing. As he looked up and saw her, he ran a hand through his sparse hair in the kind of nervous gesture that explained its current state of disarray. He did, however, try to muster a smile at the sight of his student, as he retreated behind his desk.

'Come in, Ms Schwartz.' His feet still, he started to rummage through papers instead.

'Are you . . .' Dulcie swallowed, unsure how to proceed. 'Are you all right, Mr Thorpe?'

'What?' Thorpe didn't look up, which meant Dulcie was addressing a shiny bald spot. 'Yes, yes. I'm fine. I wanted to talk with you about your latest chapter, Ms Schwartz. The one on the new manuscript?'

'My latest chapter?' This wasn't making sense.

'Yes, I'm sure I have it here, somewhere.' More rustling, as Dulcie watched dumbfounded.

A few minutes passed, and she realized she had to say something. 'Mr Thorpe?' He was looking through a drawer now, and Dulcie cleared her throat to get his attention. 'Mr Thorpe? I don't think you're going to find it there.'

He looked up, blinking. 'I'm sorry. I seem to have misplaced it.'

'No, you didn't, Mr Thorpe. I didn't turn it in yet.' She saw him take a breath as his brows lowered and rushed to cut him off. 'We talked about this last week, Mr Thorpe. That I would have it to you before the Thanksgiving break. That I should do a thorough search through the Mildon papers first. See what I can find, before I start writing.'

'Well, the pages you gave me . . .' He went back to looking. 'I had some thoughts on them. I was sure they were here.'

Dulcie watched him a little longer, unsure how to break in. 'Do you mean, the notes you gave me two weeks ago?' She asked, her voice soft. 'The ones on the chapter where I talk about finding the new pages?'

He stopped, blinking at the desktop. She kept talking.

'The notes where you point out how I keep using the word "thrilling" and I should try to mix it up a little?'

That did it. The hands that only moments before had been restlessly searching now went up, first to the already tousled hair and then to cover his face. 'I'm sorry, Ms Schwartz,' he said finally. 'You're right. I'm not – well, I'm not myself right now.' He ran a hand over his face, and Dulcie could see that it came away wet with sweat. 'I haven't been for a while.'

Dulcie watched, unsure of what to do. If he had indeed called her here mistakenly, she needed to find a way to exit gracefully. A way to make some friendly comment and stand and leave. To ignore the abject misery of the man before her.

She couldn't. 'Mr Thorpe, is something wrong?' She asked. 'Are you ill?' The pallor, that sweat. 'Is there anything I can do to help?'

He looked up, blinking, and it occurred to Dulcie just how strange this exchange was becoming. Martin Thorpe, bane of her existence. A man who only hours before she had suspected of – well, never mind. The man in front of her was in some kind of pain, physical or psychic, and she felt for him.

Dropping her voice still further, she asked. 'Is it . . . the Newman lecture tonight, Mr Thorpe?' Uncertain of how to broach the subject, she spoke so softly she wasn't sure he had even heard. 'Is it Professor Lukos?'

'No, no.' He was shaking his head sadly. 'It's not James Lukos. Even though his strictly textual reading is . . . well, it's hard to explain. Things have been building up recently.' With one hand, he removed his glasses; with the other, he rubbed his face and, at last, looked up, giving Dulcie a close-up of bloodshot eyes. 'Last night, they came to a head.'

Dulcie froze, her sympathy turning to something colder. It was his eyes. The redness was alarming. Inhuman. Partly, she realized, because of the yellowing of the surrounding irises. Thorpe might be sick. He might also, she thought, her heart beginning to race, be feral.

'Things?' Her throat was too dry to say more. She swallowed and licked her lips. At least, she realized, she had just been vindicated. 'So I did see you out on the street last night.'

'What?' He put his glasses back on and turned away. Embarrassed or self-conscious about his wild gaze. 'Yes, yes, you may well have. So much was going on . . .'

He stood and walked over to the file cabinet by the window. Dulcie realized she was being dismissed.

'So, you're okay?' It was an odd question to be asking her tutor. It was an odd situation.

Thorpe, however, had begun to act as if nothing had changed. 'Yes, yes,' he said, face buried in the top drawer. 'I'll be waiting for your pages.'

'In a few weeks.' Dulcie stood and backed toward the door. 'Getting them to you in a few weeks will be okay?'

'Let's call it one month to the day.' He looked up and smiled, giving Dulcie another look at those wild, red eyes. Those jagged teeth. 'Assuming, of course, that we're both here.'

Not even Nancy's calming presence could keep Dulcie from racing out to the street. It didn't make sense. Dulcie knew that, but she also knew that something – something horrible – was happening. Thorpe was not himself; he had admitted it. And a girl was lying in a hospital, gravely wounded.

After three blocks, Dulcie's heartbeat began to settle, and she was able to think through what she had learned. For starters, if the police were talking to the boyfriend – Josh – then they weren't looking at Thorpe. She had tried to tell Rogovoy about her adviser, about his strange appearance last night, but he hadn't understood. If all the police were looking for was a romantic entanglement, they would miss the more dangerous possibility.

She paused, breathing heavily. Rogovoy might be a dead end. She needed to reach out to the boyfriend too. He might not listen any more than the detective had, but she needed to tell him what she knew, what she had seen – and, maybe, what she suspected. He had the right to that information. It was only fair.

He also needed to know what Lloyd had said. Josh might think that his girlfriend was faithful. Maybe she was – *is*, Dulcie corrected herself. But Lloyd had thought he had been witnessing a flirtation. A flirtation with a woman who later that night had been attacked. A woman who looked – according to several sources now – like Dulcie.

As Dulcie walked in the fading light back to the apartment, she had another thought. She had been planning on attending the Newman lecture tonight anyway. All of English and American Lit would be there, and it was a chance to hear a noted scholar – the possible future department head – expound on his work. Now she had another reason to attend. Maybe it was because she felt sorry for Thorpe. Maybe she was simply hoping that no strange new development would arise to complicate her thesis. And maybe, she admitted, she had felt a little bad for Josh Blakely, too. For all his size, he had seemed earnest, if a little goofy.

Whatever the rationale, she thought, as she turned into the shadows of Cambridgeport, she was going to try something tonight. Trista would look at her funny, and Lloyd would raise an eyebrow. Nothing would happen, and Chris never had to hear of it. But tonight, Dulcie was going to put on a low-cut blouse and even some lipstick. Tonight, she was going to offer herself to the visiting Professor Lukos. Not as a potential acolyte, but as bait.

ELEVEN

C hris, blessedly, was already gone by the time Dulcie got home. Esmé, however, seemed to pick up on her plan immediately, and the little black-and-white cat clearly did not approve.

'No, kitty. No!' Dulcie lifted a white paw from the silk blouse she had just removed from the closet, gently disengaging the claws that had already found purchase in the delicate fabric. 'This is not a toy.'

'Then why are we playing?' The answer came back as the cat scampered away, only to stop and glance back at her person with wide green eyes.

'We aren't – oh, never mind.' Dulcie ducked down to retrieve a catnip mouse and tossed it. When Esmé darted after it, however, she remained in front of the mirror, contemplating mascara. This is what a girl needed girlfriends for, she realized, reaching for her phone. No, she knew what Suze would say. No mascara – and no playing games with suspected criminals. Besides, Suze was a bit of a jock. Neither of them had been particularly girly, even in their single days.

Still, they'd both ended up with loving mates. Maybe because
they hadn't played the usual games. Now that was a subject she'd
like to see the post-structuralists take on: the role of exaggerated
gender identification in undergraduate mating rituals. Or some
such.

'*Looking for a friend?*' Esmé had reappeared, and her voice –
which sounded in Dulcie's head like that of a young teen – caused
Dulcie to turn. '*I'm your friend!*'

'What did you say?' Mr Grey had mentioned friends. Surely,
there was a message here. 'Do you feel I'm ignoring you, Esmé?'

'*Chase me!*' The little cat lunged, then scooted away. '*Chase me
now!*'

'I wish I could, Esmé.' Dulcie paused to watch the adorable
creature, taking her invitation as an answer both to her query and
to her previous question. Somehow the little tuxedo cat had managed
to sum up what could have been someone else's graduate thesis in
just two words. 'It would be a lot more fun, believe me.'

That prompted another lunge as the feline bounded back to
pounce on Dulcie's bare feet and ran away again. '*Let's play . . .
at hunting!*'

'That's about it, Esmé.' Dulcie slipped the blouse on and looked
in the mirror. The green silk – the color of Esmé's eyes – really
brought out the red highlights in Dulcie's hair. 'I only wish I knew
what I was going to catch.'

With that, she grabbed her sweater. The little cat grew quiet as
she headed toward the door. '*Home soon?*' Dulcie didn't need to
hear the plea; she could see it in those round eyes.

'I promise.' She bent to stroke the smooth black back and turned
away. She and Chris had both been working too much, and
she silently vowed to play more with the young cat as soon as she
could.

'*She doesn't understand yet, little one.*' Another voice, deeper
and still, echoed in the air as Dulcie closed the door behind her.
'*She doesn't realize she's not the only one on the prowl tonight.*'

TWELVE

The hall was packed, rather to Dulcie's surprise. 'A Reinterpretation of the Depiction of Personal Ornamentation in the Late Victorian Novel' hadn't seemed like a crowd-pleaser to her, but clearly she didn't know the student body's tastes. As she stood in the back of the hall, a wave caught her eye. Trista with – yes! – an empty seat. A little awkward in her one set of heels, Dulcie made her way over the already seated spectators, their bags, and increasingly bulky, increasingly wintery outerwear to join her friend.

'You look nice.' As Dulcie stripped off her own big sweater, Trista ran her eyes down Dulcie's outfit, taking in the green blouse with its unusual amount of décolletage.

'It's not—' Dulcie caught herself. There was too much to explain. 'I figured I'd dress up for the reception after.'

'Ah.' Trista nodded thoughtfully, leaving her friend wishing she had taken the longer, more truthful route. However, at that moment, the new dean walked onto the small stage and turned on the podium mike.

'Well, hello!' The dean, a bespectacled science type, appeared a little surprised by the crowd as well. 'Thank you all for coming out on such an inclement evening. I have an announcement before we start.'

He paused, and Dulcie leaned forward to hear. This crowd didn't seem to care about bureaucratic formalities and mostly kept talking. 'Because of scheduling conflicts, our next Newman professor will be here tomorrow, as opposed to next week,' the dean was saying. 'We are lucky that this hall will again be free, although I will not be able to attend, and I hope you'll give as enthusiastic a welcome to that speaker, who will be – ah . . .' A shuffling of papers and a pushing up of glasses followed. 'Who will be Miss – ah, Professor Renée Showalter. But now, please, join me in welcoming Professor James Lukos.'

With a little more fumbling, the dean gathered up his notes to a general audience murmuring. Dulcie looked around. This was the oddest assembly she'd ever been in. While she saw faces from her department – Lloyd, Ralph, that girl in Renaissance Studies whose name she always forgot – there were a ton of strangers, too. Mostly women, she noted. And in a moment, she saw why.

James Lukos did not look like an academic. No professor this side of Hollywood had hair that glossy, like a pelt, almost, or eyes that fiery. When the visiting scholar walked – no, loped – onto the stage, he dwarfed the dean, who scurried out of his way. When he stood behind the podium and took in the crowd, slowly scanning from right to left, a general sigh followed, as if those dark eyes had personally and sequentially penetrated several hundred hearts.

'Who *is* this guy?' Trista squirmed in her seat, leaning over to ask Dulcie.

Dulcie shrugged. 'Victorian. You should know him.'

'I *wish*.' Trista tore her eyes off the front of the room briefly to reassess Dulcie's outfit. 'You knew.'

'I know he's got a reputation.' Dulcie ventured that much. 'But, really, Tris, it's not what you think. I want to find out—'

'Shh.' Trista, along with several hundred of her peers, leaned forward, mesmerized. Lukos was about to talk.

'The devil is in the details,' the visiting scholar announced. And with his own devilish grin, he began.

Forty minutes later, Dulcie still didn't get it. Partly, she told herself, that was because the Victorians always bored her, and Lukos's heavily theoretical approach didn't make it any more appealing. Didn't matter if the professor was handsome. All that bric-a-brac, all that sublimation . . . No matter how he interpreted it or what postmodern catchphrases he bandied about, there was nothing appealing about any of it. Partly, she admitted, it was because of what she suspected. Lukos wasn't just a handsome man or even an egotist. Academia certainly had its fill of the latter, if not the former – she knew from experience of several full professors who had claimed papers and even positions when everyone knew that their grad students had done the work. There was something else going on here. Something different. The visiting professor had a good portion of this audience mesmerized, and he knew it. This was a man who had a certain power, and enjoyed exerting it. That, to Dulcie's mind, made him unlikeable, if not actually villainous.

Especially if a woman he wanted had resisted him. She thought back to what Emily, the room-mate, had said. Not her comment about Josh Blakely being possessive. But that Mina wasn't the sort to cheat on her boyfriend. Besides, she might have not even been tempted. Josh might not be as prepossessing or, Dulcie admitted, as sexy as this man, but he undoubtedly had different charms. He was sincere, Dulcie could tell. Serious. And if Rogovoy couldn't see that, well then, it was her duty to point out that there were other suspects.

'Wow.' Trista's hushed voice had broken into her reverie. The talk had finally come to an end, and Dulcie had stood automatically, joining Trista and the rest of the crowd in clapping as, with one more smile, Lukos acknowledged them and left the stage. 'If he'd been the department head, I would've taken a few more years for my dissertation.'

'Trista.' Dulcie couldn't help it. This was getting silly.

'Come on,' her friend nudged her. 'Tell me you didn't get dressed up for *him*.'

'I didn't actually,' Dulcie heard herself lying. 'Though I do want to talk to him.' All around them, students were standing and retrieving coats, and the friends were carried on the tide to the end of the row. 'I think, well, I'm worried that he might be dangerous.'

'The lone wolf?' Trista was laughing. 'I bet.'

'Wolf? Why do you say that?' Dulcie grabbed her friend's arm, but just then she felt a hand on her own and, spooked, she whirled around. It was Josh Blakely, Mina's boyfriend.

'Excuse me.' He was flushed again, though that could have been the heat in the overcrowded hall. 'I didn't expect to see you here.'

'This is my department.' She didn't mean to sound so defensive; she'd been startled. 'I'm sorry, I'm Dulcie Schwartz, and I'm a doctoral candidate in English, so for me . . .' She shrugged.

'Busman's holiday?' He smiled, and she found herself warming once more to the chubby man.

'Well, professional curiosity, anyway. Though, to be honest, the Victorians are not my area of expertise. Or,' she leaned toward him, 'of interest.'

'Not that into antimacassars?' he said, to her relief. Here was one other person who hadn't fallen under the mysterious scholar's spell.

'Not at all.' Behind Josh, she saw Trista gesturing. Still, this was too good a chance to pass up. 'What brings you here?'

'Mina,' he said, and Dulcie gasped. He must have heard about his girlfriend, about the professor . . .

'You know about her and the professor?' It wasn't the smoothest move, but she couldn't help herself. 'That she and Lukos . . .'

'What?' He looked confused. 'What are you saying?'

Dulcie swallowed and took a deep breath. After that, there was nothing to do but go on. 'Mina met up with the professor yesterday. He, well, I heard he liked her.'

She watched the round-faced young man, waiting for jealousy or rage. Instead, she just saw him shake his head. 'I'm not surprised. She could give as good as she got.'

'What do you mean?' Now it was her turn to be confused.

'Mina hated all that post-everything theoretical stuff. You know, that nothing is real. That's why she switched out of the English department. Sorry, but it's true.'

'No, I can understand.' Dulcie found herself nodding. Emily had said that she and her room-mate would bring different perspectives to their common material. 'But then why did she – I mean, why are you here?'

'She loved to debunk those theories. Argue with them. And she will.' He reached into his coat pocket and pulled out a mini recorder. 'Once she's back on her feet.'

Back on her feet. From what Dulcie had heard, she was near death. 'How is she?' It sounded better than asking if she was expected to recover.

He shrugged. 'She was hurt pretty bad. Someone – somebody cut . . .' He put his hand over his mouth, his eyes tearing up, and immediately Dulcie regretted asking.

'I'm so sorry. I mean, I had heard, I just didn't know.' Trista was looking daggers at her now, but really this was more important. 'I'm sure she'll recover.' It was too weak as far as condolences went, and Dulcie realized she had more to offer.

'Look, Josh, I know it's none of my business.' He had taken his hands from his face, blinking instead to keep the tears at bay. 'I'm so, so sorry, and I'll let you go. I just want you to know, I spoke to the cops. I know the detective on the case, and I thought, maybe, there was someone else they should talk to.' She felt a bit disloyal: Thorpe was her thesis adviser, and she had only just met the young man in front of her. 'Maybe two someone elses,' she added. 'And I'm going to make sure they know.'

That made her feel a little better. The dashing professor was not only a more likely predator than Thorpe, he certainly looked more formidable than the chubby young man now standing before her. And if the young, pretty student had been arguing with the professor, she might easily have angered him – especially since he seemed so accustomed to adoration. Not that she wanted to explain any of that to Josh. 'You've got to stay strong,' she said instead. 'Okay?'

He nodded, blinking faster. But he didn't ask for details, for which Dulcie was grateful, and she let him go.

'What was that about?' Trista watched the big man lumbering out the door. Dulcie suspected, from the way he moved, that he was crying already.

'That was someone I know,' she said, unwilling to explain further. 'He's had some bad news.'

'Huh,' Trista shrugged and turned away, and Dulcie followed. The reception would be starting already, at the offices. If this crowd was any indication, the little clapboard would be packed.

'So what did you think?' Dulcie's mind was reeling with what seemed like new evidence.

'I'll be honest, I was barely listening.' Her friend turned to her with a conspiratorial grin. 'Those late Victorians are really over-the-top obsessive anyway. But who cares? Hey, there's Lloyd, heading out now.'

As they made their way out of the building, Dulcie saw the earlier clouds had disappeared, leaving the night clear. If anything, she realized, the moon was brighter tonight than it had been, although its edges were obscured by the branches overhead. Maybe tonight was the true full moon, and last night was only a build up. If so, could that mean . . .

Her thoughts were interrupted as Trista pulled her toward their friends. Lloyd and his girlfriend, Raleigh, were standing at the foot of the stairs. By the way they were holding themselves, leaning in as the exiting crowd surged around them, Dulcie figured they were having an argument – or at least an intense conversation. She pulled away from Trista's grip, ready to stop her from interrupting, but her friend surged ahead, skipping down the stairs.

'Hey, guys!' The couple split and turned toward her. 'You going to the reception?'

At that, the two exchanged a look. 'I think we *should.*' Lloyd said. Raleigh, Dulcie noted, was shaking her head slightly, her mouth set in a grim line.

'Of course you should.' Trista was too high on her own experience to notice what was going on. 'Come on. We are.'

She put her arms around the pair and started marching them off. Within a half a block, however, Raleigh had disengaged, and Dulcie had a chance to pull her away.

'Are you okay?' Dulcie had her own suspicions, but she also knew how easily she could project onto a situation.

'Yeah.' The first-year grad student sounded resigned rather than angry. 'I just hate guys like him.'

'Lukos?' She couldn't mean Lloyd. At least, Dulcie hoped she didn't.

'Yeah, everyone was in love with him. Including him. Just loves the sound of his own voice, you know?' Dulcie nodded, relieved to see that not every female had fallen under his spell. 'And I just feel so bad for Thorpe.'

That was unexpected. Dulcie opened her mouth, unsure of how to respond, but Raleigh kept talking.

'I know Thorpe's a pain. Lloyd's had a hell of a time, trying to keep up with his fussy little bureaucracies. And, well, I hope it's okay, but Lloyd's told me some of what Thorpe has put you through, too. All that nit-picky stuff. It's just that he's *our* guy, you know? Came up through the ranks just like, well, just like we are – Lloyd, too. But he doesn't have that star quality.'

'No, he doesn't.' Dulcie felt herself softening. 'I don't think he ever means to do harm.' Not in the way she had most dreaded. Thorpe was pitiable, really. Even if her worst fears were true, and he had become – No, she didn't even want to think that. Recent events had spooked her; that was all. There was no way her thesis adviser could be a creature of the—

'Hey, guys, catch up!' Trista had run up between them, this time catching Dulcie and Raleigh in her embrace. Dulcie looked at her friend, her blonde hair lit by the moonlight, and wondered if she'd been drinking. Then again, the pink in her cheeks could be attributable to the frosty night.

'Trista, what you did mean, back there?' The more she thought about it, the more likely that Thorpe was innocent. As for Mina's boyfriend, well, she didn't see him as the violent type at all.

'What? When?' She blinked at her friend. 'Back when we were talking about Professor Sexy?'

'Yeah.' Dulcie nodded. She'd never seen her friend so besotted. So entranced. 'You called him a "lone wolf," and I was wondering . . .'

'Dulcie, where's your classical education!' Trista smiled, open-mouthed, and Dulcie found herself looking at her friend's teeth. Her strong, white teeth. 'Lukos, that's his name, isn't it? Professor James Lukos? It's Greek, Dulcie. Lukos means "the wolf."'

THIRTEEN

The problem was, there was no food. Dulcie realized her mistake within minutes of entering the party. Raleigh and Lloyd had quit squabbling by then, both agreeing on the political expedience of attending. And Trista had calmed down, somewhat, as well. But by the time they reached the little clapboard, it had been packed. And although someone handed Dulcie a plastic cup of sherry as soon as she walked in, there was no refreshment of a solid kind to be seen.

She should have anticipated this, Dulcie realized. She would have if it had been any other night. Between her suspicions and her strange anxieties, however, it had slipped her mind. Besides, she had wanted to change and get out of the apartment quickly. She knew she wasn't doing anything wrong, but to explain herself to Chris would have just taken too much time. If only she'd grabbed an apple, she'd be better able to concentrate. As it was, she was sweating in a packed room, and her stomach was rumbling.

'Nancy!' She saw the departmental secretary over by the coffee maker. If anyone would know about the snack situation, it would be her. 'Nancy!' The older woman's usual confidence seemed shaken by the crowd, and she turned away. Dulcie started to go after her, when she was jostled by an overlarge teaching fellow, who nearly knocked the sherry onto her good blouse. Dulcie looked around for a surface. Not seeing one, she downed the

small cup and knelt to leave the cup on the floor. The room was
going to be trashed anyway.

'Nancy!' Despite the fact that both she and the secretary were
shorter than almost everybody there, Dulcie had managed to keep
track of her and finally caught up to the older woman over by the
coffee maker. Up close, she could see: Nancy definitely looked
upset. 'Are you okay?'

'What, dear?' Nancy was looking around. 'Did you need
something?'

'Well, I was hoping there were some snacks,' Dulcie admitted,
a little abashed.

'There was a cheese tray.' Nancy looked around in vain. 'But
those freshmen . . . I told Mr Thorpe that we should have ordered
more. But he . . .' She left it with a shrug, unwilling to bad-mouth
her boss.

'Ah.' Dulcie nodded. Now it was becoming clear. Under the guise
of being budget conscious, Thorpe was trying to sabotage the reception. 'Is he here tonight?'

'What?' She was looking around again. 'Oh, no. I don't think
he felt up to it. Poor man.'

'He'll still have a teaching position here.' Dulcie tried to summon
up some sympathy. 'I mean, if the worst happens.'

Nancy shook her head sadly. 'I don't know, Dulcie. This has been
awfully hard on him, and it's just been getting worse. These last
few days . . .'

Nancy let the thought trail off, and Dulcie nodded with what
she hoped was a sympathetic expression. Nancy was referring to the
pressure of knowing the Newmans were starting, Dulcie knew. But
Dulcie couldn't help wonder if the waxing moon had played a role
as well. At any rate, her stomach was growling loud enough to
be audible over the crowd. Before she could go in search of dinner,
however, she had a mission. 'Is Professor Lukos here?'

'I don't know if he's arrived yet.' The motherly secretary stood
on her toes, trying to see over the crowd.

'Is that whom you're looking for?' Dulcie caught herself. 'And,
may I help in any way?'

That won her a warm smile. 'No, dear. You go have fun. I was
actually looking for one of our students. She said she was going
to drop by tonight, but she was a little nervous, and I promised to
introduce her around. Maybe the crush was too much for her.'

A bad feeling came over Dulcie. 'One of our female students is missing?' She swallowed the lump in her throat. 'Who?'

'Not missing, dear. Just – not here. I believe you know her. She's an undergrad. Emily Trainor?'

It couldn't be coincidence. Another woman, the room-mate of last night's victim. Had something happened to Emily? Dulcie looked around. Neither Thorpe nor the charismatic Lukos were here, which meant either could be out there . . . in the moonlight. Without responding, Dulcie turned and left.

'There you are!' Raleigh and Lloyd seemed to have made up – over sherry. Raleigh was red cheeked, her flush strangely pretty against her dark auburn hair. On Lloyd, it was less appealing, possibly because he had a greater face to hair ratio. But despite Dulcie's murmured refusal, he reached behind him and grabbed two more plastic cups of the sweet drink.

'Did you find him?' Lloyd asked, handing her one. 'Lukos?' At the sound of his name, Raleigh made a face.

'No,' Dulcie took the cup, but kept trying to see past her friends. 'I'm actually looking for a junior who's in one of my sections. Emily, Emily Trainor. Nancy is trying to find her.'

Lloyd shook his head. 'Who could tell, in this crowd. Oh, wait!'

An excited murmur had them all turning toward the front of the room. The door had opened, letting in a blast of cold air – and the visiting scholar. For a moment, he stood in the doorway, and Dulcie could see how the moonlight illuminated his dark curls. Then he stepped inside, and the room exploded in cheers and applause. Raising one hand in a general greeting, he nodded and smiled, but seemed more interested in ducking off into a side room than greeting his admirers.

'There he is.' Dulcie looked around for a place to jettison the sherry. The surge of the crowd had moved them forward, however, and once again she ended up downing the sticky drink.

'Go get him.' Raleigh was laughing. Dulcie, however, was serious as she pushed her way through her colleagues back into the room she had just left. She found Lukos there, leaning in toward Nancy. Although he was surrounded by a wall of admiring students, the two seemed to be having a private and very serious conversation.

'If he hurt Emily . . .' Dulcie realized she was speaking out loud when one of the admiring throng turned toward her. It was Tom Jones-Smith, the department's Anglo-Saxon star, and from the look on his boyfriend's face, he'd succumbed to the visiting scholar's appeal. 'Tom, may I?' Ryan gladly pulled his partner back, allowing Dulcie to move in closer.

'Worried . . .' That was all Dulcie heard before Nancy saw her, and turned toward her with a smile that was patently false. 'Why, Dulcie, here he is. Professor Lukos? Have you met Dulcie Schwartz? She's one of our top graduate students.' Dulcie vaguely heard what Nancy was telling the visitor. Something about the newly discovered manuscript and her most recent article. What she was focusing on, however, was entirely different – and entirely silent. Professor Lukos had gone white and was staring, mouth open, at her. As if he had seen a ghost.

'But you . . . You're . . .' The speaker who had enthralled hundreds less than forty minutes earlier now seemed incapable of finishing a sentence.

'Dead? I think not.' Dulcie pulled herself up to her full five-foot-four inches, and stared at the academic. 'No thanks to—'

'Dulcie.' Nancy broke in. 'Are you feeling well? Perhaps you should sit down.'

'No, I'm fine.' Dulcie kept staring at Lukos, but he'd recovered.

'I'm sorry, Miss . . . Ms Schwartz, is it?' He had the temerity to smile at her, but she kept her eyes on his, avoiding even thinking about those big, white teeth. 'You must have confused me with someone else. I know, I thought you were—'

'Mina Love, I know.' Something was off here. He should be more unnerved.

'Yes, that's it. Ms Love. Are you her sister?' He seemed genuinely interested and not at all concerned.

'No, I'm not.' Dulcie felt herself growing bolder. 'I do know that you were one of the last people to speak to her last night.'

'Oh, that.' He started to turn away. 'Ms Shelby?' Nancy straightened up.

'Oh *that?*' Dulcie moved between them. 'A woman is attacked – is seriously injured, and that's how you respond?'

Lukos turned. Behind him, Dulcie could see Nancy, gesturing furiously, but she wasn't going to be stopped now. She looked up at the visiting scholar, trying not to notice how his teeth gleamed. He was, she realized with horror, smiling.

'I am so sorry, Ms Schwartz.' His voice had grown soft, and
colder somehow. 'Obviously, you are one of those young women
who dislike the idea of socializing between the sexes. You are also,
undoubtedly, misinformed.' He paused. Dulcie saw Nancy, behind
him, sink onto her desk.

'Yes, I met your *friend*, Mina, last night. Mina Love, such a
charming name, despite her most unaffectionate attitude. But, no, I
was not the last person to see her, since quite clearly whoever
attacked her must have seen her. I was not that person. I spent the
remainder of the evening in the very pleasant company of two of
your more *welcoming* colleagues. As I have already explained to
the police.' The smile, and its accompanying charm, were gone.
'Now, if you don't mind.' He turned away so quickly, the coat – still
draped over his arm – slapped Dulcie's face. It couldn't have been
intentional, but she stepped back as if it were, right into the arms
of her friend.

'Yikes.' Lloyd righted her as she stumbled. 'That was intense.'

'You okay, Dulce?' He looked concerned. She nodded, afraid to
turn back around. 'Don't worry, Nancy's gone after him.' Her office-
mate filled in the gaps. 'She'll smooth his feathers.'

'You heard?' Suddenly, Dulcie felt foolish. Her friend nodded.

'It was very brave. And he probably won't get the job anyway,'
added Lloyd. At that, the magnitude of what she had done – of
whom she might have just offended – kicked in, and Dulcie swayed
on her feet.

'Here.' Trista appeared, handing Dulcie yet another of those tiny
glasses. 'There's beer, but I know you don't like beer.'

'Thanks.' The warmth was welcome, and Dulcie drank down her
dose. 'But this just means . . .' The room, it was turning.

'Steady there.' Lloyd had his arm around her. 'Maybe we should
get some air.'

'I'm ready to blow this popsicle stand anyway,' said Trista. 'I
don't think Professor Charming is even going to talk to any of
us peons.' Dulcie dared a glance back. It was true. Lukos was
deep in conversation with Nancy. His arm was still covered by
his coat, only now he was holding it out as if showing her
something.

'What's he doing?' Dulcie strained to see. 'Was he hurt?
Bitten?' She started toward him, only to feel three pairs of hands
on her.

'Hang on, cowgirl.' Trista was in charge of turning her around. 'Let's let things settle, shall we?'

'But . . .' It was useless. Before she knew what was happening, Dulcie found herself out on the sidewalk.

'What was that about, anyway?' Raleigh seemed to have missed the details, and so Lloyd filled her in as they walked, huddled against the wind. 'It's my fault,' Dulcie heard him say. 'I should never have told her about seeing them at the bar.'

'It's not your fault.' Dulcie interrupted. 'He just seemed like the type. I mean, more than . . .' The wind – it had to be the wind – interrupted her, roaring down an alley. Only, she thought she'd heard something more. 'Wait,' she stopped her friends. 'What's that?'

The roar had faded, and a voice, faint but clear, was calling. A cry, saying – what?

'I hear it, too.' Raleigh was looking around them. 'It's coming from down here.' Pulling away from them, she darted into the dark between the buildings. 'Raleigh, wait!' Lloyd went after her, and so Dulcie and Trista followed. The moon, which shone so bright on the street, did little to illuminate the alley. Still, the cry was clearly audible now – a soft, mewling sound, more a whimper than a voice. And to Dulcie, there was something more: a sense of warning. Of danger . . .

'Here it is!' In the shadows, they could see Raleigh duck down. When she stood, she was holding something to her face.

'Raleigh, careful.' Lloyd moved forward as Raleigh came back into the light.

'There's no danger here,' she said. 'Look at this poor little guy.' In her hands, almost covered by them, was a tiny orange kitten. As they watched, its little pink mouth opened and they heard again the soft cry.

'Oh, kitty!' They all cooed, as Raleigh held the little creature up to her face. Even Trista lost her toughness for a second.

'Was he alone?' Dulcie had gotten that warning from something – from somewhere. 'Maybe his mother is back there, too – or other kittens from his litter?'

Raleigh shook her head, her long hair falling over the kitten's shivering body. 'I didn't see anything else.'

'We should look.' Dulcie wasn't just being practical. She had a bad feeling about this. Lloyd nodded and went back into the alley. Soon they were all there, Raleigh holding the tiny orange tabby, peering under shrubbery and in and around the two recycling bins.

'Nothing,' Lloyd concluded finally. 'He must have been dumped by someone.'

'Poor baby,' Raleigh was cooing. 'I'm going to take him home.'

Lloyd cleared his throat, and Dulcie turned. He was clearly uncomfortable. 'Um, my allergies?'

Raleigh looked up, and at that moment, Dulcie wouldn't have given much for their relationship. 'I know, honey. But just for a few nights. Just to make sure he's okay. Then we'll find a good home for him. I promise.'

An awkward silence settled on the small party. 'You'll be fostering him.' Dulcie volunteered, to break it up. 'You can even keep him isolated, in the bathroom or something. It'll be a good deed. You've probably saved that kitten's life.'

Lloyd sneezed, and Dulcie gave him a look. They had only just found the kitten, after all. He had the grace to look somewhat abashed. 'If it were just sneezing or itching,' he said. 'But I have asthma.'

Dulcie turned back to the lovers. Raleigh nodded. 'Just overnight, then. And I'll take him to the vet first thing tomorrow to have him checked out. Besides, I know who really needs a kitten.'

'Oh?' They all turned toward her. Dulcie wasn't sure how Esmé would take to another cat, and Jerry and Trista already had two rambunctious littermates in a too-small apartment.

'Thorpe,' said Raleigh. 'If ever someone could use a companion, it's our beloved leader.'

'Of course.' Trista nodded. Even Lloyd looked pleased – though that could have been relief that he wouldn't have to battle for his girlfriend's affections. Only Dulcie was left to object.

'No, you can't,' she said. That was it. The danger. The warning. An innocent kitten. But they were all looking at her. Even the kitten, its eyes clear and wide in the bright night. 'You just can't. It's not safe.'

'What do you mean?' asked Raleigh. 'I know he's not your favorite person,' Lloyd started in, but Dulcie waved him off.

'It's not what you think. It's not about my thesis, or the way he treats us. I do feel sorry for him. Really, I do, more than you can imagine.' She looked up at the sky with its bright, pale moon and thought about the wounded woman. Maybe tonight would pass without incident. Maybe another woman was already hurt, or worse. Maybe it was all a horrible dream, but she couldn't be sure. And until she was, she had to do what she could to keep one innocent safe.

'You can't give the kitten to him, Raleigh. It isn't safe,' she said finally, turning back toward her friends. 'I have reason to believe that Martin Thorpe is a werewolf.'

FOURTEEN

'**H**uh?'

'Wha?'

'Dulcie?'

All three of her friends turned toward her in surprise. Even the kitten, nestled in Raleigh's arms, looked up as if startled, its blue eyes blinking in its orange-striped face. It took Trista to articulate the question on all their minds: 'Martin Thorpe is a were-*what?*'

'*Dulcie, beware!*' Dulcie turned. The low, soft voice calling to her cut through the din, and for a moment, she wasn't sure who it was. '*There's danger here!*'

'Mr Grey?' She mouthed the words, ignoring the outcry that her pronouncement had provoked.

'Dulcie! What are you saying?' Trista had her arm and was shaking her. Lloyd was by her side, his own touch somewhat more gentle. 'Are you feeling okay?'

'She's drunk,' Trista said, turning to Lloyd. 'She doesn't have a head for alcohol.'

'No!' Dulcie shook her friends off. 'I'm not. It's just . . .' She put her hand up to her forehead, as if to push back the blinding pressure that had just begun, behind her temples.

'It's not your fault, hon.' Trista put her arm around her, more congenially this time, and started to walk her back toward the street. 'It's that cheap sherry. We may as well have been drinking cough syrup.'

'No, it's not that.' Dulcie pulled away. 'I'm not drunk. Honest.'
She looked around into three sets of disbelieving eyes. Four, if you
counted the kitten's. 'I can explain what I said about Thorpe, really.
But right now, I have to concentrate. There's danger here.'

Raleigh and Lloyd exchanged a look, and Trista took a step
forward. In one moment, Dulcie was going to be hustled away from
that alley, whether she liked it or not. She needed to explain what
she suspected and, more urgently, had heard. Mr Grey wouldn't
have warned her if there were nothing—

'What was that?' Raleigh turned back to toward the alley. The
kitten mewed softly. 'No, not that.' She pointed into the darkness.
'*That.*'

Another sound. A groan, soft but distinct. They all heard it that
time.

'Holy—' Trista turned back toward the alley, but Dulcie caught
up to her in a flash.

'Wait! There's someone back here.' Dulcie peered into the dark.
'Be careful.'

A soft sound, almost a sigh. Dulcie saw a movement. Something
pale.

'*Dulcie . . .*' Mr Grey again, but fainter, and for the moment,
Dulcie tuned him out as she heard the sound again. It was human
sound: a moan.

'Over here,' Dulcie called. Lloyd and Trista were by her side,
as she stepped forward, farther back in the shadow than they had
yet explored. There, lying against the brick wall of the building
next door, pale as a ghost in the darkness, was a woman: Emily
Trainor.

'Emily!' Dulcie ran over and knelt beside the prone student. 'Are
you hurt?'

'What? Where am I?' Emily was lying on her side and struggled
to get up. 'I thought I heard . . . I must have been . . .'

'We were just here, but you must have been out cold.' Raleigh
was behind Dulcie. 'We should just call 911.'

'No, no,' Emily protested. 'I have to get up. I have to go.'

Ignoring Raleigh, Dulcie reached out. The hands that took hers
were muddy but functional, and with only a little help, the younger
woman pulled herself to her feet.

And stumbled.

'Hang on.' Dulcie moved beside her. Emily was taller, so it was

easy for Dulcie to get under her arm and let the younger student
lean on her. 'Easy does it.'

'What happened?' Trista took her other side as they walked her
out of the alley, and Dulcie made the introductions. 'Who did this
to you?'

'I – no, I don't remember.' At the entrance of the alley, Emily
paused. The moonlight seemed to confuse her, and Raleigh, still
holding the kitten, pulled out her phone.

'You shouldn't try to walk,' she said. 'We'll get an ambulance.'

'No, please!' Disengaging from Trista, Emily reached out and
Raleigh looked up, skeptically.

'We have to, Emily. You're probably in shock now,' she said.

Lloyd nodded, adding, 'especially if you can't even remember
what happened.'

'No, I can.' Emily stepped away from Dulcie, as if to prove her
fitness. 'It was just all so sudden, you know?'

'What was?' Raleigh was testing her; Dulcie could see it. Any
sign of vagueness, and she'd finish punching in the number for
emergency services. 'Tell us.'

'I was going to the reception, you know? At the department
offices?' They all nodded. 'And then, something – no, I guess it
must have been someone grabbed me.' Emily put her hand up to
her throat. It was hard to tell in the moonlight – didn't this city
have any good street lights any more? – but Dulcie thought she saw
bruising on the girl's fair skin.

'Did you see who it was?' Trista asked the question first.

'No.' Emily rubbed her throat and swallowed. Dulcie could see
the muscles working under the pale skin. 'It – he was behind me.
It was all so fast.'

'And then?' Dulcie's voice was soft.

Emily shook her head. 'It – he pulled me back into the alley. I
think maybe someone was coming; I don't know. I tried to grab at
his hand. Tried to claw at him, but he was so strong. Then he threw
me against the wall. I think I hit my head.'

'Did he say anything? Or –' Dulcie paused, wanting to choose
her words carefully – 'make any noise?'

Emily thought about it. 'I thought I heard something. Maybe
that's why I thought somebody was coming. But I'm not sure it
was a voice. It might have been an animal.'

Dulcie felt her friends turning toward her, but a werewolf wouldn't have spoken. Would it? 'What did it sound like? I mean, did you hear any words? Anything you could make out?'

A slow shake of the head, accompanied by more rubbing of the throat.

'He grabbed me and shook me, and I hit my head pretty hard. I, maybe I heard something about "mind" or "mine."'

'Or Mina?' Lloyd had stepped closer.

'Could have been.' Emily looked up. 'You think this was the same guy who attacked my room-mate?'

'You're the room-mate?' Trista looked aghast, and Raleigh chimed in. 'That's it. I'm calling the cops.'

'No, no. Please.' Emily grabbed Raleigh's free hand. The kitten, now tucked inside her jacket mewed. '*Please*. I promise. I'll go talk to them in the morning. I just, I really want to go home now.'

'*Dulcie* . . .' The voice. There was a warning in it, almost a hiss. She didn't need the scrape of claws against the back of her hand to alert her. Somewhere, out there, danger still lurked. Dulcie spun around, as if to face the moonlight. And nearly fell.

'Whoa there.' Trista caught her. 'I think maybe we all need a good night's sleep. What do you say?'

'Please?' Emily pleaded.

Lloyd and Raleigh exchanged a glance, but after a second's silence grumbled something that sounded like assent. 'We're walking Emily home though.' Lloyd pulled himself up to his full five-six.

'Thanks.' Emily beamed at him and took his arm. 'I'd appreciate that.'

'In which case, I'm taking you home.' Trista linked her arm through Dulcie's. 'I'd say we'd all had enough adventure for one night.'

With that, Lloyd and Raleigh started off, their charge leaning heavily between them. A faint prickle at the back of her neck and the memory of that soft voice prompted Dulcie to call after them. 'Raleigh?' She turned. 'The kitten?'

Raleigh smiled, pulled her jacket open. The kitten's fuzzy head appeared, his eyes closing drowsily.

'Please don't give him to Martin Thorpe.'

Raleigh started to respond and caught herself. 'We'll talk tomorrow. Okay, Dulcie?'

'Just – please, don't do anything before we do. Okay?'

Raleigh must have heard something in her tone. 'Okay, Dulcie,' she promised. 'I won't.'

'What was that about?' Dulcie could hear Emily ask. Before she could catch the response, though, Trista had taken her arm back and was pulling her toward Mass. Ave.

'Well, that settles it,' Trista was saying. 'It's the boyfriend.'

'What?' Dulcie was still trying to eavesdrop on their departing friends. Trista, however, was quickly hustling her out of hearing range.

'I heard the cops had taken the other girl's boyfriend in for questioning.' Trista was taller than Dulcie and walking fast, and Dulcie had the distinct impression that she wanted to get her away from Raleigh and the kitten – and the remnants of the party – as soon as possible.

'I know that's what the cops suspect, but they don't have any proof.' Dulcie tried to order her thoughts, which was difficult to do at this pace. 'And besides, Josh is Mina's boyfriend, not Emily's.'

'Josh? You know the jerk?' Trista stopped suddenly, and turned toward Dulcie, her eyes growing wide. 'Dulcie, don't tell me you've gotten involved with him in any way.'

'No, I'm not.' Dulcie was grateful for the chance to catch her breath, but she still couldn't find the words. 'I'm not *involved* with him. I've met him, that's all, but I really don't think he's the type.' Before Trista could argue, Dulcie started walking again and Trista had to follow. 'I know, you think I'm a softie. But think about it, Trista. Even if he did attack Mina in a fit of jealousy, why would he go for Emily? He has no reason to be jealous of her.' She was rather proud of that bit of logic.

Trista shrugged, unimpressed. 'Guys like that don't need a reason.' At least they were walking at a more reasonable pace. 'He thinks Mina cheated on him. He thinks Emily helped. He thinks they joined forces to deceive him, or that Emily is laughing at him. Hell, maybe he thinks Mina cheated on him *with* Emily. Wouldn't be the first time. Or maybe it's not related to jealousy at all.' Trista looked over at her friend. 'Maybe he wants to scare her so she won't tell the police what she knows.'

'She doesn't *know* anything.' Dulcie thought back to her first meeting with Emily. 'She wasn't accusing him of anything. When she came to my office, she made a point of telling me that Josh and

Mina had a good relationship. That Mina was used to male attention, but that she was committed to Josh.'

'Maybe Emily only said that because she was afraid of him.' Dulcie started to interrupt, but Trista was on a roll.

'Or maybe it was true. Who knows? That still doesn't mean he didn't attack her. Maybe Josh just lost it, blamed Mina for this "male attention" she was getting.'

'Or maybe it was someone else entirely.' The fresh air had cleared Dulcie's head, and she was thinking. Professor Lukos had come late to the party. He'd have passed this way and . . . there was something else. 'Professor Lukos. Did you notice how he was holding his coat over his hand? Like he was hiding it?'

Trista gave her a half nod. 'Maybe. Or maybe he just didn't want to put a nice coat down where it would get sherry spilled on it.'

'Emily said she fought.' To Dulcie it all seemed quite reasonable. 'She might have scratched him. Drawn blood.'

'Yeah, that's true.' Trista smiled, and Dulcie realized that her friend had been holding herself back. 'I thought you were going to say he'd been bitten by a wolf.'

Dulcie opened her mouth – and shut it. That possibility had occurred to her, back at the party. 'Trista, if you'd seen Thorpe, last night. Out in the moonlight.'

'Look, I know Thorpe is a beast sometimes. Really.' Trista paused and took her friend's hand. 'I understand he's been giving you a hard time. And I know how much pressure you're under. Believe me, I know.' She stared at Dulcie until her friend nodded in agreement. That much was true: Dulcie remembered how crazy Trista had gotten as she had finished her dissertation. 'But you shouldn't – I mean, you've got to be careful what you say. You're not used to drinking, you know.'

'I'm not drunk, Trista.' She wasn't now, anyway. Though, truth be told, she did recall feeling a little dizzy and out of it. 'I'm just tired. And, well, I can explain. It all makes sense. The moon and all.'

'But it's not even a full moon.' Trista pointed and Dulcie looked. Sure enough, a slight flattening showed on the upper right of the lunar orb.

'Yesterday, however—'

'Nope.' Trista shook her head. 'Yesterday it was even further from full. I know it's been bright. I swear, it's like someone's been shining a flashlight in my window. I heard something on the news about it being particularly close to earth.' She looked up. 'But it's not full, not tonight. Though if this is any indication, it's going to be a doozy.'

'Wait, it's *going* to be?' Dulcie was looking at her friend, not up at the sky.

'Uh huh,' Trista nodded. 'The full moon is tomorrow.'

FIFTEEN

The combination of the sherry and everything else should have left Dulcie exhausted, but she felt strangely wired by the time she'd climbed the stairs. Strangely wired – and not only awake, but driven. A quick text message to Chris – *Trista walked me home. All locked up!* – and she was at her desk, that curious manuscript open before her.

'I know it doesn't make sense, Esmé, but there's something here,' she said as the young cat jumped up to peer at her laptop. 'Something in this book that ties everything together.'

As if in response, the little tuxedo cat began to wash furiously, attacking her inside hind leg as if it were possessed.

'You don't have a flea,' Dulcie looked up. 'Do you?' The cat ignored her, moving on to the pink spaces between her toes, and Dulcie returned to work.

'For dangers abound on this Road, as the bilious Moon rides to her turbulent zenith, and I would be your Friend.' Deep in the shadows, the Stranger sat, regarding her with hidden eyes. Silent, since his initial salutation, he watched steadily, as the storm beyond raged and those fiendish things, the Beasts of the Night cried their blood-curdling cries.'

'Meh.' A paw appeared, dabbing at the cursor on the screen.

'No, Esmé.' A little carelessly, Dulcie brushed the paw away. It reappeared, as Esmé batted at the cursor. Not, Dulcie told herself, at the word 'Friend.' She read on.

'Beasts of the Night cried their blood-curdling cries . . .' This was better: Dulcie needed to focus on the text, not on some vague hope that this character was some kind of precursor of her own

spiritual friend. *'Cried their blood-curdling cries?'* The awkward-ness of it hit her. Surely the author meant to revise that. The paw reappeared.

'Ravenous as wraiths, they sounded, calling for their prey in voices meant to freeze the very Blood. Only the Stranger . . .'

'Meh!' More insistent, this time.

'What?' A small fang appeared over the edge of the laptop as Esmé began to gnaw on the computer. 'No! Esmé, stop!'

Dulcie slammed the computer closed and found herself face to face with her cat. 'I know I've been busy, Esmé. But at least I'm working at home. I'm trying.' The wide green eyes stared up at her. 'You know, you can talk to me, Esmé. If you want to.' The cat tilted her head, as if to get a better view of her person. The look could have been an appraisal, leaving Dulcie feeling that in some way she had been found wanting, when it hit her: Esmé hadn't been fed.

'Of course.' Dulcie got up and headed for the kitchen. Esmé bounded ahead. 'Sorry, kitty. Everything that's happened has taken over my mind. In fact . . .' As Dulcie reached for the cat food, she realized how hungry she was, as well. That soup had been hours before, and the effects of the sherry were just about worn off. The apartment larder wasn't as well stocked with people food as it was with Fancy Feast, however, and Dulcie contemplated going out. Not yet eleven, Mary Chung's might be closed, but Hi Fi Pizza would still be open.

Dulcie was going for her sweater when the realization of what she was about to do stopped her. Another woman had been attacked tonight. Granted, both the attacks had been in Harvard Square, a full mile from where she was now. But she'd told Chris she'd be careful. Besides, as good as pizza – extra cheese, pepperoni, mushrooms – sounded, Dulcie really wanted to read more of the manuscript. It was funny how it seemed to expand. She was reading a section now that she had only the dimmest memory of transcribing. It was almost as if . . .

'Mr Grey? Are you sending me stories now?' The vague thought that she had pushed aside while reading came back to her now. 'Did you somehow appear to the author?' It made no sense; she knew that. Still, she couldn't help but wonder. But as she looked around the empty kitchen, the only sound was Esmé lapping at her dish. That was enough to remind Dulcie of her own empty belly, and soon she was digging into a monster-size bowl of Cheerios.

Of course, her phone rang. 'Mwah?' she managed, removing the spoon from her mouth.

'Dulcie! Are you okay?' It was Chris, sounding a little panicked. Rather than scare him further, Dulcie worked at swallowing the wet mouthful. 'Dulcie?'

'Sorry, Chris,' she said at last. 'I'm here. I'm fine. You just caught me with my mouth full.'

'Oh, thank god.' He sounded so relieved that Dulcie grew curious.

'Didn't you get my text?'

'I got something, but it was garbled,' her boyfriend sounded more like himself. 'All I could make out was something about "locked up." I was trying to tell myself that this was good. That whoever went after that woman had been locked up. But all I could think of was you, out there . . .'

He sounded like he could go on, but Dulcie interrupted. 'I'm fine, but Chris, there was another attack. Another student – right by the department office!'

'I *knew* it.'

Dulcie kept talking. 'It was Mina's room-mate – she's the girl who was attacked last night. Tonight it was Emily, whom I know, sort of. She's in one of my sections. But we found her. There was a kitten in the alley—'

'Wait, hang on, Dulcie. From the beginning?'

Chris didn't really mean that, Dulcie knew. It would take hours to go back over the entire evening and what she'd heard – or deduced – about the visiting professor, Thorpe, and the moon. Besides, she realized, in retrospect, she was a little embarrassed. She had accused the possible next head of the department of a horrible crime without much proof. And then she had blurted out her worst fears. Granted, to her friends, but . . .

'Dulcie?' She could make out muffled voices; he was calling from the computer lab. She should make it quick.

'Sorry, I was trying to figure out where to start.' With that, she decided that the best place was right near the end, as they were leaving the party. She told Chris about hearing something – to him, she could confide that she'd thought she'd heard a roar, and then a voice that sounded like Mr Grey – and then finding the little orange tabby. And then that feeling that something was wrong, was still very wrong – and finding Emily. 'So Lloyd and

Raleigh walked her home,' she concluded. 'And Trista walked me home.'

'Wait, you didn't call the police?'

'I wanted to, Chris. I really did – but she, Emily, wouldn't let us.' Dulcie thought back to the younger woman's resistance. 'Do you think that's weird?'

'I do, but . . .' He paused. 'You know, it makes sense.'

'What do you mean?' Esmé had finished her own dinner by then and jumped up on the kitchen table. Dulcie pushed her away as she bent to sniff at the cereal bowl. 'No, that's mine,' she mouthed. The cat turned away, with an insulted air.

'Well, the cops said it was probably a domestic, right? I bet she knew him.'

'But she said . . .' Dulcie stopped. What Chris had said fit – up to a point. 'Why wouldn't she turn this guy in?'

'Maybe she's afraid.' Dulcie wondered about that as she absently stroked the cat. 'Maybe she feels culpable in some way. Ow!' Esmé had turned and given her a sharp nip. 'Sorry, that was just Esmé. I don't think I can do anything right by her tonight.' Unless, she wondered, the little cat was trying to tell her something. 'What do you mean, "culpable"?'

'I don't know.' Chris was sounding tired, and Dulcie realized he was less interested in the details of the attack than in her own welfare. 'Maybe she was involved with him, too. Or, hey, with her room-mate. Stranger things have happened.'

Either way, it was important – and it echoed what Trista had said, too. 'Well, there's nothing like that holding me up,' she decided. 'I'm going to talk to Rogovoy first thing tomorrow. I've got to make sure he knows what's going on.'

Silence on the other end of the line. 'Chris?'

Chris's sigh was audible. 'Dulcie, do you have to? I mean, I think you did the right thing – urging this girl to come forward. You were right. She should have. But, well, she didn't. And now it really is sounding like it was something personal. Not some stray madman on the streets of Cambridge. I know you want to be a responsible member of the community. But maybe, Dulce, leave this one alone?'

'Hmm.' Dulcie took another bite of cereal. It was soggy now.

'Dulcie?' Behind him, the voices had grown louder. Chris must really be worried if he ignored his students for this long.

'I won't get in the middle of it.' She gave him that. 'I won't go to the police.' Dulcie meant that as a clarification, not an addition. She had plans.

She also had a question of her own. 'Chris, when I told you that another woman had been attacked, you said you knew it. What did you mean?'

'I didn't – I don't remember.' He was stammering. 'Hey, I should go. I've got students.'

'Chris Sorensen.' Dulcie used her best teacher voice. 'You're hiding something, aren't you?'

'I'm sorry, Dulcie. I didn't mean to.' A pause, and Dulcie knew he was considering how much to tell her.

'Chris?'

'It was Mr Grey, Dulcie.' He was speaking softly, his voice muffled as if he had his hand over the phone. 'At least, I'm pretty sure it was. I heard, well, I thought I heard a cry or a howl, or something, and then I heard his voice. *"Innocence is no protection,"* he said. *"This goes back too far."*'

SIXTEEN

'Innocence is no protection.' Dulcie mulled that one over. It could, she thought, apply to the kitten. No matter what Raleigh – or Lloyd or Trista – believed, she was determined that the little marmalade tabby was not going to fall into the wrong hands. Maybe Thorpe was blameless – she had a hard time thinking of him as innocent – but she wasn't going to take any chances. And as for the rest of it? That bit about 'going back too far'? Well, that would fit if the crime was personal – a 'domestic,' as Rogovoy had put it. Or it could have another meaning as well.

Sitting at the table, Dulcie stroked the closed lid of her laptop. This story, with its mysterious stranger, was drawing her in. Could it be connected, in some way. Could the stranger . . .?

She laughed at her own fancy. 'Esmé, I really shouldn't drink sherry,' she called. The cat had disappeared, however, leaving Dulcie to finish her cereal alone. She really should go to bed, she knew. But while she was eating . . .

Only the Stranger sat unmoved by the fiendish Cries. Only he retained a preternatural calm. Outside, the horses frothed and tossed their manes, eyes wide and frantic in the night, while the Coachman – that dark figure whose Visage lay concealed – whipped and cursed his Fury into the night.

'You have far to go.' The Voice, as soft as Velvet, reached her ear, as if by one Whisper'd by her side. 'You bear a burden of Debt to others besides yourself, to those who will follow after. And there are some who would delay you, one in particular who would take from you that which you most treasure.'

That which you most treasure? Dulcie looked up from the keyboard. A woman, pursued in a storm, who is given a lift by a mysterious stranger? This story was taking some strange turns. The first bit of the manuscript, which she had found only a few months ago among some loose papers in the Mildon rare book collection, had dealt with a murder. Someone – a young nobleman – had been found lying dead in a library.

Dulcie shivered, remembering that scene. One too close to it had really happened, in her own undergraduate house library not that long ago. She shook off the memory – what mattered now was the book.

In that first fragment, the heroine – who either had red or dark hair depending on the author's whim – had found a body. It was quite possible, Dulcie had to acknowledge, that she had killed the man described so well, whom the reader first sees lying, still and cold, on the library rug. What Dulcie hadn't known was why.

Now, in this latest bunch of pages, she was getting to a motive. Someone had been pursuing this woman – someone or something. After all, fiendish howls in the night, mysterious pursuers, and even more mysterious rescuers didn't sound like what a present-day detective would call a 'domestic.' And that, Dulcie thought with satisfaction, was one of the reasons she loved books like this. Gothic novels, and the women who wrote them, weren't bound by the dull reality of deadlines and family squabbles.

They probably weren't bound by fatigue either, Dulcie admitted when, about an hour later, she found herself face down on the warm keyboard. She'd woken to the soft touch of a paw, patting gently at her mouth.

'Was I snoring, Esmé?' Dulcie blinked up into the wide green eyes. 'Or did you think something might crawl out of my mouth?'

The little cat didn't answer, although the off-center star on her face gave her a look that Dulcie could only interpret as concern.

'Not to worry, kitty. Off to bed.' Dulcie closed the computer and pulled herself up. Tomorrow, she'd go back to the Mildon. There were more pages that she'd recently identified. Deciphering them was laborious work, and Thorpe was pushing her to work on her writing. This book, however, was too thrilling to put down.

Maybe, she thought as she brushed her teeth, she could work up an article over the winter break. 'Beyond *Umbria*,' she tried on the title. 'An Anonymous Author's Next Great Work.'

If only she could put a name to the author, she thought to herself as she slid between the sheets. She felt so close to her, as if she knew her. And yet the woman whose work had come to mean so much was still a stranger. A nameless stranger in the night.

SEVENTEEN

*T*hey were traveling fast. Too fast for the Road, the Night, or the safety of the Horses, spent as they were and mad with Fear. Too fast for Comfort, for sure, as with every bump and jolt, she gripped the seat. Hers had been no choice – Flight was the only option lest she Surrender again to him. Again – and this time, more than her Safety was at stake. Still, she wished for Peace, for a moment of blessed stillness.

'Here, this will warm you . . .' She looked up, having forgotten, for the moment, that she did not ride alone. Indeed, the Stranger – he who had hailed the Coachman and pulled over as she ran, stumbling, down that rocky path – now regarded her with cool eyes. Cool, but with compassion, she sensed, as she reached to accept the flask he offered, held out to her in one gloved hand. Dare she Drink?

'It will do you good,' came the response, though she did not believe she had spoken her Question aloud. Perhaps, in her fatigue, her thoughts were leaking into the night, much as the wind eked its way into the carriage. 'Drink,' said the Stranger. 'Then, perhaps, you can sleep.' The draught indeed was strong and sweet, with a hint of spice, and warmed her well. Mayhap she could sleep now, she mused, her very Eyes growing heavy. Maybe she would be safe.

Her lids closed, her mind drifting. The last thoughts she had were of those other Eyes, the Stranger's eyes, cool and green in the deep Shadow of the coach. Watching, and yet so calm.

Dulcie woke with a start, the taste of last night's sherry – or something stronger – warm on her tongue. Chris was snoring gently beside her, and Dulcie grabbed the clock, minutes before it was set to go off. No point waking him. After that dream, she wasn't going back to sleep.

Esmé came into the bathroom as Dulcie was brushing her teeth and rubbed against her bare legs.

'What is it, kitty?' Dulcie asked as soon as she could. 'Are you having strange dreams, too?'

The cat didn't respond, at least not verbally, and Dulcie thought about the green eyes in her dream. Clearly, her unconscious had connected the helpful stranger in the book with Mr Grey, but was it all in her mind? Her late, great cat had been reaching out to her last night; she was sure of that. Did he mean to warn her of more than the kitten? Did his message have something to do with Emily Trainor? She had to find out.

As she filled her travel mug, Dulcie considered the possibilities. She trusted Detective Rogovoy. Despite his inability to understand her concerns about Thorpe – he could be a bit concrete in his thinking – he was still a good cop. And even though Emily didn't want to talk to the police, Dulcie still felt they – or Rogovoy, at any rate – should know about the attack. However, she had promised Chris she wouldn't get involved – *more* involved, she corrected herself, and that pretty much precluded another visit to the university police. That didn't mean she couldn't drop in on Emily this morning. Maybe, now that the initial shock had passed, she could talk the young woman into going to the authorities. At the very least, Dulcie decided as she headed out the door, she might get some answers to her own questions.

'Maybe Emily can take the kitten,' Dulcie said to herself as she locked the apartment behind her. Heading down to the street, she couldn't see her own cat. But Esmé had heard her last words, as did the larger, grey shadow she seemed to cast against the apartment wall. Both of them were staring, as if still listening, at the door their person had just exited. Both had their backs arched, their tails stretched straight, and every hair standing on end.

*   *   *

As it was, Dulcie felt almost jolly as she walked toward the Square. Maybe Chris was right, she mused: the two victims were so closely related that the attacks had to be personal. While that didn't help them, it did mean that her concerns about her adviser – and the visiting scholar – were less credible. It also meant the student body at large was less at risk. And because the violence wasn't random, she reasoned, it was more likely that the police would be able to find the perpetrator. If – Dulcie picked up her pace – she could convince Emily to come forward.

What if it was Josh? Dulcie didn't know the red-faced young man and, unlike Lucy, she didn't believe she had any special powers of discernment. But she had liked him. He'd seemed guileless in his big, goofy way, and she didn't want to believe that his overlarge exterior hid some nasty violent side. Surely there was someone else in the girls' life, someone less open and friendly. For a moment, Dulcie flashed on the stranger – a dark mystery who kept himself in shadow. No, that was a book, a book that had made its way into her dreams. What was happening here on campus was something human and all too real.

Later, she promised herself, she'd pursue that particular secret as well. With the help of Griddlehaus, the head of the Mildon special collection, she'd identified several more pages of promising material from a box of uncatalogued material. If any of them advanced the story, maybe even linked that first fragment – the bit about the body in the library – to these more recent pages, she'd be in luck. What she was finding was pure gold, academically speaking.

As she made her way to the Quad, she found herself summarizing what she knew: a woman, the heroine – whom Dulcie identified for better or worse with the author – is in the grasp of someone evil. It might be the nobleman we later find dead, but it might be someone else entirely. She manages to get away and flees into the night, a wild and stormy night, only to be picked up by a coach that just happens to be driving past on the lonely mountain road. The coach belongs to – or, at least, is occupied by – the shadowy stranger, who has green eyes and some kind of reviving drink.

No, she stopped herself, the drink was part of her dream, probably the result of last night's sherry. Still, that dream had seemed so real, as if it were another part of the story. It didn't advance it enough to bring Dulcie up to that first scene in the library, however.

As she thought of the fragments she had read, Dulcie found herself wondering. She had assumed, for various reasons, that the man in the library had been murdered. She had also assumed that the heroine had killed him, perhaps in self-defense. Now, with the appearance of the stranger, another possibility presented itself. The stranger seemed to be an ally. Could he have done the killing? Was he, perhaps, the victim?

As an academic, Dulcie knew the dangers of jumping to conclusion. Even Thorpe, in one of his more lucid moments, had seen fit to warn her. Without proof, without direct ties, all she had was speculation. And speculation was fiction, not defensible fact. For all she knew, Thorpe had pointed out, she might be reading fragments of two different tales. From an academic viewpoint, that would have been wonderful: not just one, but a whole trove of previously undiscovered work! As a fan of the author, however, Dulcie found the idea disheartening. It was bad enough that her subject's best-known work, *The Ravages of Umbria*, only survived in fragments and that she would probably never get to read all of it. To find another set of partial novels was just too frustrating. Almost as bad as if she found out that the stranger was, in fact, a villain. For some reason, Dulcie found that concept disturbing. It must, she realized, have something to do with those deep green eyes.

She would have to shelve that question for later. She'd reached Winthrop House, where Emily and Mina roomed, and turned her thoughts to the room-mates as she showed her university ID and climbed to the third-floor suite marked 'Love/Trainor.'

'Hello?' She knocked. 'Emily? It's me, Dulcie Schwartz.'

Silence. For a moment, Dulcie worried. Perhaps the girl's injuries had been more severe than anyone had known. Perhaps she had lapsed into unconsciousness. Perhaps . . . the sound of movement behind the door pushed that thought aside.

'Emily?' Dulcie still felt strangely worried. 'Are you okay? May I come in?' More shuffling and a strange thudding sound. 'Emily.'

'Coming!' The sound of a voice should have reassured Dulcie, but she found she was holding her breath. Finally the lock turned and the door opened, revealing a rather bedraggled version of the student she had last seen only twelve hours before. The delay, Dulcie could see, was due to the cane on which Emily leaned.

'Emily! You're hurt.' She looked at the cane, and saw how the girl grimaced as she took a step back into the room.

'I'm a bit banged up,' she said over her shoulder, advancing toward the sofa. 'I have a bad knee. I guess I fell on it.'

'Bastard,' Dulcie muttered. Then it hit her that her early morning call hadn't helped. 'Did I wake you?'

'Yeah, but it's okay.' The sophomore pushed her hair back, giving Dulcie a view of the darkening bruises on her thin, pale neck. 'I didn't sleep that well.'

'I can imagine.' Dulcie followed Emily's slow progress back into the suite's common room, noting how thin the girl's shoulders looked under her worn T. Emily walked over to the window, dragging open the pink-patterned drapes that had kept the room in darkness, and Dulcie gasped. It wasn't just her shoulders – by daylight, the junior looked more fragile than she had only the day before, as if the attack had stolen something vital from her.

'You want some coffee?' Emily asked, propping her cane against the sofa. 'I could use a cup.'

'I drank mine on the way in. You don't have to.' Dulcie raised her travel mug, then saw how her hostess shrugged off what could have been construed as pity. 'But more's always welcome. Thanks.' Especially with Chris's schedule so disrupted, Dulcie lived on caffeine. Besides, sharing a morning ritual might encourage the younger girl to open up. Pushing aside what looked like graphs, Dulcie sat on an old armchair and looked around. The room could have been almost any undergrad dorm common area Dulcie had ever seen, down to the ratty old sofa and its Indian print throw. A trunk served as a coffee table and undoubtedly as extra storage. On top of a miniature fridge, the room-mates had a coffee maker, while one wall held the usual band posters and a Monet reprint. On the other, more of the graph, which looked like a tree of some kind.

'Do you have another room-mate?' She got up to take a look and saw names, not numbers. It was a chart of some sort. 'A mathematician?'

'What? Oh, no.' Emily came over and took Dulcie's travel mug. 'It's just us. This is just something we did for fun – I took a tutorial in genealogy, and Mina got really into it with me. Actually, it's one of the reasons Mina switched over from straight English to Hist and Lit.'

'Huh, cool.' From what Dulcie could see, the 'tree' had six levels. There had to be forty entries on its branches, most of them initials. 'Is this your family?'

'What? Oh, no.' Emily returned with Dulcie's mug and one of her own. 'Mine's boring. This is actually Mina's. She's from some old family that came over right after the Revolution. She knew – she knows a lot more of her family history than I do. I think that's why she . . .' Emily's voice faltered.

Dulcie turned from the giant chart. 'How is she, Emily?'

The student shrugged. 'She's still unconscious. The doctors say she could wake up at any time, but . . .' She bit her lip.

Dulcie ushered her back to the sofa. 'I'm so sorry. This must all be so awful.' Another shrug. 'Is that why you . . .'

The other girl looked at her, confused.

'I mean, you must just want to get back to normal.' Nothing. Dulcie kicked herself. 'I'm sorry, Emily. I came over here thinking that I wanted to get you to go to the police, to tell them what happened last night. But you must just want to forget all about it.'

'Yeah.' Emily looked down at the mug she cradled in her hands. Even her hands, Dulcie could see, were bruised.

'You fought,' she said.

'Huh? No.' Emily shook her head. 'We were friends.'

'No, not you and Mina.' Dulcie was just putting her foot in it every chance she had today. 'I mean, last night. You fought your attacker. You told us that, but I didn't know how hard until I saw your hands.'

Only then did the other girl seem to notice. Putting the mug down on the trunk, she raised her hands, palm upward. Sure enough, they were bruised, dark purple marks rising against her white skin.

'Yeah, I guess I did.' She turned her hands over as if seeing them for the first time.

'And your neck.' Emily raised one hand to her throat. She had the kind of fair skin that probably bruised easily. Still, the marks were disturbing. She covered them briefly with her hand, then quickly shoved it back down into her lap.

'That must hurt.' Dulcie interpreted the gesture. The other girl nodded. 'I was worried, when you didn't answer at first that you had been more badly hurt than you realized,' Dulcie continued. 'More than anyone had realized.' Seeing the aftermath of the attack had made her more determined. 'I know you didn't want to go to the authorities.' She intentionally avoided the word 'police.' 'I get it, I do. But Emily, you have to.'

The face that looked up at hers was blank, the dark eyes large and scared in the pale face. 'I can't,' she said, her voice barely a whisper, and looked away. 'It's my own . . .'

She stopped, and Dulcie waited. Victims often blamed themselves; she knew that. What she didn't know was how to counter it. How to get the young woman to realize that the unknown perpetrator, not her own carelessness or lack of attention, was to blame.

But Emily only shook her head, her mouth closed tight. Leaving Dulcie with the distinct feeling that she was intruding, that this girl wanted to be left alone. Dulcie was torn: Emily had already been victimized. Dulcie should respect her wishes. She should leave. If only she could get Emily to come forward. After all, there was a violent criminal out there, and she herself might be victimized again.

To give her the illusion of privacy, Dulcie turned away and drank some of her coffee. It was weak and a little bitter. Maybe Emily liked it like this. Or maybe Mina had been the one who usually made a morning pot. Thinking about Mina, Dulcie realized she had another option. She wasn't going to give up trying to convince Emily to come forward. In the meantime, however, she could do some sleuthing on her own.

'How long have you and Mina roomed together?' She got up to look at the chart. Up close, she could see that it was made up of several pages, taped together, and filled the space between the room's two windows, both of which looked out onto the Quad.

Anyone else would have been admiring the view. Three stories up, she could see the famous oaks, the last of their foliage barely hanging in. For her, the appeal was the giant chart. Larger than she'd first noticed, it extended under the bright curtain that Emily had hastily pulled open, letting in the weak November sun.

'Wow, this is huge.' Dulcie moved the curtain and heard something roll on the floor. She bent to retrieve a pencil stub, its point rounded and dull. She picked it up absently and looked at the chart. Two more branches, jutting out from the lower end – the 'trunk' – of the tree. No, she saw: three. Only the third had been scribbled over. Wild black markings obscured several names with the silvery sheen of graphite, crossing through the connecting lines. 'What's this? Black sheep?'

'Oh, that's nothing.' Emily came up beside her and took the pencil from her hand. 'I'm kind of, well, that was a mistake.' She pulled the curtain back into place, clearly embarrassed by the mess. 'I found out that Mina's not the only person in her family here at the university.'

'Oh?' It wasn't surprising, really. Emily's embarrassment about it, however . . . 'And that's bad?'

The girl shrugged. 'Turns out, she and Josh are related, way, way back. I mean, so far back it doesn't matter. But, it bothered him; I know that. I think maybe that's why she got so into all the theoretical stuff. The post-structuralist stuff. It's all so once removed, you know? Impersonal. Maybe it's . . .' She paused. 'Maybe it's safer.'

EIGHTEEN

'*Maybe it's safer.*' The words rang in Dulcie's mind. What exactly did that mean? Dulcie paused, as she tried to phrase the question for the young woman sitting beside her. Just how 'bothered' had Josh been? Was a vague fear of incest through some long-ago consanguinity enough to drive a man mad? To drive him to attack his girlfriend?

Emily was clearly fragile, and Dulcie didn't want to upset her more. Besides, the girl might not have any idea about Josh's mental state. Still, she had to ask. 'Emily,' she started to form the question. 'You don't think, maybe—'

But before she could go any further, the Memorial Church bell sounded, and Emily jumped up.

'Oh my God. It's so late! I've got to finish dressing. Get to class. I'm sorry.' She practically shoved Dulcie out the door. 'Thanks for coming by!'

'But . . .' Dulcie was backing into the hallway as she remembered her original purpose. 'Won't you consider going to the police? I'll go with you!'

'Maybe later!' Emily didn't even seem to really hear her, as she closed the door. 'Bye!'

Dulcie found herself facing the closed door as the bell continued to chime, and only the rush of other students down the hall reminded her that she, too, had obligations.

Questions continued to surface, however, through back-to-back sections. Questions other than the role of narrative non-fiction in the development of Joseph Conrad's fiction or the use of metaphor in Dickens. Would the discovery of a long-ago link upset Josh so much that he'd turn violent? Had it – or something else – spurred Mina to break off from her chubby boyfriend? Did Emily know more about what was going on between her room-mate and her boyfriend then she let on? Would she ever go to the police?

These questions were so much more immediate – and had so much more inherent drama in them – than the subjects she was supposed to be teaching. In fact, Dulcie suspected that she was sleepwalking through her classes all morning, a supposition supported by the amount of eye-rolling she witnessed when she could focus.

'It's the full moon,' she actually heard one student say as he packed up his bag. 'That's why women can't be serious academics.'

She was about to stop him – that was really going too far – when she caught herself. He was wrong, deadly wrong, about what was distracting her – and if she caught a whiff of such sexism in any of his papers, she'd make him pay for it. But he was right in that she was diverted, and, really, if she wasn't giving her all, she had no right to criticize her students.

It was a little after midday when she emerged from Emerson, and moonrise was hours away yet. But her student's comment had added another question to the list. Would the full moon tonight bring another attack?

Dulcie didn't want to think so. Tonight was the second of the Newman lectures, with Renée Showalter of McGill speaking, and Dulcie actually liked what she'd read of this scholar's work. Chris wouldn't be happy about her going out again, Dulcie knew. But really, what were her options? Stay hidden away? Even her heroine had ventured forth from the castle, only to be picked up on the road by some mysterious stranger.

Or had that only been in her dream? Standing at the base of the stairs, Dulcie shook her head. Too much had been going on, and she suspected the after-effects of the sherry weren't helping. She should, she knew, get some lunch. Food and more coffee would help clear up the confusion about the attacks and her students, the manuscript fragments, and her own dreams. But as she started to walk across the Yard, she realized that before she had lunch – and today she was going to have the three-bean burger with extra hot sauce – she needed to get some work done. Only down in the Mildon would she find answers to at least one of those questions.

'Ms Schwartz.' Thomas Griddlehaus, chief clerk of the rare book collection, looked up and nodded as Dulcie came in.

'Mr Griddlehaus,' she responded with her own nod and a smile. The two had worked together long enough that they could have dropped the formalities. They seemed right in this context, however. Despite the futuristic setting – climate controlled, clean, and white – the Mildon Rare Books Library was a time capsule. Buried deep beneath the rest of the library, it housed not only rare books and folios, but also – in a series of acid-free non-reactive folders stored in specially built boxes – the carefully preserved unidentified fragments that the university had collected over the years.

After handing the diminutive clerk her bag, Dulcie reached for the box of gloves and pulled out a pair. White and lightly powdered, they would reduce even further any chance that the oils of her skin could corrupt the aged and fragile pages she was about to read. Gloves on, Dulcie took her seat at the long white table. Although she could have found the box she wanted blindfolded, it was Griddlehaus's prerogative to retrieve it and place it, opened, before her.

'Happy hunting,' he said with something nearly approximating a wink, and with that he left her.

''Tis an entrancing light, the Moon's, fooling mortal eyes and playing shadows across our fancies.' So spake the Stranger, his own green orbs glowing in the dark. 'Such fancies may betray our deepest Hopes and yet make real our sondest Dreams.'

Sondest? No, that made no sense. Damn that 's'. Dulcie looked down at the notepad in front of her. '*Fondest*.' Yes, that was it: '*our fondest Dreams.*'

Crossing out what she had originally written, Dulcie substituted what seemed the likelier word, and then put her head in her hands to give her aching eyes a rest. Close to an hour had passed, and all she had to show for it was this paragraph.

Maybe it was time for lunch. She'd been deciphering the page before her, letter by letter, marking down the passage with the soft pencil that was the only writing implement permitted in the Mildon. Later, she'd transcribe the page into her computer, where she could begin the complicated process of trying to fit it with the other fragments. Right now, however, she needed to rest her eyes. That horrid 's'.

'*Come now, Dulcie.*' A soft voice spoke, seemingly right in her ear. '*You can do a little more.*'

'Mr Grey?' Dulcie sat up with a start and looked around. Griddlehaus was in the other room, and she was alone. Well, alone except for that voice. Unless she had fallen asleep and into a dream. 'Are you here, Mr Grey?'

A low hum began. It could have been the air-filtration system, but to Dulcie it sounded like a purr. 'Do you have a message for me?' She had lowered her voice as she glanced once more, surreptitiously, around the room. The feline spirit rarely made himself heard and visible at the same time, but Dulcie couldn't stop herself looking for those wide white whiskers or that proud plume of a tail.

'*I've left you a tale . . .*' The voice rose out of the purring hum, and Dulcie could have sworn there was a little laugh in it. '*From the dawn of our tale. Or was that a tail?*'

'Are you making a pun, Mr Grey?' The only answer was that low, rhythmic whirr.

Her spectral visitor had made his point, though. There was something in this text, something Dulcie had to find. Thoughts of lunch temporarily banished, Dulcie sat up straight in her chair. Using just the tips of her gloved fingers, she slid the page toward her. Held together, as well as protected, by the clear polypropylene sheath that encased it, the page slide silently, and Dulcie found herself wondering about the stains and creases on the paper.

'*Fondest Dreams,*' she read. Yes, that was it. Though it was no wonder she'd had trouble. In addition to her fatigue, she was hampered by the condition of this page. Even more than the others she had previously deciphered, this one was in rough shape, as if it had been through, well, through a storm. A diagonal tear had severed the word 'Dream' from the rest of the sentence, and a blotch obscured the next line.

Or did it? Dulcie reached for the magnifying glass that had become her favorite tool. Focusing on the upstroke of the letters, she had discovered, sometimes made reading them easier.

'*Those Dreams as become a Lad,*' She read. Or was it '*Lady.*' For argument's sake, since the Stranger was addressing the heroine, 'Lady' seemed more likely, Dulcie decided, scribbling down the new bit. '*Though when the Silver Orb withdraws . . .*' The next bit was gone, obscured by a dark blot that could have been ink or blood. Or even coffee or chocolate, she caught herself. The fact that she was unraveling – restoring, really – a previously unknown novel was dramatic enough, and getting her to focus might have been Mr Grey's only message. She really did not need to add her own wild imaginings to the excitement.

Method. That was what she needed, not fancy. Marking in her notebook the number of lines that seemed to be obscured, she moved down the page.

'*. . . freed by any Means from such Hateful Servitude, the disequal Bonds that would have you thus Shackled by custom and by law.*' Ah, this was good stuff. Earlier in her research, Dulcie had isolated several phrases that her author frequently used. 'Disequal bonds' was one of them, usually referring to marriage, which – in her author's world – was less likely to be a joining of souls than an unequal and purely mercenary agreement, usually decided between a woman's father and her suitor. Now that she was in a good relationship, Dulcie found this sentiment a bit sad. True, what she and Chris had was far from ideal. The few weeks when they managed to be on the same schedule they were both likely to be either fiendishly busy or sleep deprived. Still, their connection was far from 'disequal' or the kind of 'gender Servitude' that the author of *The Ravages* had railed against. Times had certainly changed.

Or had they? Dulcie shook her head. That idea had seemed to pop up from nowhere. Now that it was in her mind, however, she found herself considering it. Up till now, she had taken her author's rants at face value. Marriage in the late seventeenth and early eighteenth century was not an equal pairing between peers. She knew that, just as she knew that with marriage, women had surrendered any rights to property or legal counsel. If a woman fled a loveless – or even an abusive – marriage, she lost everything. Even her children. That, Dulcie mused, would probably be very hard. Her own father had taken off years before, and Dulcie sometimes felt that Lucy relied too much on her only child. Without her, Dulcie thought, Lucy might have really gone off the rails. Not that the difference would be that apparent, she admitted, with a twinge of guilt.

So, yes, the institution was a horrid thing: unfair and often cruel. And this author, Dulcie's heroine, was right in speaking out against it. Still, she had to wonder, where did this passion come from? Had the author of *The Ravages* been subject to an abusive mate? An unfair husband who had tried to control her – or her writing?

Is that why she had left London two hundred years before, only to surface in the fledgling United States?

Dulcie rubbed her eyes again. She was letting her imagination get away from her, and imagination, as Thorpe would be quick to remind her, was the enemy of the serious scholar. Still, it might explain the fervor of the scene that Dulcie knew was yet to come. A nobleman, handsome and yet cruel, lying dead. Could he have been based on a real, on an actual . . .?

No, she was getting ahead of herself. Another sign that it was time for lunch. But before she took her break, she would finish just this one fragment. A few lines more.

'*Shackled by custom and by law. Such Bondage would anathema be to one such as you.' The Voice, soft yet stern, reached through the howling of the winds, much as the glowing Eyes belied the very darkness of the Storm.*'

Wait. Dulcie looked around. She needed to go back and check her laptop, but Griddlehaus was nowhere to be seen. Surely, this bit of text followed on her dream, not on what she had deciphered only a few days before. The whole idea that the passenger – her heroine – was actually talking to the stranger was something she hadn't read before. Only in her dream had she heard him, the green-eyed shadow. And in her dream, she had thought . . .

She must be misremembering. She must have glimpsed the beginning of this conversation among the pages, and in her sherry-addled sleep, she'd fleshed out that first hint, creating the opening of a dialogue. If she happened to imbue the mysterious stranger with certain characteristics, well, there was precedent for that, too. There were those green eyes, for instance. And the fact that he had appeared out of nowhere to help the heroine out of a jam. And the voice . . . no, 'soft yet stern' was actually written here. Maybe she had glanced at that, too. And considering what else was going on, it only made sense that Dulcie had interpolated her own wishes on it. After all, she always identified with this author's heroines. That didn't mean . . .

She shook her head to clear it. She'd get through this one passage, then go out for lunch. Maybe even take a walk. And as the thought of one of Lala's three-bean burgers, the orange-red hot sauce dripping out the side, set her stomach to rumbling, Dulcie took a deep breath and refocused on the battered page.

She turned from Him then, unwilling to face those Eyes, so clear and green. So deep was her Regret, she could not bear to sace – sace? No, face! – face the Stranger who spoke so true. Drawing back the curtain, she peered into the Night. Darkness, only darkness, and more darkness, cut only by the demonic Howls of those pursuing.

'Fear not.' The voice, as soft as velvet, countered e'en those fiendish Howls, as one hand, glov'd in finest grey Morocco reached for hers. 'There is no Shame in what you desire, only Glory and Danger of a most Mortal kind.'

M. le Grife – Ah, the stranger had a name! Dulcie turned back her notes to see if there had been a prior reference, without success. If he had introduced himself, it was on a page she had not yet found. *M. le Grife, most Welcome are your Courtesies, and deep indeed has been your every Kindness to this lost Soul, but do not Think that though I slee* – slee? Sleep? Dulcie blinked and looked again. The passage broke off here, the page torn.

Dulcie sat back and pressed her fingertips to her eyelids. She was tired. She was hungry. This really was time to stop. She looked up: Griddlehaus was visible behind the front desk. She should call him over to replace this precious fragment. That was the tail end of their ritual, speaking of tails; the signal that her work was done for the day.

'*Slee.*' If only she could just finish this fragment – and it hit her: Not '*slee, flee!*' She'd been having trouble with those miserable letters all day. '*But do not Think though I flee . . .*' Yes, that made sense.

Dulcie moved to close her notebook, Mr Griddlehaus's name on her lips, when another thought caught her. She'd been mixing up 'f' and 's' throughout the day. What if . . . no . . .

She looked at the top of her page. M le Grife – that was the name of the stranger with the green eyes. He was a Frenchman – M had to be for 'Monsieur.' But what if she'd done it again,

with this stranger. The one with the green eyes who appeared out
of the darkness to help a lost and embattled female. She squinted,
made the substitution: Not *M. le Grife*, but *M. le Grise*. Monsieur
le Grise – or, to an American, Mister Grey.

NINETEEN

'This is getting confusing.' Dulcie addressed the squirrel. She
had emerged from the Mildon only minutes before, hurrying
out before Thomas Griddlehaus could ask her about the
day's finds. She'd been headed toward Lala's when the reality of
what she'd just uncovered stopped her in her tracks. Halfway across
the Yard, she found herself staring at the little grey rodent and
wondering just what was going on.

'I mean, is the stranger Mr Grey? Are you?' The squirrel, who
had been interrupted burying an acorn, didn't answer. Not that Dulcie
would necessarily have trusted anything he said anyway. 'Is this his
tale – or tail – or mine? Am I dreaming about what I've seen in the
Mildon, or are pages appearing that mirror my dreams?

'Am I completely losing it?' Dulcie raised her arms and then
dropped them, and that probably more than the futility of her questions was what caused the little creature to scurry up the nearest
oak. Still, the rapid retreat of the squirrel didn't make Dulcie feel
any better. Or less hungry.

'Maybe,' she addressed herself as much as any unseen spirits,
'I'm hallucinating. Severe hunger, combined with delayed alcohol
poisoning from cheap sherry.'

Lala's was the answer, though for once Dulcie was grateful that
the authoritarian proprietor was absent. As much as she appreciated
Lala's efforts – slipping her into a seat ahead of the line or coming
up with just the right dish to salve her mood – Dulcie couldn't deal
with any interaction right now. A burger, the noise of congenial
strangers . . . No, not even strangers. Just a burger and she'd tune
everything out.

Luckily, by the time she walked in the café's door it was past
two. The lunch crowd had dispersed, and Dulcie treated herself to
a table rather than a counter seat. A small table, way in the back,

promised the privacy she craved, and when she gave her order to one of the newer, unfamiliar waitrons, she felt like maybe she'd be getting the peaceful break she needed.

When her burger arrived, practically steaming, she was sure of it. Squeezing the squirt bottle of sauce on top of the patty was about all she was up for. Lifting the burger, she closed her eyes, the better to savor that hot-sweet first bite.

'Dulcie?' The burger was calling her name. 'Dulcie Schwartz?'

No, the burger did not have to sound so uncertain, of that she was sure. Chewing, Dulcie opened her eyes to see Josh Blakely standing uncertainly behind the empty chair. Only the fact that her mouth was full kept her from crying out in alarm. As it was, she nearly choked. But as she managed to both chew again and breathe, she reminded herself that she was in a crowded restaurant. In the back, certainly, but in full view of a dozen other late lunchers. She'd heard Rogovoy's suspicions; she knew what Josh may have done. But whatever this man's game was, she should be safe – at least long enough to finish her burger.

'It's me, Josh,' he said, misreading her hesitation. She nodded nervously, acknowledging that it was in fact him. Unfortunately, he took this as permission of some sort and pulled out the chair. She swallowed, about to tell him that she was off duty. Not really here. Just about to leave when he sat down and leaned toward her.

'I'm really glad to have found you, Ms Schwartz.' His voice was soft and possibly, she thought, scared. 'I really need to talk to you.'

'Sure,' she said. She could hear her voice tremble and tried to cover. 'What's up?'

She took another bite, while he fidgeted, and thought about what she had learned. He didn't *look* like a villain. He was too large, for starters, and those pink cheeks. That was silly, though. Bad guys came in all shapes and sizes. Hadn't she just been wondering about the role of the handsome young lord? He probably didn't look evil either. Then again, had the lord been bad? Wasn't it just as likely that the stranger was somehow involved? Just because he had green eyes and a vaguely familiar name . . .

'. . . notes about the family.' Dulcie realized that Josh had been speaking. Softly and more toward the paper napkin he was currently shredding than to her. Still, it behooved her to catch up.

'I'm sorry.' She reached for her own napkin. That hot sauce really did get everywhere. 'I'm afraid I was distracted. You were talking about some notes?' As she wiped her mouth, Dulcie tried to remember if she had Josh in any of her sections. That would be the simplest explanation, and the easiest to deal with. If, in addition to being Mina Love's boyfriend, he were also another student looking to make an excuse about why he wasn't going to make a deadline, she'd be overjoyed. Unfortunately, she was pretty sure she had never seen him before yesterday. His problem, he confirmed, was of a touchier nature.

'Not my notes,' he told the napkin. 'I mean, I shouldn't even be asking for them. But, well, they're important.'

'Whose notes are they, Josh?' She just couldn't be afraid of this man. He couldn't even look her in the eye. 'What are you talking about?' She left the question open and took another bite.

'They're Mina's.' The name came out so soft that at first Dulcie didn't hear it. 'Mina's,' he repeated before she could ask. 'Mina was working on something – on the history of someone, well, of a woman, and the notes are important. At least, I think they are. I mean, she said they could be a vital part of her research.'

The chart. Suddenly the burger turned to dust in Dulcie's mouth, and she reached for her water glass to choke down the bite. She'd seen the branch that represented Josh's family. She'd seen the angry scribbles that obscured it, the pencil dropped – or thrown to the floor in anger. That was damning evidence, and he wanted it.

'Her research?' Now she was the one barely making a sound. She couldn't help it, though. She had no breath left, and as soon as the words were out she wished she could swallow them back.

He nodded, and Dulcie managed to swallow, her mouth now as dry as that burger. He was still staring at the napkin, and so she turned to it as well. In light of what he'd just admitted, it took on a different meaning. Not the nervous fiddling of a worried suitor, but an act of destruction. He had literally taken the napkin apart. Destroyed it with those admittedly pale and soft-looking but still quite large hands.

So much for judging by appearances.

'I know about the research, about the family.' Dulcie was whispering. She didn't know why – nor did she know why she had just admitted to what could be dangerous knowledge. 'I mean, I saw it.

Just this morning,' she tried to cover. 'I went over to see Emily, because . . .'

She stopped herself. Of course Josh would know that Emily had been attacked.

'She's upset, isn't she?' He looked up at her, his eyes big and blue. Seemingly guileless.

'Well, yes, and she . . .' Dulcie stopped. Emily hadn't wanted to report the attack last night, and this could be why. She might be afraid of Josh. Dulcie couldn't let on. 'She's upset over all that happened, and she was supposed to lead a section for me.'

Josh nodded, and Dulcie found herself exhaling some of her tension. 'She's very attached to Mina, I know. I think that's why she took it so badly. Why she was so shocked . . .' Now it was his turn to let a sentence trail off, only Dulcie wasn't going to let him get off so easily.

'So shocked at what, Josh?' She leaned over her plate, her cooling burger forgotten. 'Shocked that you . . .' It was the hot sauce. It had to be. Just as Dulcie was about to drop the bomb, she hiccuped. ''Scuse me!' The apology was automatic, but it gave Dulcie a moment to think. If Emily didn't want Josh Blakely to know that she knew who had jumped her, she certainly wouldn't want him to know that she'd revealed his strange fixation with his girlfriend's genealogy.

'That you are so upset about Mina.' It was a lame save, but it was the best she could do. In the meantime, she dabbed at her mouth with her own napkin, hoping that would camouflage any obvious embarrassment.

To add to her confusion, he nodded again, and when he looked up, he had tears in his eyes. 'I just hope I'm wrong about it all. It's just so terrible.'

Dulcie nodded. It was terrible. Terrible that a young man could get so obsessed about his girlfriend that he would hurt her rather than lose her. Terrible that he would take some connection between their ancestors so seriously. Unless, it occurred to her, the distant connection had just been an excuse. Maybe Mina had wanted to break off from this chubby, awkward man. Maybe she wanted to accept someone else's attention. Emily had said that Josh was very attached to Mina – not vice versa.

'Were you trying to get the chart from Emily?' Dulcie kept her voice soft. She didn't want to give anything away, but she did want to get at the truth. 'Is that what happened last night?'

'What?' He shook his head. 'Last night? No. We spoke, remember? I taped Lukos's talk. There's another one tonight, right?'

She nodded, remembering what Josh had said. How Josh had assumed his girlfriend wasn't attracted to the dashing professor. 'Does Mina hate Renée Showalter, too?'

He shook his head. 'No, all that connectedness stuff? She loves it. She says she really likes to see the author as a person. I guess that's not considered a good thing in the English department any more. That's one of the reasons why she . . . Why she . . .' He buried his face in his hands.

Dulcie had to resist the urge to comfort him. Instead, she waited.

Finally, Josh looked up. 'It's been so hard,' he said. 'They aren't allowing visitors. She's still unconscious, and they say they don't know if . . . When . . .' He reached for another napkin and blew his nose. 'But I know Mina. She's tough. She's from hardy stock.' He smiled, as if at a private joke, and Dulcie found herself shrinking back. Everything he said: about fury, about toughness, it all could be interpreted against him. And she'd been about to pet this monster's hand.

She needed him to say more. To dig himself in deeper. 'Anyway,' he was still talking. 'I wanted to ask if maybe you could help me get those notes. I know Mina would want them to be safe.'

Dulcie was confused. If this was a scheme to enlist her help in destroying the family tree, it was pretty elaborate.

Josh kept talking. 'I don't know the details, but there's something important she's found. A letter or something – she called it a primary source – about a woman, about her family history. She wanted to get some advice about it. Not from Lukos; you know what she thought of him. But she thought if this other professor, the one speaking tonight, gets the position, she might be more open to helping her with it. Maybe she'd even switch back to English.'

'Hold on.' He was getting off track, and Dulcie needed to rein him in. 'She found out something about *her* family history?' She paused, letting him reconsider his own words. 'Or yours?'

Josh shook his head in apparent confusion. 'I'm not explaining it well,' he said. 'It has something to do with blood.'

'And Emily?' Dulcie tried to quell the shiver that word – 'blood' – sent through her. She had to be strong about this, if she was going to get him to say something – anything – that was real.

'Oh, Emily doesn't understand any of it.' Josh was shaking his head. 'She just doesn't get why Mina cares, so I'm hoping to keep this quiet.'

'Keep *it* quiet?' She was close to a confession; she could sense it. But even as she phrased the words, she heard a familiar ring. Her phone. And even as she dug into her bag to turn it off, she caught the looks from her fellow diners. 'Hang on,' she opened her bag, hoping to find the offending instrument. When she did, the number of the incoming call reminded her of what she had promised.

It was time for some fast thinking.

'Detective Rogovoy!' She looked at Josh as she spoke.

'No, Dulcie. This is Chris.' Her boyfriend, on the other end, sounded mildly confused.

'Detective Rogovoy, how good of you to call.' She'd explain later. 'I'm having the most interesting conversation with Josh Blakely at Lala's Café in the Square, but I was thinking of calling you.'

Just as she suspected, Josh froze, his pink cheeks turning white as he shook his head. 'No,' his lips formed the word, silently.

'Dulcie . . .' Chris was talking, but Dulcie had more of her charade to play.

'You'll be right down, Detective?' She wasn't letting the young man out of her sight. 'Is that what you said?'

'Dulcie!' A little louder this time.

Josh, meanwhile, had gone silent, though she could see him shaking his head and repeating the word: 'No.' As she watched, he raised his hands and stood up. She stood too. 'Not yet,' he said, and started backing away. She stepped around the table, still holding the phone. For a big man, Josh was moving quickly through the crowded room.

'Miss? Oh, Miss?' She turned. The waitron was standing over her table, a peevish look on his face. 'Did we forget something?' He was waving her bill, and she reached back into her bag for her wallet.

'Dulcie Schwartz!' The voice in her ear startled her as she threw a five on the table. Chris sounded angry. 'Didn't you promise me you weren't going to mess with this? Isn't that what you promised me just last night?'

'Yes, but . . .' She looked up. Everyone in the café was staring at her. And Josh Blakely was gone.

TWENTY

'Chris, it's not what you think.' Taking her phone out to the sidewalk, Dulcie tried to placate her boyfriend. 'I've been trying to disengage. You see, I had just spoken to Emily.' She heard him start to interrupt and cut him off. 'She's my student, Chris, and I just dropped by to make sure she was okay.'

'Just dropped by?' Chris knew her too well. 'And, what, you couldn't talk her into going to the cops?'

'Well, no. And she really should have.' Dulcie gave up any pretense. 'But I left it at that. Honest, Chris.' The silence on the other end of the line reminded her that he didn't know everything. 'She did say something that made me wonder about her room-mate's boyfriend, though. And then I ran into him – I was at Lala's and he walked in. He sat down at my table, Chris. So I pretended you were the police. And it worked – he took off.'

'Was he threatening you? Dulcie, this is why I didn't want you to get involved.'

'He wasn't threatening me, per se.' Dulcie thought back over the brief, strange interaction. 'He just wanted me to help him with something. I think he wanted me to get something for him out of Emily and Mina's suite.'

'Dulcie, I don't like this.' In the background, Dulcie could hear an aggrieved 'mew'. Maybe Esmé was chiming in. More likely, Chris had been distracted from filling her food dish.

'I don't either, Chris. I said I wouldn't do it.' Pedestrians were weaving around her. 'And he started to get weird. That's why I pretended you were Detective Rogovoy.'

That's when Chris surprised her. 'Maybe you should really call him,' he said. 'I mean, if this guy is dangerous and he thinks you're talking to the cops, well, Dulcie, I didn't want you to get in deeper. But maybe you already are.'

'I don't know.' Dulcie heard what Chris was saying with a sinking feeling. She didn't want this to be happening. Now that their brief, strange conversation was behind her, she found she still couldn't see Josh as a violent man.

'Dulce, don't tell me it's because you're still thinking . . . you know.' The sidewalk was getting loud, and Chris's voice trailed off.

'What?' Dulcie put her hand up to cover her other ear. 'Did I miss something?'

'You know, your other theory? About Thorpe being some kind of, I don't know . . .'

'A werewolf, Chris?' A woman stopped at that, which caused the bearded man behind her to plow into her. Dulcie turned to face the wall. 'Weren't you trying to convince me there were no werewolves?' If there were other pedestrian pile-ups behind her, Dulcie didn't want to see them.

'Yes . . .' Chris sounded tentative. 'I didn't know if it had worked, though.'

'Well, something was odd.' Dulcie thought of the howls she had heard – and of Thorpe's disheveled appearance. 'But the attacks happened over the last two nights, and neither of those were the full moon.'

They also weren't fatal attacks. The voice, so soft and yet so close, caused Dulcie to spin around.

'. . . thinking rationally.' Chris had started to respond.

'What? I'm sorry.' Dulcie turned back toward the shelter of the wall. 'It's noisy out here.'

'I just said, I'm glad that you're using your brain, Dulcie. That you're not letting Lucy get to you.' Chris paused, and Dulcie knew she was supposed to respond. 'Dulcie, you're not are you?'

'What? No.' Not Lucy, but that voice . . .

'So, maybe you should go talk to Rogovoy? Since you're involved anyway.'

Unless Josh really was innocent, and someone – or something – else was responsible for the attacks. 'I don't know, Chris.' Dulcie couldn't tell him what she was thinking. Not yet. 'Maybe you were right the first time. I should just let it be.'

He didn't sound happy, but he had let her go, and Dulcie found herself wandering back toward her office, mulling over what she'd learned. Emily had been shaken up. Scared. That was true. But because of that, she might not be the best judge of character right now. And no matter how you sliced it, genealogy wasn't a likely motive for attempted murder. Was it?

Halfway through the Yard, Dulcie stopped. She'd intended to get back to work. She hadn't yet entered the strange fragment from this morning's research into her computer, and tonight she'd be going to hear the second Newman lecture. But maybe, just maybe, this time, work could wait. In truth, she knew little about the initial attack, and none of it first hand. She'd gone to visit Emily this morning. Was there any reason she shouldn't try to see Mina? Josh hadn't been able to see her, but that didn't mean the same prohibition would still apply – or, at any rate, apply to a non-suspect like Dulcie. Maybe the girl would be talking by now, and all of this would be cleared up. At the very least, maybe Dulcie could get some answers. Then she'd be able to concentrate on her own mystery: the puzzle of that tantalizing manuscript.

'I'm sorry.' The orderly on duty didn't look apologetic. 'What did you say your name was?'

Dulcie had made it up to the fifth floor of the university health services. It didn't look like she was going to get any further.

'Dulcie. Dulcie Schwartz.' She repeated for the third time. 'I'm Mina Love's section leader and . . . a friend.' If the girl were healthy enough to rebut this, then Dulcie would gladly retreat. 'I was hoping to visit her.'

The orderly looked at his clipboard. 'You're not on the approved list.'

'There's a list?' Dulcie tried to peek, but the blue-clad man held the clipboard to his chest.

'Family and approved visitors only.' He glared at her. 'By order of the university police.'

'Oh, of course.' Dulcie hadn't thought of that. Whoever had attacked Mina once might be looking to finish the job, and if no one person had been officially charged then the police would have to keep everyone away. 'But maybe you can tell me how she is? I mean, how she's doing?' She put on her best winsome smile.

Another scowl told her it wasn't working. 'I'll have to check.' He backed away. 'I'm not sure if we're releasing status updates.'

With that, he walked away, leaving Dulcie to wonder if she should even wait. Within a minute, however, he was back, accompanied by a grey-haired woman in a white coat whose mouth fell open the moment she saw Dulcie.

'Excuse me, are you—?' Whatever the woman was about to ask Dulcie was interrupted by the orderly, who grabbed her arm and whispered in her ear. 'I'm sorry,' she said after he was done. 'I didn't know you weren't family. I'm afraid we're keeping aspects of this case confidential.' Her smile softened the words, but Dulcie still felt frustrated.

'Can you tell me how she's doing?' She bit her lip, unsure of how to ask. 'If she's going to . . . you know . . .'

'We're doing everything we can for her.' Another smile, this one a little sad. 'And she's a strong young woman. I'm afraid at this point, we all have to wait.'

Dulcie nodded. 'Thanks.' She turned to go when the doctor called to her.

'Wait.' Dulcie turned back. 'You're a friend?' she asked.

'Well, she's one of my students.' Something about the doctor compelled honesty.

The doctor nodded, as if confirming something to herself. 'May I give you a bit of advice?' Her voice was warm and soft, and Dulcie nodded. 'Please take care of yourself. Someone hurt this young woman, very badly, and he – or she – is still out there. If he sees you, well . . . he might get the wrong idea and come after you, too.'

TWENTY-ONE

Great. Just great. Dulcie was trembling a bit as she headed back toward the Square, despite her efforts to dismiss this latest pronouncement. It wasn't like the doctor had said anything new; Rogovoy had already told her that she looked like Mina Love. But to hear it from another person, a stranger, made it more real. Of course, she had had the resemblance confirmed by Josh – the way he had done a double take when he'd first seen her . . .

She stopped in her tracks. Could that be why Josh had approached her at Lala's? Was he following her? Obsessing about her, in Mina's absence?

Dulcie started walking again, a little faster. If he was fixated on her, he'd done a good job of hiding it. The young man who had sat at her lunch table had seemed utterly focused on his girlfriend. Then again, if Josh had attacked Mina, and if Emily's chart was why, then he might do anything to get his hands on it. But why approach her? Did Josh know that she had just visited Emily? Maybe he'd been watching the room-mate's entrance. Maybe it hadn't been a coincidence that he'd wandered into Lala's right after she did. He'd said that he'd been glad he found her; he didn't say whether or not he'd been stalking her.

Suddenly, the idea of descending into her lonely basement office lost its appeal. There was a security gate in place, but anybody with a valid student ID could get in. And if Lloyd weren't there, she'd be alone.

Maybe this would be a good time to make use of her privileges at the departmental office. She could undoubtedly find a corner to work in. At the very least, Nancy would be there, and her presence was always comforting.

But the departmental secretary wasn't her usual self when Dulcie greeted her. Instead of calmly making one of the endless pots of coffee that the grad students relied upon her for – or even sitting tranquil and a little resigned behind her desk behind reams of paper – the stout secretary was hurrying to and fro, moving chairs and looking rather as if she had lost something important.

'Nancy, what's up?' Dulcie dropped her bag by the stairwell and rushed over to the older woman. 'May I help?'

'What?' Nancy looked at her over her half-glasses. 'That chair, dear. Do you think it needs a pillow?'

'The chair?' The furnishings of the small student lounge were of an age that made Dulcie wonder if they had ever been comfortable. They were, however, the same as they'd always been. 'Why? Do we have new pillows?'

'No, no.' Nancy looked despondent. 'No, we don't.'

'Nancy?' Dulcie stepped in front of her and took her hands. 'Why don't you have a seat?'

She led the secretary over to the threadbare couch and sat down next to her. 'What,' Dulcie asked, once it was apparent that no explanation would be volunteered, 'is bothering you?'

'I don't like to say.' Nancy's voice had dropped to a whisper.

Dulcie took her hands again. 'Nancy?'

'It's Mr Thorpe,' she said, finally, in a near whisper. 'He's very upset.'

'With you?' Dulcie started to rise. Thorpe might yell at her. After all, he was her adviser. But Nancy Shelby was not only the highly efficient hub of the department, she served as its den mother as well – supplying endless caffeine and sympathy. 'Thorpe has no right . . .'

'No, no, please. Sit down.' Only Nancy's agitation caused Dulcie to settle back onto the sofa. Her face, however, must have revealed her intent. 'It's not his fault. It's the whole situation.' She looked around as if the acting chief might have appeared in the last moment. 'The Newman lectures.' She was whispering now. 'I've been trying to set up, and yet not bother him. And the place is a mess. And he's been, well, agitated all day, and it's only getting worse.'

'He's here?' Dulcie started to rise again; only this time Nancy grabbed her arm and pulled her down.

'Don't go up there.' Her whisper had an urgency to it, and Dulcie thought she heard the edge of fear. 'He's gone wild, Dulcie. I swear; he was really quite brusque.'

'He has no right.' Dulcie repeated. She felt protective of Nancy. All the grad students did, but there was something else nibbling at her consciousness. Something Nancy had said. 'So, what? He's barricaded himself in his office?'

Nancy nodded, a little too eagerly, Dulcie thought. 'He said he is not to be disturbed, at any cost. And that he might be there all night.' She sighed, some of the tension coming off her. 'I guess he really doesn't want to hear about the lecture. But we've got the reception afterward, too, and I really don't know what to do.'

'Keep everyone downstairs, I guess.' What was it? 'Though I don't know how you'll do that. If tonight is anything like last night, you'll have your hands full.'

Nancy nodded. 'That's why I was trying to do what I could. To get everything ready. And then I thought, maybe he'd like a nice soothing cup of tea. You know, before everyone gets here. And that's when he, well, I wouldn't say he yelled. Mr Thorpe is much too much of a gentleman to do that. But, Dulcie,' she looked up, her eyes filled with tears. 'He was very short. I was only trying to be friendly, and he positively barked at me.'

Barked? Dulcie wondered. Or howled?

TWENTY-TWO

With Dulcie as a steadying presence, Nancy settled down a bit, at least enough to make coffee and go back to the exam-room scheduling she seemed to have started hours before. Dulcie found it difficult, at first, to follow suit – the idea of her adviser, agitated and possibly moonstruck one floor above her, making concentration elusive. But as Nancy's quiet bustling re-established an air of normalcy, before too long she was able to immerse herself, once again, in the text.

'*And do not Think that though I flee . . .*' She had copied the new segment into her laptop. It seemed to follow the earlier passage, with both the heroine and the mysterious M. le Gris in the carriage. The wolves were still howling outside, and the carriage hurtling along.

'*Those Night-time Terrors spring full-throated from the world both Seen and Unseen.*' Dulcie had copied that bit down a few days ago, and it seemed to belong here. With a little cut and paste, she fit the passage into place. '*What do you know of my Plight? What may a Stranger know of one who races forth?' Her breath, returning, gave her courage to speak up, despite the howling fierce of both Wind and Wolf. 'What would you know of a Woman in the Night, who needs must take shelter with a Stranger, as did I, neither knowing nor being Known beyond the kinship of the Dark?*'

It was strong stuff, but there was still something missing.

'Where do you introduce yourself, mysterious stranger?' Dulcie scrolled back over the old text, muttering to herself. Her comments didn't provoke any response from Nancy, but she didn't find what she was looking for, either. Instead, it was another voice that ultimately interrupted her search, causing her to look up with something almost like relief.

'There you are!' It was Lloyd, with a big grin on his face. 'I was hoping you'd come by the office, and when you didn't, I tried calling.'

'Sorry, I guess I turned my phone off.' Dulcie pulled it from her bag: three messages. Two from Suze. Damn. 'What's up?'

'My recognizance has paid off. Professor Showalter has checked into the Commodore also. She's going to be meeting with students at the bar.'

Dulcie looked down at her notes. She should keep working. But she was, she suspected, at a bit of a dead end until she could go back to the Mildon and locate that missing passage. Besides, the opportunity to chat with Renée Showalter, a scholar who actually focused on eighteenth- and early nineteenth-century fiction and who cared about authorship to an unfashionable degree was too tempting. She looked over at Nancy, who had regained some color in her round cheeks.

'Go on, Dulcie.' The older woman seemed to have recovered her composure as well. 'I'll be fine here. I just won't beard the lion in his den again.'

'Don't say "lion".' Lloyd was shaking his head. 'Too much like "cat".'

'Just as well, Nancy. It's probably better if you don't.' Dulcie forced a smile. She didn't like leaving Nancy alone. It wasn't a wild cat she was concerned about. However, she couldn't resist Lloyd's invitation. Renée Showalter was as close as Dulcie was likely to come to a role model: a specialist in her century, and a woman to boot. If she actually got the chairmanship, well, that could mean a world of difference for Dulcie.

'How's the kitten?' Dulcie asked as they hit the sidewalk. In response, Lloyd took out a handkerchief and blew his nose. 'Fine, I think.'

'That bad?' She waited while he dabbed at his eyes. 'But you've visited at our place.'

He shook his head. 'I've taken antihistamines every time I've come over.' He shoved the handkerchief in his pocket. 'I never wanted you to know. It seemed unfriendly somehow.'

'And that's not an option now?' Lloyd turned a sorrowful gaze on her, and even in the afternoon dusk she could see how red his eyes were. 'Sorry. But, please, can you hang on a little longer? I promise, I'll come up with another home for the kitten. It's just—'

His sneeze cut her off, and she let the thought lie. Someone must need a kitten. Someone besides Martin Thorpe.

'So, Dulcie.' Lloyd interrupted her thoughts. They were walking quickly, heading toward the Common. The Commodore was right across the public space, and Dulcie could see its canopied front entrance through the leafless trees. 'May I ask you something?'

There was an edge of anxiety in his voice that his earlier confession didn't explain. She turned toward him and nodded, and once they'd crossed the street, he continued. 'Do you think Showalter would be good for you?'

'For me?' Dulcie was a little startled by the question. 'Or the department?' Surely Lloyd wasn't questioning the ability of a woman to head their little fiefdom – or was it her area of expertise? Dulcie had thought Lloyd above that kind of prejudice, though the institutional bias against the Gothic novelists was widespread.

'For you.' Lloyd was watching her. 'I mean, she's pretty much an unreconstructed structuralist, if that's a term, and that's your thing. And she's eighteenth-century fiction, too, right? So if she's here, doesn't that mean the university wouldn't need another expert? I mean, unless she decided not to teach or something.'

'Oh.' Dulcie hadn't thought about that possibility. Then again, she rarely thought about life after her dissertation. It all seemed so impossibly far away at this point. 'I guess I was just thinking about how great it would be to have someone who shared my interest.'

'Poor Dulcie.' Lloyd smiled at her. 'You really are alone out there, aren't you?'

She shrugged. 'I'm kind of used to it.' It was true: she'd been one of very few children at the commune, and, among them, she'd been the only bookworm. With only Lucy and no brothers or sisters, she'd grown used to following her interests by herself. Even Chris, as dear as he was, only vaguely understood her area of expertise. He certainly had never read *The Ravages of Umbria*, or anything like it. Before she could explain, however, they crossed over from the Common, and Lloyd was pulling the door open.

'Hey, kids.' Trista was at the bar, holding what looked like a Martini. Beyond her, a small crowd had gathered, and as they approached, Dulcie looked to see if she could identify Professor Showalter.

'What are you having?' Trista seemed more interested in her cocktail than the candidate, leaning forward to get the barman's attention.

'PBR,' said Lloyd. 'Uh, if they have it. Otherwise, whatever's on draft.'

'Diet coke?' Dulcie thought she made out the professor, but with this crowd it was hard to tell. Sure, she recognized several of her colleagues, but it seemed the bar attracted an older clientele than the People's Republik, their usual hang. Several tweedy men held down one end of the bar, and three women, all with short hair and minimal make-up, sat at one of the few tables beyond its end. Between them and the bar, however, there was one woman – greying, reddish hair in a bun. Could that be Renée Showalter?

'Thanks.' Dulcie took the glass from Trista and nodded toward the end of the bar. 'Is that her?'

'What? Oh, Showalter?' Trista turned to stare. 'Yeah. She needs to color her hair, or something. Redheads going grey just look faded.'

'Huh.' Dulcie paused, thinking of her mother. Lucy used so much henna that her hair had taken on an odd purplish hue. Maybe she agreed with Trista. Maybe that was also why Dulcie's author had opted out of using red hair in this latest manuscript, not that her characters ever got past their prime.

'Dulcie?' She looked up. Trista seemed to be waiting for something. 'I asked if you want an introduction.'

'Oh, sorry. No, not yet.' Dulcie grabbed an empty bar stool and took a sip of her soda. It was funny. She'd been so involved with her latest find that she'd nearly forgotten the big question her initial discovery had raised.

In that first fragment, her heroine had been fighting with – and then possibly standing over the dead body of – a man. A man whose hair color had seemed to change in various versions from red to black and back again. At the time, it had infuriated her, not being able to figure out which version the author had intended. That was a problem with rough drafts, though. And over time, the hair question had been overwhelmed by others surrounding the young lord's role in the heroine's life – and her possible role in his death.

'Come on, Dulcie.' This time it was Lloyd who was talking. 'It won't be that bad.'

'What?' Clearly, Dulcie was missing something. Luckily, Lloyd was filling Trista in.

'I shouldn't have said anything.' He was talking softly and his nose was stuffy, but through some trick of the bar, Dulcie could hear him clearly. 'I pointed out that if Showalter gets the gig, she might take all the eighteenth-century fiction courses for herself. And, really, how many Goths does a department need?'

'A few anyway.' Dulcie broke in, forcing the happy tone into her voice. She really didn't need her friends' pity. Not yet anyway.

'So, I can introduce you?' Trista slid off her stool, leaving her empty glass on the bar.

'Uh, sure.' Maybe she needed to go back to that original fragment. Maybe she needed to focus on what that hair color meant. If only . . . Dulcie caught herself. This was nerves. What Lloyd had said in combination with her own hopes was making her anxious. She was being silly. And so she followed as Trista weaved her way through the bar crowd.

'*Dulcie* . . .' What was that? Dulcie turned, and Lloyd bumped into her. '*Listen to* . . .'

'Sorry.' Lloyd had been holding his beer, which now slopped onto the floor.

'Dulcie, are you okay?' Lloyd transferred his pint to his other hand and reached back to the bar for a napkin. All the while, he was watching Dulcie. 'You look, I don't know, distracted. Do you really not want to meet this woman?'

'No, I do.' Dulcie nodded to stress her point, and turned around. Trista was a few people ahead of them, now, and Dulcie made to follow her. It beat trying to explain.

'Professor Showalter.' Trista was talking to the red-haired woman. 'I'd like to introduce my friends,' she was saying. 'They're both doctoral candidates in the department, and Dulcie . . .'

Her way was blocked. A suit jacket, presumably occupied by one of those older regulars, had stepped in front of her. Only instead of tweed, this was grey flannel, probably a business suit. A little corporate, but soft, which Dulcie noticed because she had stepped right into it.

'*Pay attention, Dulcie.*' The suit knew her name?

'Oh, I'm sorry.' She stepped back and looked up – but the man was gone. When she turned back, Trista was gesturing to her. And the red-haired professor was looking up with a smile.

'Professor Showalter.' Dulcie squeezed between two more drinkers. 'Hi, I'm Dulcie Schwartz. I'm very interested in hearing you speak tonight.'

'Will you be dealing with Nathaniel Hawthorne?' To her right, Sean Cafferty butted in.

'He's a little late for me,' the professor responded. 'Though I am very interested in American Romanticism and its origins.'

'Like the Gothics?' Dulcie wasn't going to let her chance go.

'Why, yes.' She had the professor's attention again. 'Ms Dunlop here was just telling me that you are writing about the period.' The professor had the most piercing eyes. Not green, exactly, but greenish gold. 'You're focusing on one of the English novelists?'

'Yes, but actually, she—' Dulcie didn't get a chance to finish. Sean, tall and confident, was leaning in again as if he owned the professor.

'If you're looking for a research associate in the Romantics, I've been working on a paper.' Of course, count on Sean to position himself as a research associate. He wasn't the sort to be taken advantage of. 'I'm writing about the rise of Dark Romanticism for the *Literary Compendium . . .*'

Well, that was it. Sean could go on for hours, and soon it would be time for the professor to prepare for her talk. No wonder Mr Grey had warned her. If she'd been paying attention, maybe she wouldn't have missed her chance. But as Dulcie turned away, she felt a hand on her sleeve. The professor's – and Dulcie turned back, a little startled.

'I'm sorry,' she was saying to Sean. 'I need to ask your colleague about something.'

Sean looked stunned. Handsome and self-assured, he was used to being the center of attention. Certainly, he'd never lost out to Dulcie.

She didn't have long to savor her victory, however. Professor Showalter was looking at her again, and her gaze was intense. 'What were you saying, Ms Schwartz?'

'Oh,' Dulcie struggled to remember. That stranger, the soft grey cloth. What had the voice being telling her to do? 'Just that, yes, I am writing about an English novelist. But I think she emigrated. Are you familiar with *The Ravages of Umbria?*' It was an awkward question. One would assume that any properly credentialed academic – especially one being considered for the chairmanship of the department – would know the work. But Dulcie had learned by long experience that many otherwise quite well read scholars skimped on the Gothics. And *The Ravages* was hardly *The Castle of Otranto*.

'Of course.' Renée Showalter was nodding. 'The two surviving fragments are a testimony to the importance of the women authors of the era. In fact, there was something, if only I could remember. A paper looking at the political significance of the author's work. Wait – that was you. You've been tracking essays you think she wrote.'

'Yes, that was me. I, I mean.' Dulcie felt herself flushing with pride, as well as embarrassment over her awkward response. She was flustered: so few of her colleagues even cared about this anonymous author's best-known work. 'Those essays are why I think she may have emigrated.' Best to move on. 'There are some fascinating pieces that I believe I can connect to her. And that's not all. Just in the last few months, I've found some fragments . . .' She was about to explain, to tell this professor about the manuscript, but something about the situation – the intensity of the professor's gaze – stopped her. It was as if she was looking into Dulcie for some reason. Or looking *for* something . . .

What if Lloyd was right? What if this professor – this Renée Showalter – was looking not only to head the department, but also dominate its studies of eighteenth-century fiction? Should Dulcie share her discovery? That might be all she had when she left the university to seek her fortune. And until she published, the work was fair game. Dulcie didn't want to end up one of those graduate students who got credit only as a research assistant when a paper, or worse, a book, came out.

'Yes?' The professor was leaning in.

'Well, I'm hoping to maybe finally put a name to the author.' That was true, though it was also far more speculative than her other work. 'You know, if I can actually trace her work.'

'That's it.' Showalter snapped her fingers. Her hands, Dulcie saw, were large and strong, and she didn't wear any nail polish. 'I knew there was something. You've been looking for the lost Gothic Thomas Paine referred to, am I right? You found something in the rare book collection here?'

Dulcie nodded, a knot forming in her stomach. She had gotten ahead of herself, mentioning that first fragment in her paper. But it was too late now. The professor's hand was on her forearm now, as if the older woman could sense her desire to flee.

'We have to talk. I've read something – something that was given to me. And I was contacted recently by a student, an undergrad, who wanted information about a source she'd found while on an unrelated search. I'm not sure, but there are some extremely intriguing possibilities. Highly speculative, I assure you, but we should discuss them.' She glanced around, and Dulcie found herself following her gaze. To her left, Trista was saying something to Lloyd, and Lloyd was smiling at Dulcie, happy that he had facilitated the meeting. To her right, Sean Cafferty had a look on his face like a stymied puppy. Dulcie doubted that women ever cut him out of their conversations.

Not that he lacked persistence. Taking the professor's pause as an opportunity, he tried again. 'Professor Showalter, if you're interested in our rare book collection, I'd be happy to show you around. The Mildon Collection—'

She raised her hand, silencing him, all her attention back on Dulcie. 'In private. Are you free tomorrow morning?'

'I – I can be.' She had one section. That wasn't enough of an excuse. 'I have a section, but after eleven . . .'

'Good.' The professor sounded like she wouldn't take no for an answer anyway. 'Let's meet here at quarter after. Trust me.' She reached for her bag. 'This will be worth your while.'

With that, she turned to the assembled students. 'Time for me to get ready. Thank you all for this warm university welcome,' she said, and headed toward the elevator.

'Well, that was something,' said Lloyd as he and Trista flanked her to get the news.

'It was something all right.' Dulcie couldn't feel as sanguine. 'I wish I knew exactly what.' Ignoring Sean, who was openly glaring at her, she led her friends out of the bar. This time, she wasn't going to be stupid. 'House of Pizza?' She affected a lighter tone than she felt. 'I'd say we have time for a large with everything before Professor Showalter takes the podium.'

'Sean?' Lloyd was a peacemaker. It was one of his endearing traits. Their colleague, however, simply turned away.

'I guess not everyone likes pepperoni,' said Dulcie, trying not to sound too relieved.

TWENTY-THREE

Raleigh joined the friends at the House of Pizza, and Dulcie couldn't help but notice how apologetic the younger girl looked.

'How's the kitten?' Dulcie asked, as soon as Lloyd got up for more napkins. They were all on their second slices by this point, and slowing down enough to converse. 'Is he just adorable?'

'He's great. A little marmalade fluff ball. But Lloyd . . .' She shook her head and put down her crust. 'I finally had to put the kitten in the bathroom, just so he'd stop sneezing and be able to sleep. I made a vet appointment for him, but I really should have brought him to the shelter today.'

'No, please.' Dulcie countered her. 'Don't do that. I'll – I'll find a home for him.'

'Are you still against me giving him to Thorpe?' Raleigh leaned over the table to steal some of her boyfriend's soda. 'Because, if not . . .'

'No, Dulcie's right.' Trista broke in, to Dulcie's surprise. 'I mean, I don't agree with what you said, Dulcie, but there's something going on with him. Something a kitten can't cure.'

'A kitten cure?' Lloyd was sitting back down. As if on cue, he sneezed again and grabbed one of the new napkins.

'Never mind.' Dulcie wanted to change the subject. 'Here.' She slid the remaining slice onto Lloyd's plate before turning to his girlfriend. 'Just, please hang in there.'

'No problem,' said Raleigh. Lloyd blew his nose, but didn't disagree.

With some reluctance on Dulcie's part, the group decided to forego cannoli. It was getting close to seven, and if last night's lecture was any indication, the hall would be packed.

The four piled out of the pizza house into a true November night, very brisk but also very clear, and without any discussion, they started walking quickly. As they headed toward the lecture hall, Dulcie checked her messages. The ones from Suze were friendly, but distracted. '*Sorry we keep missing, Dulce,*' her friend had said in the second one. '*Life will get simpler after this stupid test.*' The tone was warm, but that just made it worse. The third call had been a blank – someone hanging up. Suze must have gotten frustrated, Dulcie decided, and turned her attention back to the friends by her side.

'Although, let's face it, Professor Showalter doesn't have the charisma that Lukos had,' Trista was saying.

'To men, she might,' chimed in Dulcie. When Lloyd didn't join in, she amended that. 'Or to eighteenth-century fiction specialists.'

None of her friends responded to that, and Dulcie shivered. Here in the Square, there were plenty of street lights to illuminate the night. It was the cold that was getting to her, she decided. Not the full moon, bright overhead. Still, she found herself wondering. 'Does anyone know if Lukos is going to be there?'

Trista turned toward her with a sly grin that reflected the night's blue-white glow. 'You felt it, too. Huh?'

'No,' Dulcie shook her head, unwilling to let Trista explain. Clearly, she had missed something while checking her voicemail. 'He's good looking, but there's something creepy about him. I just wanted a chance to talk to him.' She remembered the professor standing with Nancy. The way he'd hid his hand, as if he'd hurt it, perhaps in a struggle.

'He took off.' Trista had the word. 'I saw him get into a cab and heard him say Logan.'

Dulcie looked at her friend. She wasn't sure she wanted to know why Trista had been so close to the visiting professor. In this light, a combination of street lights and store windows, she looked foreign – different somehow. 'Are you sure he made it to the airport? I had some questions for him.'

'I didn't see him come back, if that's what you mean. If I had known you were looking out for him, too . . .' Trista's grin only grew.

'Not like that, Trista.' Dulcie's patience was wearing thin. 'But, don't you think it's odd that he arrived at the party so late? I mean, first he was seen with Mina. Then he's not where he's supposed to be – and Mina's room-mate gets attacked?'

'Does this mean you don't think it's Thorpe any more?' Raleigh looked hopeful. The kitten, of course.

'I don't know.' Dulcie shook her head. 'They're both acting

weird. But someone is attacking women – women who are in our department.'

'Well, I'm happy to escort any of you home tonight,' said Lloyd. 'Or anywhere after dark.' His voice was still somewhat nasal, but it was such a gallant offer that Raleigh grabbed him for a kiss.

'Thanks, Lloyd.' Dulcie smiled her thanks, as did Trista. Though Trista, Dulcie thought to herself, was probably more formidable in a fight than her office-mate. 'I will say,' she added, 'that this is one reason why I wouldn't mind a woman taking over.'

Raleigh turned toward her. 'More attention to women's safety?'

'More attention to women novelists,' Trista suggested. And before Lloyd could jump in, Dulcie added her own caveat.

'And, yes, I do know that if Showalter gets it, that probably fills the requirement for a specialist in the Gothic canon. And, yes, I'm fine with it.' She sensed her friends' surprise. 'I just think that maybe she would be a better choice for the university. Better for the department, anyway.'

'Showalter wouldn't necessarily edge you out. She really wanted to talk with you.' Lloyd noted. Dulcie didn't know how much he had heard. 'She seemed really interested in your work.' He looked up at Raleigh and Trista. 'Showalter had read Dulcie's paper.'

'That's great, Dulcie,' said Raleigh, and Trista chimed in. 'Cool!'

'I don't know.' Dulcie shrugged, pulling the collar of her big sweater closer. From what the visiting scholar had said, it sounded like maybe she had already uncovered the book Dulcie was seeking. Or worse – proof that her author hadn't written it. 'Maybe.'

'Dulcie's just gun shy,' Lloyd decided. 'She's had bad luck with advisers. Can you blame her if she just wants everyone to leave her alone?'

'Good luck with that. Oh, speak of the devil.' Trista had dropped her voice, but they all looked. About a block ahead of them stood Martin Thorpe. He was facing away from them, staring at the darkness between two buildings. Dulcie couldn't help but remember what had happened the night before. Was he hearing a cry – of a kitten or a wounded woman – in that alley? Or was he contemplating the darkness for another reason?

Dulcie's sweater, thick as it was, was no match for the November night. She was shivering, her teeth clenched to keep them from chattering. It wasn't just the cold, though. She knew that – and she knew what she had to do.

'Mr Thorpe,' she called, affecting a jollity she didn't feel. 'Over here!' She waved.

'Dulcie, what are you doing?' Trista reached for her arm and pulled it down. 'You *want* him to join us?'

'I want some answers.' Dulcie hissed through her teeth.

He didn't hear her. He couldn't have; he was still too far away. It didn't matter, though, what he heard or what Dulcie wanted. As the friends stood, rooted to the sidewalk, the acting head of the English and American Literature and Language department turned and stared. His remaining hair was wild, glowing like steel wool under the street lamp, and his eyes were shadowed. Dulcie knew he recognized them, though. She was positive she could see a spark in his hooded eyes. Her friends didn't seem so sure.

'Maybe he can't see us,' Raleigh suggested. 'We're kind of in shadow here.'

'Mr Thorpe!' Dulcie called again. 'It's me. I mean, it's I!'

It didn't matter. Even as they started walking again, he straightened up, pulled down the edges of his jacket as if to neaten it. And then he took off, in a long, loping run down the street and away from them.

TWENTY-FOUR

'That was weird.' Lloyd sniffed.

'He's a weird dude.' Trista just sounded peeved. 'But that was rude.'

'Come on, guys.' It was up to Raleigh to play the peacemaker. 'He's under enormous stress. And it's pretty obvious where we're going: to Emerson to hear Showalter. Maybe he was on his way there. Maybe he was hoping to sneak in, without anyone seeing him or something.'

'He could've said something.' Trista was not going to be mollified. 'He could have walked with us at least.'

Dulcie turned toward her friend. A moment ago, Trista hadn't wanted the attention of the balding scholar. Now that he had fled, however, she was looking after him. He'd run, Dulcie noticed, up toward the Common.

'Well, he's not heading toward Emerson any longer,' she noted, slowly. 'In fact, I think he was coming from there when we saw him.'

Her adviser had been standing when they saw him, but he'd been facing them – as if walking away from the Yard.

'Maybe his nerve failed him,' said Raleigh.

'Maybe the room was too full and everyone was too excited to hear Showalter.' Trista definitely had an axe to grind.

'Whatever, we should get moving.' Lloyd urged them forward, but Dulcie trailed behind. Thorpe had had a haunted look, and he'd definitely been coming from the Yard. Now he was heading toward the Common – and toward the Commodore.

'You don't think he'd wait for her, do you?' She caught up to Trista and whispered her question.

'Wait for whom? Showalter?' Dulcie nodded.

'You mean, at her hotel?' Trista had noticed the direction Thorpe had taken, too. Dulcie nodded again.

'What a creep.' Trista shuddered, and Dulcie didn't think it was from the cold.

'Maybe we should warn her,' Dulcie suggested.

'She wanted to talk with you anyway, so maybe you two could chat on the way to the lecture hall.' Lloyd had obviously heard the speculation. 'I mean, I don't think Thorpe would do anything, but, you know, you could say something.'

'Just tell her that he's been under tremendous stress,' suggested Raleigh. 'Surely, she'll understand that.'

With that, they turned the corner. The gate on this side was unguarded, and Dulcie looked around, suddenly aware of the openness and vulnerability of the campus.

'You okay?' Trista was looking at her funny.

'Yeah,' she nodded. 'I keep thinking of Emily and Mina.'

'They weren't in the Yard.' Trista threw an arm around her friend. 'There are people here, and you're with friends.'

'Yeah.' Dulcie shivered and crossed her arms. 'I'll be glad to get inside, though.'

'New England.' Trista smiled over at her as they made for the building. 'It always sneaks up on you, doesn't it?'

Suddenly aware of the time, the friends dashed up the steps. They needn't have worried. Although a respectable crowd had gathered in the first-floor lecture hall, they were able to find four seats together only halfway back.

'Well, I'm still glad we got here when we did,' said Lloyd.

'I'm glad the heat's working,' added Trista. 'Dulcie here is like ice.'

'I'm fine.' Dulcie forced a smile. 'I just have to get my parka out of storage.'

'I don't know, Dulcie.' Trista looked over at her. 'Your hands – if I didn't know better, I'd have said you were the SoCal girl, not me.'

Raleigh looked concerned. 'Should we share a cab home?'

'No, I'll be fine,' said Dulcie. 'Besides, we're going to the reception after, right?'

'Mos def,' said Trista. 'Nancy will expect us.'

Dulcie felt a stab of worry. She hadn't thought about the secretary in over an hour. They'd left her alone – with Thorpe. Was she okay? Should they go check on her now? Dulcie found herself fidgeting and forced herself to stop. After the lecture would be soon enough. If only it would start. If only Showalter didn't talk too long. She took off her sweater. Folded it. Then refolded it. Time seemed to slow down.

'I wonder what's holding things up?' It was Raleigh. So the delay wasn't just in Dulcie's mind. Nor was Raleigh the only one wondering. Dulcie looked around and saw that the rest of the hall – nearly full, finally – was fidgeting. The noise level was growing, too, as students started questioning with increasing impatience.

'Where is she?' Dulcie heard a woman ask. She craned her head around as other voices took up the query. 'Did they reschedule again?'

Suddenly, the room grew quiet, and Dulcie turned back around. A woman was walking to the podium. Nancy, Dulcie saw with a wave of relief. The departmental secretary was wearing the same plaid skirt she'd had on earlier, the same turtleneck sweater, but she looked beautiful just then. Dulcie could have run up and kissed her.

'Good evening,' she said, too quietly. Then, reaching for the microphone, she made some adjustments and her voice boomed out. 'Good evening – oh!' She stepped back a bit. 'Thank you all for coming tonight.'

Dulcie smiled. It was good that they were giving Nancy a little more responsibility. They should have let her practice, though, if they were going to have her announce Professor Showalter.

'I'm afraid I have an announcement,' Nancy was saying. A murmur rose from the crowd. 'It seems that tonight's lecture will not be happening as planned,' she said, and the murmur grew into a hum. Nancy waited until it died down a bit and then leaned into the mic. 'We hope to reschedule, of course. I mean, we *will* reschedule.' Nancy looked around. The room was now silent. 'But the second Newman lecture will not be happening tonight,' she said. 'I'm afraid Professor Showalter, tonight's honored guest, has gone missing.'

TWENTY-FIVE

The hall erupted, and Dulcie jumped out of her seat. Her first concern was for Nancy. The poor woman looked flustered, and Dulcie pushed her way to the front to be with her.

'Nancy!' Dulcie waved over a sea of students. 'This way!'

It took the secretary several minutes, as it seemed every student in the hall had a question or concern to share.

'My word.' She finally met Dulcie in the hall. By then, the attendees had begun to file out, although the noise level had hardly abated. 'I think, perhaps, I handled that badly.'

'What else could you have said?' Trista had made her way over, too.

'Maybe I should simply have announced that she had canceled or that there had been a technical difficulty.' The older woman was breathing heavily. Dulcie took her arm and led her to the back stairs, where she could sit. 'I'm afraid I panicked.'

'You did fine.' Dulcie sat beside her.

'Why was it up to you, anyway?' Trista asked. Dulcie looked up: it was a good question.

'Nobody else was there.' Nancy shrugged. 'The dean was only scheduled for last night, for the first lecture, and, well, I gather Mr Thorpe was supposed to make arrangements. The student from technical services came to ask where everyone was. He had the PA all set up and he wanted to do a sound check.'

'That's why Thorpe was running toward the street.' Dulcie was thinking out loud. 'He must have been searching for her – or going to meet her.'

'What? Mr Thorpe?' Nancy was looking at her funny. 'You saw him?'

'Well, yes.' A sliver of doubt began to creep up Dulcie's spine. 'We saw him out on the street. He was heading in the direction of her hotel. He looked a little frazzled.'

Nancy was shaking her head. 'I wish he'd said something. Left a note for me.' She paused, biting her lip. 'I hope he's not upset with me. As it was, I called the hotel, and they tried her room. I didn't know what else to do.'

They all turned to her.

'If he'd had word from Professor Showalter, I wish he'd have let me know,' Nancy continued. 'But he didn't. He took off almost immediately after you left, Dulcie. Thundered down the stairs like some kind of wild animal. I didn't dare ask him where he was going, he'd been in such a mood – and I haven't seen him since.'

For lack of anything better to do, the friends escorted Nancy back to the departmental headquarters. The door was locked when they got there – and the alarm had been set – but Dulcie didn't relax until she and Trista had checked the upper floors.

'No sign of him.' Dulcie announced, coming down the stairs. 'Or her, either.'

'I was wondering if I should contact someone in the administration,' Nancy had taken the reception cheese plate out of the office's small refrigerator, and Trista was digging in. 'But I didn't want to do anything – do the wrong thing – without Mr Thorpe's permission. Still, this is highly unusual. She could have met with an accident.'

'Or something,' Dulcie added. She picked up a square of Cheddar – and put it down again. Even Trista had stopped after two slices of Brie. They were all thinking the same thing. Two nights before, Mina Love had been stabbed. Last night, Emily Trainor had been attacked, and they hadn't reported it. Tonight, a visiting scholar was missing. As far as anyone knew, she might be lying in an alley hurt

– or worse. In some way, they might be to blame. 'We should call the police.'

Nancy looked like she was about to protest, and so Dulcie continued.

'She's not at her hotel. She's not here. You haven't heard anything.' She looked at her friends, unsure of whether to continue. 'And you heard that a young woman was attacked not far from here two nights ago?'

Nancy nodded once, a short, terse nod. 'You're right.' She got up and headed toward the phone.

'If you want, I could call.' Dulcie stood, too. 'I have the cell number of the detective on the case.'

'That would be great.' Nancy's relief showed in her face, and Dulcie pulled out her phone. As she looked up Rogovoy's cell, another thought hit her.

'Nancy, you didn't *hear* anything out there tonight,' she asked. 'Did you?'

Dulcie could feel her friends' eyes on her. Still, she had to know.

'Hear anything like what?' Nancy asked, eyes wide.

'Like, an animal?' Dulcie sensed Trista coming up behind her, about to cut her off. 'A dog?'

Nancy only shook her head. 'To be honest, I've been so distracted, I don't know if I would have.'

'Dulcie . . .' Trista was about to interrupt, when Dulcie found the number. She raised her hand for silence as the detective's cell rang.

'*You've reached Detective Milo Rogovoy . . .*' His first name was Milo? She turned away from her friends, preparing to leave a message.

'Detective Rogovoy, this is Dulcie. Dulcie Schwartz,' she started. Behind her, Lloyd yelled something. Then Raleigh was talking, too. Dulcie spoke louder. 'We have a situation at the English Department headquarters. It seems our visiting scholar, Renée Showalter, has gone missing—'

'No, she hasn't.' The voice behind her caused her to turn. 'I'm here. I made it.'

Dulcie turned to see the professor standing in the doorway. Her face was dirty, and her hair had come down from its neat bun. Raleigh was brushing leaves off the professor's jacket sleeve, and Lloyd was leading her in by her other hand.

'I'm afraid I messed up my hair though.' She put one hand up to smooth it, and stared with dismay when it came away bloody. 'Oh my. This is going to put a crimp in my lecture.'

TWENTY-SIX

Dulcie left another message for Rogovoy while Trista was calling 911, and Lloyd and Raleigh got the professor settled on the sofa.

Nancy, meanwhile, was fretting. 'I shouldn't have waited. She was out there. Hurt. Alone.' Dulcie longed to comfort her – and to question the professor. But even as she was talking to voice mail, they heard a car pull up and suddenly the large detective was filling the doorway. Within minutes, he had gotten the basics and was sitting down with the professor to take her statement.

'I don't know what happened,' she was telling Rogovoy. He had folded his ungainly body onto the sofa next to her and tried to banish the students and Nancy from the room. They had retreated as far as the open doorway, where they now stood, listening. 'That's what's so maddening,' Showalter was saying. 'The last thing I remember was crossing the Common. I know I shouldn't have – the concierge warned me. The moon was so bright, though. It was like daylight, and I thought it would be safe.'

Raleigh shook her head. They'd all been warned as undergraduates: the city Common, once used to graze cattle, was larger than it first appeared. And despite its pasture origin, it held enough trees and shrubbery to shield any number of evil-doers.

'So, you set off across the Common.' Rogovoy was writing on a pad, but Dulcie had the strong impression that he was also committing her words to memory. 'And this was around six thirty?'

'Maybe six forty.' The scholar couldn't stop reaching up to touch the top of her head. Nancy had wrapped some ice in a dish rag for her, and Showalter had immediately applied it to the spot where her bun had been. She'd taken it off a few moments before, though, and Dulcie could sense Nancy's impatience to intervene – to offer fresh ice or a larger pack.

'Six forty?' Rogovoy must have sensed something, too. He glanced up at the spectators in the doorway: a warning glance – be still. 'You had your bag.' He did glance at his notes then. 'A large leather briefcase on a shoulder strap. And you were heading to Emerson lecture hall?'

Showalter nodded and winced. Nancy started forward, and Rogovoy held up one ham-like hand, stopping her in her tracks. He did, however, pick up the discarded ice pack and offer it to the professor. She took it gratefully and held it to the back of her head.

'Yes, I was giving tonight's Newman.' She looked over at Nancy. 'I'm so sorry. It was very foolish of me. Careless. I hope the nominating committee won't hold it against me.'

'I'm sure they won't,' Nancy said, before Rogovoy's hand went up again.

'Let's proceed,' he said, his gruff voice as much a bark as a command. 'You were walking across the Common. It was bright out. Did you see anything?'

'That's what's so foolish.' She was shaking her head, slowly. 'I should have been more careful. I knew I was distracted. You see, I'd found something. Stumbled across it, really, which was occupying my mind. I needed to talk to someone – to talk to . . .' She stopped, tongue-tied. To Dulcie, it looked like she was in pain, her face white and her hand, where it pressed the ice pack to her hair, trembling. 'I had something in my bag. Not money – a document. A letter? No, it's hopeless. I feel like it's on the tip of my tongue, but I can't remember.'

'Let's go back to what you do remember.' Rogovoy was nothing if not thorough. 'You're walking through the Common. How far did you get? Did you see the big statue? Or were you under the trees?'

'Did you hear anything?' Dulcie couldn't resist. This woman had been hit – by someone or something – not bitten or stabbed. Still, she couldn't forget what she had heard, out on the street the night Mina Love had been attacked, or the series of warnings.

'Ms Schwartz, please.' It was a command, and Dulcie shut up. Still, Renée Showalter had heard her.

'I did.' She seemed to be working hard at something. Trying to remember. 'I did hear something – like a dog. Or, no, wilder. Louder. Like a wolf.' She looked up at the detective. 'That's not possible. Is it?'

'Coyotes have been spotted in some wooded areas.' The detective sounded very matter-of-fact. 'But there are no known cases of any animals attacking an adult in this city.' From his tone of voice, they wouldn't dare.

'No, I didn't think so.' The professor's face was screwed up, though with the pain or the effort to remember, Dulcie couldn't tell. 'I feel like it's important, what I was thinking about. It wasn't just the lecture.' She shot a glance at Nancy. 'Though of course I was thinking about that, too. Mentally going over my notes.'

'And then?' Rogovoy was trying to keep her on track.

She just shook her head again. 'Nothing,' she said, sadly. 'No, that's not entirely true. I heard something – I think I heard something – coming up behind me. But then he – it – it must have hit me. Hard. I went down, and all I remember is looking straight up. All I could see was the moon.'

TWENTY-SEVEN

'It was you, Dulcie.' Lloyd was talking, but Dulcie only half heard him. 'It was you whom Professor Showalter wanted to talk to. She had something she wanted to tell you about, she said. Maybe something that would help you with your thesis. Another part of that manuscript.'

Dulcie looked at him, mildly surprised. They had shared an office for nearly five years. Still, she often felt like she was working in a vacuum.

'Showalter had something for Dulcie?' Trista leaned in, and Lloyd filled her in on the conversation. Trista had been just a little too far away, Dulcie realized, to hear either the professor's words or the sense of urgency in her voice.

The friends were still sitting in the departmental headquarters. Rogovoy had finally gotten his statement and agreed to let the EMTs – who had shown up by then – take the visiting scholar to the infirmary. She had protested: 'It's just a bump. I knew there was a reason I had so much hair,' but Rogovoy had insisted. Dulcie had wanted to tag along, but he'd stopped her, literally blocking her way with an arm like a fallen tree.

'Let's let the good professor get checked out, shall we?' From his tone, Dulcie could tell he suspected that she knew more than she'd let on. She was spared from an interrogation, though, when another call came in. A uniform had found what might have been the professor's bag, and Rogovoy took off, leaving the students with a warning.

'You live in a city, kids. Not the Forest of Arden or something.' Dulcie couldn't suppress a smile at that. 'Please, be sensible. I'm busy enough as it is.'

'Exeunt, pursued by a bear.' Lloyd had muttered as he left. 'Okay, exit bear.'

Now the four of them sat in the student lounge, while Nancy made phone calls and generally fidgeted. The cheese plate was long gone. Dulcie wanted to take off, too – she had questions that none of her friends could answer. As she looked around at them, however, she realized that she was the center of attention.

'I don't know what she wanted to talk to me about,' she said. 'Honestly, I was actually a little worried. You know, she's in my field, I may have made a discovery . . .' She left it open. They knew the risks and the rewards of working with senior scholars.

'I think she had something she wanted to show you.' Lloyd was determined. 'Something about her voice. But, hey, she'll probably remember tomorrow, right? And if someone coshed her over her head for her bag, he probably wouldn't care about a bunch of papers, right?'

'If it was an ordinary mugging.' Nothing about this sat right for Dulcie.

'You're thinking it was the same guy.' Raleigh was watching her more closely than her boyfriend was. Dulcie nodded. 'But what's the connection? Mina, well, maybe it was her boyfriend – or someone who wanted to be. Emily was the room-mate. She knew something, or had seen something. Maybe he only wanted to scare her. But Professor Showalter?'

'If I knew that . . .' Dulcie could only shake her head. Before any of the friends could chime in again, they heard Nancy, softly clearing her throat.

'I've reached the dean,' she said. 'I've explained everything. He was very understanding, actually. Said I behaved admirably.' She smiled a little, the first time all evening Dulcie had seen her do so.

'He'll handle everything from here. And now, I think I'd like to lock up and go home. It's been a tiring evening.'

'Of course!' Lloyd was the first to jump up. 'Shall we walk you home?'

'You could walk me to the Harvard Square cab stand,' she said, her smile widening with gratitude. 'And thank you. I trust you will all take care getting home?'

'Definitely,' said Raleigh, giving Trista and Dulcie a pointed look.

'I'll walk her back home, and grab a cab,' said Trista. Dulcie doubted she would, but by the time they reached the apartment Dulcie shared with Chris, Trista would be almost to her place anyway.

The four gathered on the sidewalk as Nancy locked up and set the alarm.

'Well, that's that,' she said, coming down the steps. 'I daresay we'll be fielding calls all morning.'

'We?' Dulcie turned to the secretary, her words sparking a thought. 'I hope you'll have some help, Nancy. I hope . . .' She stopped, the reality of the situation coming home. 'Martin Thorpe never showed up. Were you able to reach him? Was the dean?'

Nancy only shook her head. 'I tried, several times. The dean tried, too.' They turned the corner, the lights of the Square bright ahead of them. That's when Dulcie noticed that the moon had reappeared, after a brief eclipse by a fleeting cloud. 'Nobody's seen or heard of him since dusk. No sign of hide nor hair.'

TWENTY-EIGHT

'*Look not to your accustomed Havens, your usual sources of Refuge and Succor. For they may betray you.' The Voice, though quiet, carried clear and stern despite the Howlings of the night. 'Be wary, for that which you carry endangers you greatly, and those who would be near to you, more greatly still. Such is the threat, lying as it does within the very Promise of your Burden.'*

'*My Burden? What do you know of my Burden?' She clasped the edge of the carriage's leather-cushioned seat, one hand reaching*

*blindly toward the rattling door. 'I would know, Sir, who you are
and how come you to be so most Familiar toward that which is
most private unto me?'*

*Those eyes, brilliant as Emeralds, bore deep within her and yet
with Warmth. Her hand came away from the door, and the Coach,
that vile conveyance, ceased for a moment its tumultuous sway.
Almost in that moment, she knew Peace, the Stranger's words
confirming in her what she must do. Dire deeds awaited along one
path. If she could flee, if this carriage could carry her beyond His
reach, she would be safe. She would be freed of the Burden. Those
nefarious Acts which she feared she must do, she most dreaded.
And yet . . .*

Dulcie woke with a start. It was happening again: she was seeing
herself in the dream. She was not only reading, she *was* the heroine,
the mysterious woman in flight. Well, she thought, reaching for the
sleeping cat, maybe that made sense. As Esmé murmured and shifted
to a more comfortable position, Dulcie thought it through: the reason
she loved this author – the reason she was able to devote so much of
herself to studying her writing – was that she related so strongly to
her. Unlike so many other novelists from the past, this writer's stories
had always felt contemporary to Dulcie. Never mind the language –
that was just the style of the times. The emotion, the motivations
underneath, had rung true through the centuries. As vital as a call from
the sister she never had.

Suze. She hadn't called her friend back, and she missed her now.
Well, this was a rough time for both of them. They were both so
busy. Actually, considering everything on her plate, the dream made
even more sense. Despite all that had happened yesterday, Dulcie's
mind was clearly still on her work, and the fragment she had just
deciphered had featured her heroine talking in a familiar way to her
strange fellow passenger. In some sleeping part of her mind, Dulcie
figured, she had simply carried the conversation one step further.
The stranger had picked her up for a reason and was helping her
figure a way out of a tough situation. Maybe he was trying to warn
her about something – or about someone.

Maybe, she admitted, he was trying to warn her about her own
future choices. As much as she might like to, Dulcie couldn't forget
that first fragment she had located, only a few months back. That
scene, which seemed to be from a later part of the book, had shown
her heroine standing over a dead body – the body of the man Dulcie

had identified as Esteban the Young Lord. Because of what had then occurred in Dulcie's own life, she had wondered about the heroine's role in that scene: had she uncovered a murder, or had she been culpable, in some way, herself? Dulcie didn't want to believe that this strong-willed heroine was capable of violence. That's what the stranger seemed to be suggesting, however: that at some point, in one of the book's upcoming scenes, the heroine might find herself forced to do something – those 'nefarious acts' – that would forever alter the course of her life.

Esmé squirmed, and Dulcie let her down. Caught up in her dream, she'd been holding the little cat too tightly, and as she watched her pet begin to groom, a sense of normalcy resumed. Yes, maybe her heroine would end up involved in the mysterious death of the young lord. This was a Gothic novel, and as much as Dulcie related to its heroine – and its anonymous author – she should understand the conventions. The horrible storm, the mysterious stranger, the handsome young lord – these were all standard features of the popular genre, although fancy theorists like Lukos would undoubtedly have some wordier explanation tying it in with the death rate of the era or the sublimated rage of the oppressed female. It had been a violent time, with wars and revolutions on both sides of the Atlantic. But to Dulcie – and, she was pretty sure, to her author's contemporaries – a murder, or some kind of demonic monster, was just a bit of spice added to the mix. If only Dulcie didn't relate so strongly to this book.

Maybe, she thought as she got out of bed, it was because she was uncovering this long-lost novel page by page. Paragraph by paragraph, sometimes. That could amplify the emotional impact. Now that she was awake, the apartment seemed peaceful. Chris was still at work, and Esmé had curled herself back up to resume her sleep. Dulcie would try to follow suit, as soon as she'd had a glass of water.

Maybe, she acknowledged as she let the tap run, she'd had the dream as a follow-up to that last phone call with Chris.

'I'm worried, Dulcie.' Her boyfriend had said. 'This just sounds bad. I don't think you should go out after dark alone any more. Not until this is resolved.'

'Chris.' Dulcie knew she was whining. She couldn't help it: he hadn't even let her finish. 'You're not listening. I'm telling you, this isn't some random maniac. I don't think it's a mugger either. I saw

Thorpe – all of us did – and he was definitely acting strange. And he never showed up. I mean, he is the acting head of the department.'

'And maybe he went home and unplugged his phone.' Chris wasn't buying it. 'Maybe he went out and got drunk. Who could blame him? Look, Dulcie, I know he's been hard on you. Okay, I know he's been a real jerk. But the way you're thinking doesn't make sense. It's like you're thinking: "Thorpe is a jerk. Women are getting hurt. Therefore, Thorpe is hurting women." In terms of logic strings, it just doesn't—'

'Chris!' Dulcie hated when he got all mathematical on her. 'I *am* being logical. I mean, I thought that maybe Professor Lukos was involved. He'd been hitting on Mina, after all. But Trista saw him leave.'

'Trista saw him get into a cab.' Chris was speaking slowly, as if she wouldn't understand otherwise. 'Excuse me, Trista *says* she saw him get into a cab. Do you see the possible loopholes, Dulcie?'

'Yes, Professor.' She couldn't help her tone. He had brought it on herself. But she had one more argument – one he couldn't simply bat away. 'You're forgetting one thing, though, Chris: Mr Grey. If I were really in danger . . . I mean, if someone was close to hurting me, don't you think I'd have gotten a warning? We both know that I'm not alone out there.'

'I don't know, Dulcie.' Chris didn't sound convinced, but Dulcie knew she'd won. He had no case against her spectral feline protector. 'But there's one more variable you're not taking into consideration.' Or did he? 'Maybe everything you've been hearing *is* a warning,' he said. 'The voices you hear, the dreams you've been having? After all, there's only so much that one ghost cat can do.'

There was no answer to that. Either one had faith, as Dulcie did, or one didn't, and she had ended the conversation with her boyfriend on an unsatisfactory note. The dream had come after, and Dulcie, awake in the pre-dawn, found herself wondering about its meaning. *'Be wary,'* the stranger had warned. Well, that was what Chris had been saying, more or less, so it was quite possible that she had simply let his message into her dream. Then again, he had also warned her about Trista. He couldn't really suspect Trista, could he? No, it was more likely that he was just pointing out the flaws in Dulcie's humanities-oriented logic. Still, his words had put the idea in her head, and standing in the cool half-dark of the kitchen, Dulcie couldn't quite rule them out. *'Your usual sources of Refuge and Succor,'* the stranger had also said. Granted, Dulcie had felt angry – and a little betrayed – by that last phone call with Chris. That could have sparked those dream warnings. Unless it was more. Dulcie stared out of the kitchen window, taking in the sleeping city and its wide-awake moon.

Maybe it was the light. Somehow, the moon managed to shine around the sides of the bedroom shade. Maybe it was Esmé. The little tuxedo had gotten up again at dawn, pawing at the window at the birdsong outside. More likely it was the cold pizza Dulcie had finished off before returning to bed. Whatever the cause, Dulcie's sleep had been fitful, and she'd woken early, still tired and alone.

It wasn't Chris's fault. She checked the clock; he'd be in the Science Center for another half hour. Still, after that last conversation, she had no desire to wait up for him. Instead, she fed Esmé, who seemed particularly affectionate this morning, and got dressed.

'Play!' As Dulcie reached for her sneakers, Esmé pounced, grabbing the loose end of the lace. *'Hunt!'*

'That's what I'm going to do, kitty.' Dulcie removed the lace, and then extricated her hand from the cat's playful grasp. 'Maybe that's what you're trying to tell me?'

'Play with me!' The cat pounced again, this time using her claws.

'Oh, no!' Dulcie drew back. 'This is not how you get someone to play with you.' Dulcie looked at her pet, the off-center white star on her nose making her look a little lopsided and confused. 'Even though you are adorable.'

She reached for her cat to give her one more quick pet, and Esmé reared up, wrapping her front paws around Dulcie's wrist and nipping at her hand. 'No, Esmé! No!' Dulcie pulled away, shaking her head. 'Chris has got to stop rough-housing with you,' she said, as she grabbed her sweater and headed for the door.

'But it's not Chris I worry about.' The little cat's voice was lost to Dulcie as she clambered down the steps. *'It's you.'*

TWENTY-NINE

C hris was wrong, and Dulcie knew it. Something very odd was going on, and Thorpe was at the heart of it. Still, Chris had a point that she should leave things to the police. Dulcie had already told all she knew to Detective Rogovoy. At least, all she could tell the big policeman without breaking a confidence or getting herself locked up in a psych ward. Better she should visit the University Health Services of her own volition, she thought as she walked into the Square. She had almost an hour before her first section, anyway. And while it was arguably too early to call the hotel to see if Professor Showalter had returned to her own room last night, it was not too early to pay a visit to the visiting scholar if she had been admitted. Besides, Dulcie was itching to know what the professor had been going to tell her. Surely, after a night's rest, the professor's memory would have returned.

Pushing open the big glass doors of the student infirmary, Dulcie was thinking of the visiting scholar. Perhaps she'd been too suspicious; this had been an odd week. If the professor really did have information – or even a lead on a juicy document – she'd take back everything she had said. In truth, it would be great to work with a senior scholar who actually valued the same books she did.

Distracted by such a tantalizing idea, Dulcie was taken up short to hear her name. She was even more surprised to turn and see Nancy, the departmental secretary, standing by the front desk.

'Nancy! Are you okay?' Dulcie rushed over. 'Were you hurt? I knew we shouldn't have left you. Even the cab stand isn't . . .'

'No, no, dear.' The stout woman took Dulcie's outstretched hands in her own. 'I'm fine. Honest. Though I'm glad to see you here.'

'Really?' Dulcie couldn't remember what she and her colleagues had talked about in front of Nancy. Someone must have said something about Professor Showalter's interest. 'Because, last night, the professor couldn't remember . . .'

Nancy was shaking her head. 'Oh, dear. You haven't heard.'

Dulcie gasped. Had the head injury been more severe than they had realized? 'She's not . . .'

Nancy smiled. 'No, Dulcie. She's fine. I believe they only kept her overnight for observation.'

Dulcie looked up, quizzical. 'And you're escorting her back to the hotel?'

'I'm here for Mr Thorpe, Dulcie.' Her voice was warm and concerned. 'This is why we couldn't locate him last night. I assumed you knew.'

'No, I . . .' Dulcie was calculating. If Thorpe had been here last night, he couldn't have been the attacker. If he had also been victimized, that threw all her theories out. Unless Trista had been wrong, and Lukos had doubled back, his eye on the competition . . .

'Ms Shelby?' A man in a white coat, surely too young to be a doctor, was standing behind the receptionist. 'We can take you in now.'

'Dulcie?' Nancy turned toward her, clearly inviting her along. 'Will you join me? I'm sure he would appreciate the company.'

'Sure.' Was Thorpe beaten? Bloody? Dulcie braced herself for the worst.

The aide – he couldn't be a doctor – ushered them off into a consulting room. 'Mr Thorpe has had a good night's sleep,' he was saying. 'He says he feels much better today. I know he appreciates you coming in, and he gave his permission for this visit. Please keep in mind, however, that the circumstances surrounding his admission are sensitive, and that he may not be ready to discuss them yet.'

'What happened?' As he led them out of the room, Dulcie mouthed her question to Nancy.

'Mr Thorpe . . . He, well, he has been under enormous stress.' Nancy whispered back. 'All I know for sure is that he came here. He told the doctor on call that he was afraid. Afraid of what he'd do, and—'

'Mr Thorpe is ready to receive you now.' An older white coat had stepped into the hall beside them, pushing some kind of large metal cart. Perhaps he was the aide? But as Dulcie's eye followed the older man, the younger ushered them inside the room. There, looking a little less sweaty and a lot less frenzied than the last time she had seen him, lay Martin Thorpe, her adviser and the acting head of the department, dolled up in a hospital johnny with a bowl of oatmeal before him.

'Good morning, Mr Thorpe.' Nancy slid right in to nursing mode.

Dulcie almost expected her to start spooning up Thorpe's cereal for him. 'I hope you're feeling better this morning.'

'I am. Thank you, Nancy.' His voice sounded less strained, Dulcie noted, though it did rise in surprise as he greeted you. 'And good morning, Ms Schwartz. I didn't know you had come along with Nancy.'

'Well, actually, I didn't.' Dulcie was thinking fast. Thorpe had not been attacked; he'd checked himself in. If he'd come in before moonrise, before Professor Showalter had been attacked, then it really might just have been stress. If, however, he'd come in later . . . She had to chance it. 'Nancy told me you were here and, of course, I wanted to visit.' She swallowed and took the leap. 'But I actually came by to visit Professor Showalter. You must have heard: she was attacked last night.'

'What? No.' The spoon clattered down on the tray, and Nancy turned toward Dulcie.

'I don't think we have to upset Mr Thorpe with all of that right now, Dulcie,' she was saying. 'After all, Professor Showalter will be perfectly all right—'

'Where did this happen?' Thorpe was gripping the bed rails. 'And . . . when?'

'Before she could give her lecture.' Dulcie ignored Nancy, focusing instead on her adviser. 'Not long after Trista, Lloyd, Raleigh, and I saw you out on DeWolfe Street.'

Thorpe lay there, his new-found color gone, his mouth slightly open. 'You saw me?'

'Right as the moon was rising.' Dulcie's voice was soft. Suddenly, she didn't want her suspicions to be true. It was too horrible. 'You must have been headed here, then. About, oh, six thirty?'

'What?' Thorpe was staring into space. 'No, not then. I, well, I wandered for a while, I'm afraid. I gather I was really not myself. I only came here when I realized that I wouldn't – that I couldn't sleep. It must have been late. Maybe near dawn.'

'Dulcie.' Nancy's voice had progressed from kindly to stern. 'That is enough now. Mr Thorpe has had an understandably trying experience. We are here to visit and to comfort him, and if you cannot let him recuperate, then you should leave.'

'Yes, yes.' Thorpe was reaching for something – a call button, Dulcie could now see. 'Maybe you should both go. I'm really not myself yet.'

'I'm so sorry, Mr Thorpe.' Nancy was up and nearly dragging Dulcie out of her seat. 'Please, don't worry about anything. You just get some rest now.'

Outside, she turned surprisingly fierce eyes on Dulcie. 'What was that about?'

'You don't think it odd: Thorpe "isn't himself" and one of the claimants for his position is brutally attacked?' Dulcie was whispering, but such was her excitement that two orderlies in blue scrubs looked over. 'We saw him, Nancy. He was heading toward the hotel. Toward the Common.'

'Dulcie, I never . . .' Nancy was shaking her head, a look of profound sadness on her face. 'I know that Mr Thorpe can be difficult to deal with. Lord knows, I've been a little discomfited by his behavior recently. But to accuse him of . . . of . . . I don't even know what.'

'It's not his fault, Nancy.' Dulcie leaned in. 'Not if he can't help himself.'

Nancy only kept on shaking her head. 'Your books, Dulcie. I fear you've taken them too much to heart. This is simply the case of an ordinary man. An extraordinary man in some ways, perhaps, but an ordinary man when it comes to fear and stress. Don't you know, he was on the verge of killing himself last night? And here you are, accusing him of I don't know what.'

'Killing himself?' She hadn't gotten that from what her adviser had said. 'He didn't say that.' She was sure of it. 'He said he was afraid of *what he might do*. And, Nancy? I'm afraid that maybe he did it.'

THIRTY

N ancy wouldn't talk about it any more. Nor did she want Dulcie's help with sorting out the various appointments and commitments Thorpe's absence had thrown into disarray.

'I wonder if you need a break, too, Dulcie,' she had said, with unaccustomed sternness, after Dulcie's umpteenth attempt to get her to understand. 'You are confusing yourself, with your books and your stories. We're not like that, dear. We live in a much simpler world.'

They'd been out on the plaza by then, and the workday bustle around them almost convinced Dulcie that Nancy was right. At any rate, she knew she didn't want to make an enemy of her.

'I'm sorry,' Dulcie said finally, despite her conviction to the contrary. 'Sorry for upsetting you, anyway. May I treat you to a muffin?' The coffee shop on the plaza was known for its muffins and scones.

'No. No, thank you, dear.' Nancy relaxed, looking tired, rather than defensive, but she mustered a smile. 'Why don't you treat yourself, though? Take some time for yourself, dear. Here in the sun, outside of the library.'

Dulcie nodded and tried to return the smile as she watched Nancy walk off. Nancy had always been reliable. Comforting and solid. Had she just alienated the one warm member of the departmental staff? Or was the secretary just too grounded to comprehend a supernatural threat? Whatever the older woman believed, Dulcie had to find out the truth.

She turned to go back in. No, she told herself. It wouldn't do to question Martin Thorpe further, even assuming she was allowed in to see him. However, if she were lucky, Renée Showalter would be well enough to receive visitors – and maybe her memory would have returned.

Fearing repercussions from her brief visit with Thorpe, Dulcie kept her head low as she re-entered the infirmary.

'Renée Showalter, please?' She was speaking softly, her eyes darting.

'Excuse me?' The receptionist narrowed her eyes. 'And who are you?'

'Dulcie Schwartz.' Dulcie tried to speak up, but she heard the hesitation in her voice. 'I'm a grad student, and Professor Showalter and I were speaking last night, before, well, you know . . .'

The receptionist, her mouth set in a grim line, considered the young woman before her. Dulcie did her best to look innocuous, even going so far as to bat her eyes.

'Do you need a tissue?' The receptionist pulled several Kleenex from a box. It wasn't what Dulcie had intended, but she accepted them as a peace offering, and thirty seconds later, the receptionist looked back up.

'She's in room three-oh-four. Take the elevator up to three.' She checked her monitor again. 'She's being discharged this morning, so hurry if you don't want to miss her.'

With a quick thanks, Dulcie trotted over to the elevator. This was great news. Surely, the professor must now remember whatever it was she had meant to tell Dulcie. They did have an appointment to meet, but since she was here anyway, Dulcie saw no reason to wait. Besides, Showalter might appreciate her dropping by.

The door to room 304 was open when Dulcie arrived, but the white privacy curtain was pulled shut. Behind it, Dulcie could hear several voices. A doctor, probably, with some last-minute care instructions, or maybe an orderly helping her dress. Dulcie hung back, thinking she'd wait for quiet before announcing herself.

'There you go, Professor.' A cheery woman's voice. 'I hope that doesn't hurt too much.' She was right: someone was helping the scholar dress.

'Thank you.' Dulcie recognized the professor's voice. 'I hope you catch him – or her.'

'Do you remember any more details?' Not an aide, then. A cop. 'You would be doing a service for the community.'

'I don't know.' A pause. 'I wish I could be sure.' Dulcie leaned in. If the professor mentioned seeing anyone who sounded even remotely like Thorpe, she'd have her proof.

'You said that you had been talking to someone who had behaved strangely?' The cop was pushing.

'Yes.' Showalter drew the word out. 'But I don't want to cast aspersions.' There was a rustle of clothing, before she resumed. 'It was odd, though. I had thought that it would be generous to share what I had found. That what I had uncovered was important and would be appreciated. I don't understand what went wrong. I mean, no, I can't say with any certainty, Officer. I'm sorry. But I do know that poor girl did seem somewhat unhinged.'

THIRTY-ONE

ulcie couldn't believe it. But even as she felt frozen to the spot, she realized she couldn't stay. Flattening herself back against the wall, she eyed the elevators. If the professor and the cop stepped out now, she was cooked. She had come to talk to Showalter when she already had an appointment in a little over an hour; it certainly could seem like she was stalking her.

But – wait – any building of this height would have an emergency exit. Did she dare open those doors? Try for the stairs? No, there was too great a chance that she'd set off an alarm. Instead, in a mad dash that she hoped was open to a more conventional interpretation, she bolted into the ladies' room, where she lingered for a good twenty minutes before daring to venture out.

By then, the coast was clear. She was also late for her section. Though by now the early epistolary novel was the furthest thing from her mind.

Clearly, her students felt the same way. 'I don't know, Ms Schwartz.' Forty minutes in, Roz, slumped in her seat, was whining. 'It just seems to go on and on.'

Dulcie nodded in sympathy before realizing that she should counter the sophomore's impression with some context.

'It does, doesn't it?' She might as well admit that much. 'But think of what the author is trying to do. Before texting and emails, before the telephone, you caught people up by writing letters. Everything important, anything you needed to tell someone, you would write. Richardson is trying to duplicate the rhythm of those letters. Remember, these women haven't spoken in ages, so everything is fair game. Besides, they had no electronic devices.' Dulcie nodded toward Julie, in the corner, who was clearly texting under the edge of the table. 'And no TV, so they had more time on their hands for things like reading and writing.'

'Maybe it's the formatting.' Julie shoved her phone in her bag. 'It's so hard to understand who's speaking to who.'

'Whom,' corrected Dulcie. Julie was trying to pretend she'd been reading, that much was obvious. However, that didn't mean Dulcie couldn't use the moment. 'What you're noticing is the voice. While the language is more formal than what we'd use today, it is a casual, intimate voice. The author is trying to re-create a real chain of letters back and forth between friends. He wants you to see that each writer knows the other, and so they don't need to explain too much.

'But they don't tell you who's talking – writing – half the time.' Julie wasn't giving up. 'It's confusing.'

And even as Dulcie answered her – 'this kind of reading does require a little more concentration than a text message' – it hit her. Dulcie didn't know for sure whom Professor Showalter had been talking about. Granted, it sounded like the professor was talking about her, but maybe she had jumped to the wrong conclusion.

The question then was: whom had she been complaining about? Showalter had been surrounded by students at the bar, and both Lloyd and Trista had been with her. Trista. Dulcie stopped, unwilling to let the thought form. Trista had been at the hotel, waiting for Showalter to arrive. She and Chris had discussed that because Chris had doubted the blonde postgrad as a source of information, and Dulcie had defended her. But why had Trista been so eager?

One possibility came to her immediately. Her friend had a one-year post-doc position, nothing more. Trista always appeared relaxed or at least in control, but Dulcie knew how hard her friend worked. If she thought she had a shot at permanent position under a new department head, she might come on a little strong. And – what? Attack her? No, that made no—

'Ms Schwartz?' She looked around. Her students were looking at her.

'I'm sorry,' she smiled at them. 'Julie, did you have any more to add?'

With an eloquent roll of her eyes, the sophomore let Dulcie know she had missed something important. But right at that moment, the chimes of Memorial Church sounded.

'Well, we'll pick this up next week,' Dulcie said, trying not to sound too grateful. She had communications of her own to explore.

*   *   *

Trista wasn't answering when Dulcie called. She didn't respond to a text either, though that didn't mean anything. Trista had her own teaching assignments, and Dulcie knew that she was also working hard on a paper for a spring quarterly. That was how postgrads got jobs, Dulcie reminded herself. Not by intimidating professors.

But if it wasn't Trista whom Showalter had been talking about, and it wasn't Dulcie, then whom? Dulcie tried to remember the other faces at the bar. Raleigh hadn't joined them until after. Besides, Lloyd's girlfriend still had years to go on her thesis, and that meant even less motive for an attack.

Maybe the hotel staff would know. Considering what had happened, Dulcie doubted that the visiting scholar would want to keep their appointment – even if she wasn't avoiding Dulcie. But Dulcie should show up. And then, maybe, she could ask some questions.

She might even clear Martin Thorpe, Dulcie thought as she headed toward the Common. Rather to her surprise, Dulcie realized, she wanted her adviser proven innocent. Part of that was practical. Dulcie had already been forced to find a new adviser once. To have to go through that again would almost guarantee her thesis would be delayed another year, if not more. But also, if she were being honest with herself, it was that she felt bad for the man. He had looked so frail in his hospital johnny, and that had brought home to her how vulnerable he must feel. Maybe Raleigh was right. Maybe he did need a kitten. If only Dulcie could be sure that the little orange creature would be safe with him.

Chris might not think that she had a logical mind. Certainly, compared to his years of training with computational Xs and Os, she didn't, but she could follow a train of thought. And one thing kept coming back to her. Professor Showalter's words strongly suggested that she had been bothered by a woman, another student or a rival scholar. But that did not mean that whoever – or whatever – had struck down Mina Love and attempted to hurt Emily Trainor wasn't something much more dangerous. And much more wild.

This was not a pleasant thought to have as she crossed the Common. But in the broad light of day, the open space looked empty rather than threatening, and the leafless trees barely cast any shadow on the asphalt path. In fact, Dulcie could see all the way across the public park, to where another figure was making its slower way up toward the hotel.

'Emily?' As she gained on the other person, Dulcie saw a cane and recognized the slow, limping gait. 'Is that you?'

'Ms Schwartz.' The student turned with a smile, and Dulcie was pleased to see that the younger woman had a little more color in her cheeks. 'What brings you here?'

'I was heading to the Commodore.' Dulcie pointed to the building ahead of them. 'I was hoping to talk to someone there.'

'That's funny.' Emily turned toward the building, giving Dulcie a glimpse of her bruised neck. 'I am, too. But I don't know if she's still there.'

'You're not . . .' Dulcie paused. This was a strange coincidence. 'You're not looking for Renée Showalter, are you?'

'Yeah.' The junior's head bobbed. 'I am. I missed her talk last night. And I – well, it may be a while before I go out at night again. But I know that Mina would want . . .' She stopped and bit her lip so hard the color went out of it.

'I know Mina was a fan,' said Dulcie, trying to make her voice as gentle as possible. 'I am, too.'

'She . . . No.' Emily shook her head. 'Mina would want to confront her. All those outdated ideas . . .'

'Oh. Sorry.' Dulcie apologized, suddenly reluctant to mention her appointment with the scholar. 'I thought Mina was into the whole new historicism thing, the connectivity. Josh said—'

'Josh? You were talking to Josh?' The girl's welcoming smile turned to a glare. 'No surprise there. He was just jealous of Professor Lukos. Not to mention . . .' She shut down, shaking her head again.

'What? Emily?' Dulcie tried to get in front, to look into the girl's face. But Emily kept her face averted.

'It's funny,' she said, finally looking up. 'You'd think he'd be the one to want to drop the whole "connectivity" thing, right? But now he's pushing for it, like it gives him some hold over her.'

Dulcie didn't know how to respond. Clearly, this went beyond literary theory.

'Has there been any change?' Dulcie hesitated even asking.

Emily only shook her head.

'I'm so sorry.' Dulcie couldn't help it. She had to ask. 'So, she hasn't been able to tell anyone what happened?'

Another slow shake. 'They keep saying she could wake up at any moment. That's why I thought, if I could reach the professor, maybe get her notes, it would be something Mina could work on while she recovers. You know, finding the holes – discrediting Showalter, getting her out of the running.'

'I see.' Dulcie didn't, not really. Clearly Emily had an exaggerated idea of what any undergraduate's impact would be. Still, it was a kind gesture – and Dulcie didn't have to respond in more detail. Even at Emily's slower pace, they had arrived at the hotel.

Emily reached for the door, only to have a uniformed doorman pull it open. 'Well, it was nice seeing you.'

Dulcie let the injured student go ahead of her and watched her walk to the bank of elevators. Well, so much for mutual areas of interest. Maybe it was just as well Mina had left the department. For now, Dulcie advanced on the front desk – and then stopped. If Emily Trainor could go directly to Renée Showalter's room, why couldn't Dulcie? She knew she wasn't the annoying student about whom the scholar had been complaining. And the visiting scholar *had* said she had something to share only yesterday.

'Wait!' She turned as she saw Emily step into an elevator. 'Hold that, please?'

Too late. The doors closed, sending Dulcie back to the front desk. Without Emily, she didn't even know where the professor was staying.

'I'm here to visit Professor Showalter,' she said, trying to sound confident.

'I'm sorry. That guest is no longer with us.'

Dulcie gasped. So much had been happening that for a moment, she had put the worst possible spin on the desk clerk's words. 'She . . . she . . .'

'She checked out this morning.' The clerk was looking at her quizzically. 'A little less than an hour ago.'

'Of course.' Dulcie nearly collapsed against the counter with relief. After leaving the health services, the visiting scholar probably wanted to get home. It was possible she didn't even remember their appointment. 'Did she leave any messages? Any way to get in touch?'

'No, I'm sorry.' The clerk made a cursory pass over what must have been an electronic note pad. 'I don't see anything. Would you like to leave your name, in case she calls back?'

'No, thanks.' In case the professor had wanted to duck her, Dulcie didn't want to sound like a stalker. Besides, Showalter was an academic. Dulcie could find her email online. Once she was back at McGill, the professor would be free to tell Dulcie whatever it was that had been on her mind at the bar last night. If she still wanted to. Still, Dulcie thought, she may as well wait. Emily would doubtless be down soon, and even though the sun was shining, Dulcie worried. Emily looked frail and was clearly still shaken up by what had happened. Dulcie would walk her back to her dorm room. Maybe, along the way, she could get her to talk a little more about her room-mate's studies.

In the meantime, she walked over to the elevators. It couldn't be long now.

'Ms Schwartz.' A gruff but familiar voice caused her to spin around. 'Why am I not surprised to see you here?'

'Detective Rogovoy!' Dulcie kicked herself. Of course, the university police would be following up. 'I'm glad to see you.'

'Why?' His big face wrinkled in concern. 'Are you okay? Has anything happened?'

'No, I'm fine.' She was almost laughing. 'In fact, I just came over to see if Professor Showalter was still here. I was hoping maybe she might remember something.'

That big face scrunched up some more, and Dulcie realized she was talking herself into a corner. She wasn't supposed to have heard what the professor had told Rogovoy's officer at the infirmary. Nor, she realized, could she say anything about waiting for Emily. The junior hadn't reported the attack against her, and Dulcie couldn't out her against her wishes, not so long after the fact.

'She had some information for me. A paper or a lead or something.' It was true as well as expedient. 'She and I were going to talk this morning.' Dulcie shrugged.

Rogovoy seemed to chew her words over. 'I'm sure she'll be in touch, Ms Schwartz. If what you're saying is true.'

'Detective! Why would I lie?' That was probably pushing it, but it worked. Rogovoy broke into a smile that transformed his whole face.

'Because you fancy yourself an investigator.' The grin faded as quickly as it had appeared. 'And that gets you into trouble.'

'Well, why are *you* here?' He was going to tell her to leave any moment. She had to act fast.

'Official business.' He was looking at her. 'There's something more going on, Ms Schwartz. Out with it.'

She opened her mouth to protest – and shut it again. Rogovoy was a good cop, with good cop instincts. She had to give him something. 'Do you think what happened last night might have had something to do with what she was going to talk about last night?' Even as the words formed, Dulcie realized that she was wondering about this. 'Maybe with what she was going to tell me?'

'And it's not something hinky with this adviser of yours?' He was testing her, she could tell.

'Well, it is true that we saw him near the Common last night. And he didn't check himself into the university health services until much later. Plus, he sort of had motive – more motive than for the other two attacks, anyway. But—'

'Dulcie Schwartz.' Rogovoy was shaking his large head slowly. 'You really hate that guy, don't you?'

'No, I don't, actually.'

It was no use. 'Come on, Ms Schwartz. Go back to class. Or go to the library. Just, please, stay out of trouble, and let me do my job.'

THIRTY-TWO

She would, Dulcie told herself. If only she could trust the burly detective to follow up. Not about the troublesome student – he was too good a cop to leave that be – but her idea that the attack was connected to the subject of her talk. Without the professor, or any notes, though, she was at a loss to decipher what exactly the professor had uncovered. She would, she decided, wait for Emily Trainor and ask her a few more questions. At the very least, she could walk the junior back to the Square. After her fright, she might appreciate the company.

Taking up a position on the sidewalk, away from the hotel entrance, Dulcie called Trista. No matter what Chris said, she didn't doubt her friend. However, she did have some questions that the pierced postgrad could answer.

She was just leaving a message when Emily appeared, leaning

heavily on her cane. Dulcie rushed over to help. The doorman, apparently, was busy answering Rogovoy's questions.

'Hey, I yelled over to you,' Dulcie said. 'But you were already going up.'

'Sorry.' Emily could have shrugged, or it could have been the cane. 'I saw you go over to the front desk, so I figured maybe Showalter had left something for you.' She glanced over at Dulcie to see if she had guessed correctly. 'Besides,' Emily continued, 'I was really hoping to catch her. It would have been a coup for Mina. If only I could've gotten over here more quickly.'

That was it, her cue. 'Emily?' Dulcie hesitated, but this was what had been bothering her. 'How did you know what room Professor Showalter was staying in?'

The girl looked at her with a blank stare. 'What? I told you.' Dulcie shook her head. 'I spoke with her, with the professor, before her talk. I told her about Mina being in the hospital. I knew I wasn't going to make it to her lecture, so she'd told me I could come by today.'

'Ah.' It was all Dulcie could muster. So much for her own special connection with the scholar. They walked on in silence, and Dulcie couldn't help noticing that each step Emily took seemed to hurt more.

'Have you had your leg looked at?' She asked gently.

Emily shook her head. 'It's an old problem. Sometimes it acts up. Getting thrown . . .' She let the sentence trail off and sighed. 'I was really hoping to get the professor's notes.'

'That's really sweet of you.' Dulcie thought of Suze. They had both helped each other, too. 'You must be close.'

A nod this time. 'We've roomed together since freshman year. I know that most people end up hating their freshman room-mates. But with us, it was like fate or something. We do everything together. Or did . . .'

'Until Josh?' It was a guess.

'Yeah, he's one of those guys.' Emily kept her eyes on the sidewalk, but Dulcie could hear the bitterness in her voice. 'You know, the type who doesn't like it when his girlfriend has any other friends. It's happened before.'

Dulcie turned to stare at the other girl. If Josh had a record of harassment, she wanted to know. And Detective Rogovoy needed to know. 'Josh has done this with other girls?'

Emily shook her head. 'No, sorry.' Walking seemed to be exhausting her. 'Mina. She's had boyfriends before who want to cut me – cut all her friends – out. She attracts that type.'

'Some guys think that's what intimacy is all about.' She turned toward the junior as they walked. 'I guess your research showed him that someone can be too close.'

Emily paused at that, and Dulcie couldn't read the look that the junior gave her. 'I don't mean that the attack is your fault,' Dulcie rushed in to explain. 'I mean, you just did the research.'

'Yeah,' said Emily, hobbling along. 'I guess.'

Could that have been why she was jumped? From the set of Emily's mouth, Dulcie could tell that she didn't want to talk any more, and Dulcie was a little relieved when her phone rang. Trista, calling her back, she saw, and when she turned to Emily, she saw that the junior was grateful for the break as well.

'Take it,' she said. 'I'm fine. Really.'

As if to prove her point, she sped up and was almost half a block away before Dulcie could pick up the call.

'Hey, Tris, thanks for calling me back.' She hesitated. What she really wanted to know was why Trista had pursued Showalter so ardently, but she couldn't figure out how to ask that without it sounding like an accusation. 'I'm over by the Commodore,' she volunteered, hoping it would prime the pump. 'I came by hoping to catch Showalter, but she had already checked out.'

'Yeah, about an hour ago.' Trista seemed to know everything. 'She'll be back in a few weeks, though. I think they must consider her a serious candidate.'

'You know this?' Dulcie was taken aback.

'Pretty sure.' Her friend sounded so casual. Not at all what Dulcie would consider stalker-ish. 'At least, I'm hoping.'

Now she was getting somewhere. 'What's it to you, Tris? I mean, she's not in your field.'

'Exactly,' said her friend. 'But speaking of . . . you might want to get down to the Mildon. I was just on Level Three and I saw your new best friend, Josh Whatsisname – the boyfriend? – he was talking with that mousy little librarian. I think they were coming close to blows.'

THIRTY-THREE

There was clearly a lot that Dulcie didn't understand. Trista's answer, for example. That one word – 'Exactly' – was ringing through her head. However, one thing she did know for sure was that Thomas Griddlehaus was an ally. Not only that, he was her friend. And if he was being threatened by a potentially dangerous student, she was going to his defense.

Turning to cut back through the Common, Dulcie weighed the option of calling the university police – or, at least, of alerting her friend Mona, who worked upstairs from Griddlehaus in the circulation department. Maybe she could gather some of her colleagues. Rush downstairs, and – what? Break up a possibly heated discussion between an undergraduate and the senior clerk of the Mildon Rare Books Collection? Maybe she could draw Griddlehaus aside and explain that Josh Blakely was being questioned in connection with the attack on his girlfriend a few nights before. Even that, however, was questionable. Josh was innocent until proven guilty. And Dulcie herself, she remembered with a sinking feeling, had found the young man likeable.

Better she should just hurry over and see if she could help sort things out.

'Mr Griddlehaus!' Dulcie called out as soon as the elevator door opened. The subterranean hallway was artificially and overly lit, but Dulcie thought the mousy clerk brightened at the sight of her, hurrying down the hall.

'Ms Schwartz!' He was definitely smiling. 'You seem quite exuberant today.'

'Oh, yes.' She stopped short. The passage was deserted, the entrance to the collection its usual quiet self: no conflict – and no Josh – in sight. 'I am, of course. But I was wondering, did you happen to see an undergraduate? A Josh Blakely?'

'Ah, of course.' Griddlehaus tipped his head back, as if to peer out of the bottom of his glasses. 'I should have known. I thought I saw your compatriot, over by the reshelving area.'

'She called me,' Dulcie confessed. 'She thought maybe you were having a disagreement?'

What came next was either a snort or a laugh, Dulcie couldn't tell. What she could tell was that Griddlehaus was pleased with himself. 'Some people,' he said, with evident pride, 'need the rules explained to them. More than once.'

Before she could ask another question, he waved her in. Out of habit, Dulcie dropped her bag by the front; Griddlehaus would lock it away when he checked her in, but for now, she followed him back to the reading room. There, she saw Josh Blakely sitting quietly and clearly waiting. His hands, clad in the white archivist's gloves, were clasped on the table top before him. At their approach, he turned and the expression on his round face could only be described as beaten. Considering the setting, Dulcie realized once again that whatever physical deficits the diminutive librarian might have, on this turf, he was the master.

Dulcie nodded back, unsure of how to respond. 'What did he come for?' she asked, keeping her voice low.

'That's just it, Ms Schwartz.' Griddlehaus walked her back to the entrance, where she filled out the visitor's log. 'He had no idea what he wanted, not really, or even how we work here. This is not simply a lending library.' He pronounced the penultimate word with distaste.

'He wanted to take something with him?' Dulcie looked up in disbelief.

'Indeed.' Griddlehaus handed her the slip of paper that served as a pass. 'He was asking about some "information" from the early nineteenth century. He wanted to, ahem, "see if he could check them out."'

'Maybe he meant he wanted to look at them?' Dulcie wasn't sure how conversant the librarian was with contemporary slang.

'Please.' He stared at her over his glasses. 'He even asked if he could renew online.'

'Well, it looks like he understands now.' Dulcie couldn't resist peeking back at the well-lit room. 'Do you think he'll mind if I do some work, too?'

Griddlehaus didn't even honor that with a response. Instead, he led her back and saw her seated, before going off to the archives.

Dulcie pulled a pair of gloves from the box in the table's center and nodded to Josh. 'You've discovered my secret hideaway,' she said. It was a little disconcerting to have someone else here, especially someone she'd just been discussing.

'It's a very cool place.' He looked around. 'I, uh, didn't understand how it worked.'

'Read you the riot act?' If you weren't dating him, Dulcie thought, Josh Blakely seemed like a nice guy.

'Kinda.' He leaned across the table. 'I thought I could take some stuff out. You know, for Mina. Make up for not having the lecture to play back for her.'

Dulcie looked at him. His round, red cheeks were positively cherubic, and she couldn't help but wonder: was he really hoping to cheer up his girlfriend, or was this another way of controlling her life? 'You're looking for some early American documents, Mr Griddlehaus said?'

Josh nodded. 'I've heard there are some really rare things here, and well . . . Didn't I tell you about Mina's research?'

'You mentioned it.' Dulcie waited. Was this more about Mina's family tree? But Josh kept talking.

'Mina found something – a letter, or part of a letter in the history department archives. Something about a woman from back then. She might have been a writer; we don't know. But what grabbed Mina was finding out about her life. This woman had it kind of rough, and I guess she was a real survivor. She's really taken with her – I mean, Mina is – and I thought if I could surprise her with something original – something that would help her figure out who this woman was – it would be a real treat.'

'I'm sure it would.' Dulcie found herself drawing back. A woman writer – a 'survivor'? She shook her head. It had to be coincidence. As unlikely as an undergrad being able to 'take out' a document from the Mildon. Dulcie began to understand Griddlehaus's pique. 'Well, I'll leave you to it, then.'

As if on cue, Griddlehaus had come back with a box, which he placed in front of Dulcie. As she sat back, he opened it with a flourish, taking out the polypropylene-enclosed sheets one by one and placing them, carefully, side by side on the tabletop before her. When he got to the third, he stopped. 'I believe this is where we left off, Ms Schwartz,' he said, and walked away. He hadn't even looked at Josh.

'Sorry,' Dulcie whispered, feeling a bit abashed. Griddlehaus was making her feel bad for the poor boy. Still, since she was here . . . Maneuvering the large magnifying glass over the page, she began.

'But do not think that though I flee,' Dulcie smiled to think that

as recently as yesterday, this one word had given her so much
trouble. *'I fear He who would contain me within Tyranny's walls.
E'en though I reject most vehemently those Disequal bonds, so too
would I o'erthrow his claim on she who –'*
'Ahem.' Dulcie looked up. Josh was turned toward the front desk,
where Griddlehaus was hunched over his own book. The space
before Josh was empty. Griddlehaus was a harsh taskmaster when
he had a lesson to teach. Well, it was his library, and Dulcie's time
was limited. She leaned back over the brown and wrinkled page.
The magnifying glass stand was already at the edge of the table, so
carefully, barely touching the edge of the polypropylene covering,
she nudged the page a bit further up to better see the bottom. That
was better.
    *'O'erthrow his claim on she who will come after, for though Body
she may be yet not Spirit of the oppressor, and ne'er shall I relinquish to him that which equally is os mine.'*
    Josh was fidgeting. And while Dulcie was trying to concentrate,
writing down the words she deciphered one at a time, his move-
ments didn't make it easier. He had one of the pencils out now,
and was spinning it slowly from hand to hand. Dulcie looked
down at her pad. 'Is os? Is *of.*' So the line would read: 'That
which equally is of mine?' Even now that she had the words right
their meaning remained elusive. She needed to concentrate. *'That
which . . .'*
    Josh dropped the pencil. Dulcie looked up, prepared to snap, but
the undergrad looked mortified and she instantly felt ashamed.
Instead, she nodded. The time to intercede had come.
    'Mr Griddlehaus?' She gently pushed the magnifying glass back,
so it no longer hung precipitously over the fragile document, and
standing, approached the front desk.
    'Ms Schwartz!' He looked up, as wide-eyed and innocent as a
child. 'Are you done with that box already? I thought, surely, that
page alone would take you an hour.'
    'Mr Griddlehaus.' She lowered her voice and leaned in. 'Do you
think, maybe, you can help that poor guy out?'
    'I would if he asked correctly.' From the clerk's voice, Dulcie
suspected he didn't care if Josh heard him. On second thought, she
corrected herself, he wanted the undergrad to hear. 'All he said was
that he wanted to see manuscripts from the area around Philadelphia
for 1800 to 1850. And then he looked at me. I waited for him to

clarify, and when he didn't, I assumed he was still figuring out what years, or which townships, or whether he was seeking manuscripts of novels, of biographies, or even of sermons. And I went on with more urgent requests.'

Once again, Dulcie thanked Lucy's Great Goddess for her better luck in life. Griddlehaus was a wonderful ally. As an enemy, however, he was formidable.

'I suspect it might be biographies,' she said, thinking of what Emily had said. 'Family histories, or the like. But do you think,' she offered, 'I could ask him?' She had no desire to get on the clerk's bad side, but it seemed like some mediation was in order. Otherwise, she might not get much work done either.

Griddlehaus sighed with such drama that Dulcie had to work to suppress a giggle. 'If you want to bother,' he said. Then he leaned toward her so only she could see his wicked grin. 'I think I've made him suffer enough.'

'Mr Blakely?' She couldn't help it: the formality of the archive was as much a habit as the white gloves. 'Do you think together we could perhaps narrow down your search?' As she worked at framing the question, she turned, aware that the librarian was looking over her shoulder. 'Mr – Josh!'

Dulcie fell against the wall as she was rudely shoved aside. Griddlehaus was charging by her, arms raised high and yelling.

'Stop! Stop right there! You, sir! What are you doing?'

THIRTY-FOUR

They reached him before he could do any damage. In fact, as both Griddlehaus and Dulcie yelled, Josh froze, and by the time Dulcie had raced back around to her side of the table, she was wondering if he would ever move again. The shock on his face was enough to make her almost feel guilty.

'What were you thinking?' Dulcie gently moved the pages out of the undergrad's reach.

'I – I had the gloves on.' He stammered, holding up his hands as evidence, his eyes wide and quite possibly tear filled.

'That's not enough,' she said, shaking her head sadly. 'These are very fragile pages. They're more than two hundred years old. Didn't you see Mr Griddlehaus removing them from the box for me?'

'But – but I thought I saw you—'

'Ms Schwartz has *earned* the right to handle certain documents.' Griddlehaus, recovering from his shock, interrupted, his voice laced with venom. 'She is a scholar, who comes to the Mildon with respect. While you—'

'Come on.' Dulcie darted around the table and grabbed Josh's arm. 'Mr Griddlehaus, why don't we just leave for a while?'

'I'm sorry,' Josh called, as she ushered him out of the collection. 'Really!' As the elevator door closed, he turned to Dulcie. 'I thought he was going to attack me.'

Interesting choice of words, Dulcie thought. 'It wasn't you I was worried about,' was all she said. 'I've never seen him that worked up. The Mildon is his baby.'

The elevator opened onto the main floor. Dulcie couldn't tell from the look on the guard's face if Griddlehaus had called up any instructions. Still, she figured, better safe than sorry. 'Have you had any lunch?' She asked the red-cheeked junior, as they stepped into the lobby.

'What?' He stopped to reply. 'No. It's only—'

'Come on,' Dulcie pulled him along. Eleven forty-five wasn't that early. In fact, it was the perfect time to get a seat at Lala's.

For a potential batterer, Josh went quietly, and as Dulcie led him through the Yard and out to the street, she took advantage of his silence to school him a bit in the ways of the Mildon.

'It's not a regular library,' she said, still holding onto his arm. 'It's the pre-eminent rare books depository in North America.' She checked out the traffic before dragging him into the street. 'Perhaps in the world.'

'But . . .' They made it to the sidewalk, and she maneuvered him to the right. It was a bit, she figured, like walking a large dog. A large, not overly intelligent dog. 'But,' he tried again, as she pulled him by a couple with a stroller, 'why didn't he tell me? I would've followed the rules.'

At that, Dulcie paused. The only answer she had wasn't complimentary, to any of the participants. 'You annoyed him, Josh,' she said finally. 'Thomas Griddlehaus is a brilliant man, and you came onto his turf with all sorts of demands about what he should do for you and what you wanted. And you didn't respect the collection.'

'Oh.' Josh shut up after that and let himself be walked down to the little café. Even at this hour, most of the tables were full.

'There.' Dulcie pointed. 'In the back.' When Josh hesitated, she grabbed his arm again. Tables at Lala's were first come, first served, and she wasn't missing her chance.

'Lunch?' A moment after they sat down, Lala herself was there, and from the way she looked down her prominent nose, Dulcie sensed that she didn't approve.

'Yes, please.' Dulcie smiled up at the beetle-browed proprietor. She would explain later that she hadn't been hanging onto Josh out of affection – Lala was very loyal to Chris. Unless, of course, the chef had heard that Josh was under suspicion for the attack on Mina. Maybe it was the constant stream of both community and university personnel who came through here, or maybe she had powers of her own, but Lala managed to be surprisingly well informed about most doings in Cambridge.

'Wow, is that really—?' Josh was staring up at the large proprietor.

'Three-bean burger, extra sauce.' Dulcie cut him off. 'And a diet Coke for me. Josh?'

'Uh, the same.' He looked up as Lala plucked the menu from his hands. There were not going to be any extras – no bowls of soup, no spicy-sweet roasted nuts – brought to the table today.

'I think you should give Mr Griddlehaus a day to cool off.' While they waited, Dulcie concluded her lecture. 'Go by tomorrow, apologize, and tell him that you'd like to learn the proper protocol for using the collection. He'll be flattered, and you'll make an invaluable friend.'

From the look on his face, Josh didn't seem convinced. 'Maybe I'd just better avoid the place. I only have another year and a half.'

'Come on,' Dulcie responded. 'He's not that bad.'

'It's not like I need anything he's got down there for myself.' Josh wasn't looking at her.

'You never do research?' Unable to see his face, Dulcie couldn't tell if he was still afraid of Griddlehaus or if something else was going on. Then she remembered what Emily had said. 'You're sick of genealogy, is that it?'

'What?' He turned back to face her. 'No, that was never my thing anyway. I'm poli sci.'

'Oh.' She nodded. There was something here, something she wasn't getting. 'But you don't want Mina looking too closely into family histories.'

He was staring at her quizzically, his brow knotted up. 'Wait, did I tell you?'

Dulcie froze. This was it. He was going to confess. But just then they were interrupted by the appearance of two baskets, lined with waxed paper that was quickly becoming translucent as a red-orange sauce dripped from the edges of the burgers each held.

'Wow.' Josh hefted the burger, which took two hands. Dulcie reached out to stop him, and caught herself. He'd been talking. She needed him to stay relaxed if he was going to continue.

'Sorry. What were you going to say?' She heard the tension in her voice, and picked up her own burger to cover.

'The woman . . .' He took a bite. 'Oh, wow, this is great.'

Dulcie did the same. For the first time ever, she barely tasted Lala's special. 'The woman?' It was hard to sound casual, especially with a full mouth.

Josh nodded and reached for a napkin. 'It's all still really speculative,' he said. 'But there's this strange chance that they're related.'

'*They?*' Dulcie took a second bite, a small one, in case she needed to launch another question fast.

Josh nodded, chewing. 'Mina,' he said finally. 'And the woman. I mean, probably not. That was another of Emily's things.' He took another bite, but Dulcie still managed to hear what sounded like, 'That's how she is.'

'They, not you?' This was where Josh had stonewalled her before, and she found herself trying to read his face. The fact that his cheeks were distended with food made it difficult, so she bit into her own burger, this time letting herself savor the spicy patty and the hot sauce. It really would be a shame not to enjoy one of Lala's specials. Besides, chewing gave her a chance to regroup. And if Josh was going to deny any interest in genealogy, or in Mina's research, she was going to have to find another way to come at him.

'Tell me.' She tried again, taking a sip of soda. 'How did you and Mina meet?'

'Contemporary political theory.' Josh brightened up at the mention of a course that Dulcie had barely survived. 'We both took it last year. That's when I realized I wanted to concentrate in poli sci. Mina was considering switching into women's studies back then.'

'Really.' Dulcie took another bite and considered. She needed to draw Josh out, make him feel like they were having a friendly chat. 'My room-mate minored in women's studies,' she offered. It was an odd conversational gambit. From what Dulcie remembered, Suze's classmates had been a very tough, self-aware group. Not the sort to fall victim to abusive men. Then again, there was often a gap between theory and practice.

'What's her name?' Josh sounded eager, although that could be its own warning sign. 'I wonder if Mina knows her.'

'Not likely. She and I graduated, oh, what is it? Five years ago.' Sometimes Dulcie couldn't believe it.

'Tell me anyway.' He was working his way through the burger, but he seemed to have mastered the art of tackling the two-handed meal and talking. 'Mina's got a lot of friends, still, from women's studies. She says they're a really cohesive group.'

'They are.' Dulcie remembered regular late-night study sessions, when Suze would bring her classmates over. The talk could get heated, but it always ended on a supportive note. In a way, Suze's minor had helped Dulcie focus on her thesis topic: the female friendships that were key to *The Ravages of Umbria*. Then again, Suze hadn't had a possessive boyfriend at the time, and she might not appreciate this one being interested in her now. 'So, what do you think of that crowd?' Dulcie deflected his question.

'What crowd?' He blinked, his round eyes so innocent in his red face. 'The women's studies people? They're great. I even thought about changing my major, well, for a little while.'

Dulcie felt her internal alarms go off. For a few minutes there, Josh hadn't sounded like an abuser. She had noticed that he hadn't insisted on Dulcie giving him Suze's name. But this could be another red flag. It was unusual for men to be that interested in women's studies – but it would fit with some kind of odd attempt to co-opt Mina from the start, to move in on her territory and show her that he would always be around. Always watching. Unless . . . perhaps it was the effect of the warm meal, or the fact that he seemed so happy to be sitting, eating, and talking, but Dulcie wondered, once again, if Josh truly was as clueless – and innocent of the charges – as, well, Esmé.

And if he was, did that put the spotlight back on Thorpe? Dulcie couldn't forget how wild eyed – and wild haired – her adviser had looked both nights she had seen him on the street. On one night, Mina Love had been brutally attacked, her throat reportedly cut open. On the other, two nights later, Professor Showalter had been felled by a blow. Granted, hitting someone on the head wasn't particularly lupine, but Dulcie didn't know the details. Perhaps Thorpe hadn't completed his transformation. Perhaps he wanted to subdue her before sinking his fangs into her tender flesh.

Or perhaps Thorpe was the attacker, but he was not a werewolf. Could job stress lead a man – a noted if not famous academic – to attack women around the full moon?

'Ms Schwartz? Dulcie?' Dulcie blinked. Josh was staring at her, his round face worried. 'Are you okay?'

'Sorry, I was caught up in a thought.' Dulcie shook her head to clear it, and Josh settled back into his seat. For that moment, he had seemed honestly concerned, and that spoke well of him. Then again, there had to be something attractive about him, or else Mina would never have fallen for him – either for good or ill.

'I was remembering my room-mate's undergrad experience.' Suze would forgive her, she knew, if she used her as a sort of stalking horse. 'There was one girl, one woman, who came from some kind of horrible background. She took all these feminist theory courses, was really involved in political action. But I guess it was really some kind of compensation.' She paused, ostensibly to reach for a napkin. 'Suze reached out to her, but this girl didn't respond. Or maybe she couldn't. She really needed someone to take care of her.'

Josh was nodding as he finished the last of her burger, and Dulcie felt a flash of revulsion as he licked his greasy fingers. That was it – that was his rationale. Reaching for another bunch of napkins, he wiped his hands.

'I hate to say it, but I know the type.'

She held her breath. He was going to confess. Maybe not to attacking her. Maybe not to trying to run her life. But to finding her weak or wanting. *He who would contain me within Tyranny's walls . . .*

'Women who are, well, I don't want to say handicapped, but who are dealing with other issues. Still, those classes can be great. I think a lot of those women find strength in the political action groups.' He balled up the napkins. 'I know Mina did.'

THIRTY-FIVE

Dulcie left lunch more confused than ever, despite the warm feeling that comes from indulging in a tasty – and even moderately healthy – meal. As she had struggled to come up with another, more probing question, Josh had excused himself to use the restroom. Then he'd paid and grabbed his coat, all the while thanking Dulcie for her help at the Mildon. She hadn't had a rejoinder for that, and had watched him go, unsure of what to think.

At least, she told herself as she followed him out to the street, Mr Grey would have approved of what she did. Though what she meant by that – whether she meant rescuing Josh from the angry Griddlehaus or grilling him afterward – she wasn't sure. It was simply a thought that had popped into her head. One that put her in a cheery mood as her phone started to ring.

'Nancy!' Dulcie was surprised. 'Are you okay? Was there another . . . incident?' The secretary rarely called.

'Thank you, dear, I'm fine.' The warm voice was calm, but Dulcie wasn't quite reassured. 'I am not sure everything is as it should be, though.'

'Oh?' The warm feeling was dissipating fast, and she turned toward the buildings to hear better.

'It's Mr Thorpe, Dulcie.' In the pause that followed, Dulcie began to envision scenarios. Her adviser was dead. Her adviser had lashed out, clawing a nurse. He was . . .

'He's very upset, Dulcie.' Nancy broke in before her imaginings could get worse. 'He checked out a little after you left, and he has come into the office. But he's not himself. He's under enormous strain right now, and I don't think your little outburst at the health

services helped. I understand that he is not always easy to work
with, and I do know he has his faults. But frankly, Dulcie, I believe
you owe Mr Thorpe an apology.'

'I'm sorry, Nancy,' she replied. 'I really am.' The good feeling
was gone, and with it, the sense that Mr Grey would approve of
her actions. The secretary was right. She had acted on assumptions.
Even if she were to be proven correct, the balding scholar would
be more to be pitied than hated. It wouldn't be his fault if he had
been turned into some sort of horrible, homicidal creature. She
shivered at the thought, despite the broad daylight, and had a thought:
daylight and an invitation. She had her opening to find out more.
Trying to sound more contrite than curious, she added to her
response. 'I'll come by and talk to him.'

'I'm glad, Dulcie,' Nancy's voice registered her approval. 'I knew
you'd do the right thing. I know he's difficult. Please keep in mind,
he's only human.'

Dulcie hoped she was right.

On Nancy's advice, Dulcie headed over to the departmental offices.
The motherly secretary had suggested she just 'pop in,' rather than
make an appointment ('you'll only scare him, dear'). And Dulcie,
who had been wondering if her adviser would decide to take off if
he knew she was coming, agreed.

There was so much going on that she just couldn't get a handle
on. What she really needed was time to think it all through – ideally
with the aid and comfort of either Esmé or Mr Grey. Josh, for
example. At first the junior had seemed like a nice guy, a fairly
ordinary blend of geeky and sincere. Then again, Dulcie acknowledged, that would be what an abusive boyfriend would look like
– until one got caught up in his nets. If that were the case, well,
then it was possible he had attacked Mina and then Emily, and then
switched back into his current caring mode. He might even be in
some form of denial about it and not realize he had been the one
to hurt them. But if that was the case, how did Professor Showalter
fit into it all? Was it that Mina had been interested in her research
– even if just to discredit it? Or did it somehow touch on the ancient
connection Emily had uncovered between Mina and her boyfriend?
No, Dulcie shook her head as she walked. It all seemed too tenuous.

Then again, was it any more likely, really, that Martin Thorpe
was the would-be killer? Logic said no, and a small, persistent voice

in the back of her head pointed out that someone who didn't read Gothic fiction every day would not even have considered the possibility of a lycanthropic malefactor. That voice – which bore a sneaking resemblance to the low, quiet voice of a certain feline specter – also warned Dulcie that she needed to be aware of her own prejudices in the matter.

'I am, Mr Grey.' She said under her breath. A passing pedestrian turned and looked. 'At least, I'm trying to be. That is why I'm going to meet with Thorpe now.'

The response – a sense of questioning, mixed with a bit of doubt if not humor – was not phrased in words, exactly. It didn't need to be. 'Well, part of the reason,' amended Dulcie, ignoring the looks she received as she turned from the busy avenue onto DeWolfe. 'I'm *trying* to be fair, Mr Grey. It's just that . . .'

She stopped. This is where it had happened, that first night. Where she had heard that howl – that strange unearthly howl – and then, moments later, seen Martin Thorpe emerge wild and disheveled from the shadows. This was where, although she didn't know it at the time, a young woman – a student – had been mauled.

Dulcie took a deep breath, looked around, and made up her mind. She might not understand how, exactly, this had all happened. But she had to keep her wits about her. Something strange was going on, and whether or not he was culpable, Martin Thorpe was involved. It only made sense for her to be careful.

THIRTY-SIX

'But the problem is, I don't know if I'll ever find the section that explains what happened exactly.' She looked up, breathless and lost. 'It may never be resolved.'

Forty minutes later, Dulcie was deep in a different dilemma. Despite her fears, Martin Thorpe had indeed been in his office when Dulcie climbed the rickety stairs. At his invitation, she had trundled into his office and, somewhat unwillingly, into the guest chair opposite his desk. She'd found herself studying the bookshelves that lined the wall as she forced out the words she had promised Nancy she would say. The words that, she knew, were only polite, even if they just might be terribly, tragically wrong.

'I'm sorry if I sounded like I was accusing you of anything untoward, Mr Thorpe.' She switched her focus to her hands as she spoke. She really needed to stop biting her nails. 'I know that you are innocent of any wrongdoing.'

It sounded formal, fake and stiff, but it was the best she could do. And Thorpe seemed content to have it over with.

'That's fine, that's fine,' he said. 'Everyone gets a little hot-headed when things go wrong around here.' His acceptance of her rote apology was both so vague and all-encompassing, it led Dulcie to believe that Nancy had primed him for this scene as well, and that he had been as unwilling as she was.

By the time she was able to look at her adviser directly, his complexion had even returned to something like its normal pallor, leading Dulcie to wonder if she had indeed imagined both those odd episodes.

When Thorpe had then followed up by asking her to tell him about her latest findings, she was, if not convinced, at least distracted. It was so much more pleasant to discuss the pages she had found, the bits of story she was piecing together. And to have her adviser actually listen with apparent interest . . . well, it was like catnip would be to Esmé.

Only now, she had arrived at the crux of her problem: 'I haven't yet found the connecting link in the story,' she continued. 'So maybe I never will know how it all works out.'

Thorpe was watching her silently, but Dulcie had more or less forgotten he was there, so deep was she in thought. 'I wish I knew how the protagonist is involved with Esteban, the young lord,' Dulcie said. She'd already explained about the strange carriage that appeared to pick her up. And while she had glossed over the howling wolves outside – 'some kind of threatening noises, probably supernatural,' she had said – she had let her emotions temper her reaction to the stranger inside the carriage. 'He's a good guy, I think. I'm pretty sure,' she had said. 'After all, he picks her up and rescues her from . . . whatever is out there. And he seems to be warning her.'

'About what?' Thorpe's voice interrupted her reverie, and she looked up. 'Couldn't he be warning her about himself? After all, he seems rather . . . demonic.'

'What?' It took Dulcie a moment to reorient. 'No, he's not demonic.'

Thorpe shrugged and looked away, muttering something like 'as if it were immediately apparent.' And Dulcie caught her breath. Could Thorpe be talking about himself? But his next question caught her even more off guard.

'Is it truly vital to keep looking for more pages?' He had switched to his pedantic voice, a little dismissive and little haughty. 'These so-called "linking pages" may no longer exist. In truth, we have little evidence that a complete manuscript has survived at all.'

'But the Paine letter refers to a complete book. A masterwork, and if it is by my author . . .' She caught herself. 'By the author I'm studying, then its worth would be incalculable.'

'Yes, yes, but time has a very real value as well, and a scholar could spend a lifetime looking for a complete lost work and then proving attribution to a particular author. Could lose a lifetime, too, if the search proved fruitless.' He seemed much more himself again, in this mode, making notes on a pad even as he spoke. 'As your adviser, I would be remiss if I didn't point this out, Ms Schwartz.'

'But—' Her protest was stopped by his raised hand.

'I understand the appeal of the hunt, so to speak.' Dulcie swallowed her response, and he kept talking. 'When the blood is up I, too, have sought to track down the elusive . . .' He paused, finished writing whatever it was he was writing, and pushed the paper aside. 'The elusive prey. But, really, Ms Schwartz, what have you to gain? You've already uncovered significant portions of new prose, and you've also gone far in making a strong case that these new fragments were indeed penned by the author of *The Rampages.*'

'*The Ravages.*' She couldn't stop herself. He looked up, eyes bloodshot over his glasses, and she shut her mouth.

'*The Ravages.*' He looked back down. 'In fact, if I do recall your précis correctly, your thesis focuses on that earlier, better-established work. What there is of it. This later work, if indeed it is by the same author, was simply going to be a chapter, a speculative chapter posing some hypotheticals about the future life and work of this unknown author.'

'But I want to know what happens!' Dulcie couldn't hold it in any longer. 'I've read the later bit, where she's standing over the body. And these pages seem to be earlier, when she's fleeing from someone – probably from Esteban. I want to know how she got from here to there. What happened between them to cause her to run? Why was the stranger warning her? Did she –' Dulcie licked her lips, her mouth suddenly dry – 'kill him?'

It was the wrong kind of question. Unscholarly in the extreme, and in the silence that followed Dulcie felt herself shrinking down in her seat. But although her adviser seemed momentarily taken aback by her outburst, he soon closed his mouth and his eyebrows returned to their customary place behind his glasses. And, wonder of wonders, he smiled.

'You are quite taken with this fragment, aren't you?' She nodded, even though the question was rhetorical. 'That speaks well of your dedication, even if it is a misplaced enthusiasm.' Those eyebrows arched again, wrinkling his prematurely high forehead in a particularly unattractive manner. 'And it confirms my initial impression that you have already spent enough – more than enough – time on what will most likely prove a wild-goose chase.

'After all, as a scholar you need to be looking at how this character was created. What literary devices were employed by your putative author that could link her with the dramatic personae of the known work. Not on whether this character – this nameless, fleeing woman – was good or bad, or whether someone killed one person or another. Such distinctions are irrelevant to our purposes – and, ultimately, to your thesis. You need to pursue this as a scholar, Ms Schwartz. You are not, after all, reading for fun.'

THIRTY-SEVEN

D ulcie had left soon after that, her spirits as dim as the darkening sky. Thorpe was right, of course. The search for a missing novel could be a scholar's life work. It might, he had even suggested in a belated effort to cheer her up, become hers. But such a quest would take years, rather than months. And, odds were, it would take the kind of resources that neither Dulcie, nor even the Mildon, could provide. To piece together an entire novel, she'd probably have to search archives up and down the Eastern Seaboard. Even abroad, if she counted in the collectors who might have bought the book when it was first published or the scholars who may have salvaged bits of it in the ensuing centuries. She wouldn't be able to find the entire book. Not in a year or two, and not here, and if she kept on looking, before she knew it, she'd be entirely off track with her thesis. Instead of a PhD, she'd end up Dulcinea Schwartz, ABD – all but dissertation – looking for teaching jobs at private secondary schools, and wondering where she'd gone wrong.

The day was giving way to dusk as she made her way home, and the evening chill made her wrap her sweater close. The street was empty, and for a moment she thought of heading back into the Square. She could grab a cab there, or maybe find someone to walk with. The way Thorpe had talked about stalking, about prey, had left her with an unsettled feeling, as had his casual dismissal of her heroine's involvement in the young lord's violent death. Yes, it did matter, she wanted to yell out. It mattered a lot.

She turned the corner and lowered her head as a blast of wind buffeted her, bringing tears to her eyes. She blinked them away, sniffing. Thorpe was more than temporarily off balance, she thought. He was truly a strange man. How could he say it didn't matter if someone had killed someone else? Yes, these were fictional characters. But even to *say* that . . .

Another gust, this time carrying grit that swiped at her face like claws. Like the claws of a particular ghost, she realized, ducking into the wind. 'Mr Grey? Am I that far off base?' She closed her eyes against the grit, willing a response. The only answer was the wind, which swirled around her, hurrying her along like the clouds it was whipping into the sky.

It could have been a warning. The full moon may have passed, but an empty street at dusk was not the place to be. Not when women were being attacked, being hurt, and the attacker might be a mere human, evil but mortal. The sky darkened, the clouds gathered . . .

And just like that, the wind died away, leaving Dulcie alone and, for now, unmolested. She nodded to herself. 'You're right, Mr Grey,' she said to the fading light. All her fears and fancies were simply her way of avoiding the real issue. She knew that. Martin Thorpe's main job was to keep her on track. Just because she resisted his discipline didn't make him an abuser of women . . . or worse. It just made him her adviser.

THIRTY-EIGHT

'**S**urprise!' Chris greeted her at the door. 'I have the night off.'

'That's great.' Dulcie tried to muster a smile. 'Something smells fantastic.'

'It's just spaghetti.' He followed her into the kitchen, where Esmé was already dining. 'But I made garlic bread, too. Did Trista walk you home again?'

'No, I didn't ask her to.' Dulcie threw her sweater over the back of a chair, causing the cat to look up, and headed toward the fridge. 'Do we have any wine?'

'Wine?' Chris sounded taken aback. 'Maybe. From the other week.' He watched as she rummaged around, emerging finally with a half-empty bottle. 'So, did you take a cab?'

'No, I walked.' Dulcie poured herself a glass. It tasted a little sour. She drank it anyway. 'It wasn't even full dark when I left the Square, Chris.' She took another sip, then poured the rest of the glass down the sink.

'I would have met you, you know.' Chris was hovering behind her as she rinsed the glass and filled it with water. 'I'd have walked back with you.'

'I know you would have.' She turned and willed that smile into place. 'Because you love me. I know that, and I love you for it. But really, I'm fine.'

He started to speak, and she put her hand over his mouth. 'Look, Chris, we're dealing with one of two possibilities here. The first – okay, the most likely – is that this was a domestic issue. Someone, probably Josh Blakely, attacked his girlfriend and then her room-mate for whatever crazy reason abusive guys have. The second is that Martin Thorpe either is or has been convinced that he is a werewolf. If it's the first, well, I'm not involved with Josh. And if it's the latter, well, the moon is past full. So we're all safe for another couple of weeks. And as for Professor Showalter . . . well, she was probably simply mugged.'

'Wait, a professor was mugged?' It wasn't the question Dulcie had been expecting. That was the problem with their crazy schedule. She and Chris stayed in touch on all the important things, but the day-to-day stuff tended to get lost.

'Yeah, Professor Showalter. She was supposed to give the Newman lecture.' Dulcie explained everything – focusing on the fact that the visiting scholar had been walking across the Common at night and had been relieved of her bag. As she was telling Chris about how Thorpe had gone missing, leaving Nancy in charge, Esmé finished her meal and came over to be pet, which Dulcie did. By the time she and Chris finally sat down to eat, she'd caught him up on Thorpe's hospitalization, too.

'Poor guy.' Chris served out the salad. 'I can't imagine the search committee will count this in his favor.'

'The search committee?' Dulcie grabbed a piece of bread. 'They can't hold it against him. Not if they were the reason he got sick. Or whatever.'

Chris didn't say anything.

'Can they?' Dulcie crunched the garlicky toast without even tasting it.

'Let me put it this way,' Chris reached for his own slice. 'By the time this is through, Thorpe might wish he really could turn into a wolf.'

Dulcie mulled this over as she ate her pasta. By the time they had polished off seconds, she was glad she had made peace with her adviser. His actual advice, however, still bothered her.

'What do you think, Esmé?' Despite the occasional splash, the little tuxedo cat had remained in the kitchen as Dulcie did the dishes. Clearly, she had been wanting more company. 'Do you think I should make do with what I've already found and get back to writing?'

'Isn't that a loaded question?' Chris was drying. Esmé only looked up at her person, head tilted at a quizzical angle. 'I mean, if it were a logic chain . . .'

Dulcie let him go on. He meant well. Besides, as he talked over the mindless occupation of soaping and rinsing, she could think. What if she went back to writing, but kept looking through the Mildon papers in her spare time? Wouldn't the chance of finding more be worth such risk? *Worth such risk* . . . those words brought up an echo of something, if only she could remember . . .

'Dulcie!' Chris reached over and turned the tap off. Only then

did Dulcie realize that the sink was nearly full and that Esmé
had fled from the spray. 'Look,' her boyfriend continued. 'I can
finish up here. You've been scrubbing that saucepan for ten
minutes now. I'll just rinse it, set it out to dry, and join you in
a few.'

'Thanks, sweetie.' She didn't even try to explain. It wasn't
anything logical anyway. Instead, she took her laptop into the living
room and began to type in the few lines she'd managed to decipher
before lunch. *'Ne'er shall I relinquish to him that which equally is
of mine,'* she read, once she'd typed it in. That was a puzzler, and
even when she went back a line, it didn't become more clear: *'though
Body she may be yet not Spirit of the oppressor.'*

She'd gotten it wrong. Misread – or mistranscribed – what had
been written. There was no other answer. She'd been working
quickly, distracted by Josh's bored antics even before his brash act
had caused her to usher him away from Griddlehaus. Unless . . .
no. It didn't make sense. It might never make sense. She should
give it up, and get back to work.

Dulcie almost laughed. Only a few months before, this author's
best-known – and only verified – work, *The Ravages of Umbria*,
had been her favorite piece of fiction. She'd been thrilled to unravel
its themes and characters, and she'd been overjoyed when her appli-
cation to write her thesis on the little known, fragmentary book had
been approved. Now here she was, looking back on the nearly
complete novel as 'work.'

Chris had come into the living room by then, with Esmé. But
seeing her at her laptop, he'd gone over to switch on the game. The
Red Sox, Dulcie had picked up, were not the team that had won
the World Series. Not any more, but Chris and Jerry seemed to take
pleasure even in their defeat. Male bonding, she thought, as Esmé
rubbed against her ankles.

'Well, we have our own sisterhood, don't we?' She pulled the
cat onto her lap and massaged the base of her ears. The lines on
the screen didn't turn any less opaque, but the purring warmth of
the little creature calmed her.

It also gave her an idea. 'Is this from you, Esmé?' She looked
down at the cat. Esmé, however, was staring over at the TV. For
once, it seemed, the Sox batter had managed to hit something, and
the cat's eyes were following the televised flight of the ball. 'Go,'
Dulcie placed Esmé back on the floor. Instead of running for the

television, though, the little cat jumped onto the couch – and onto Chris. In a moment, they were both lying there transfixed by something Dulcie simply did not understand.

'Enjoy,' she said softly, and turned back to the screen. Whether it had come from the little cat or not, the memory of another woman, one who might be able to help, was encouraging. Punching open her email, Dulcie did a quick search. There was no obvious link to Professor Showalter in any of her earlier contacts. That didn't dissuade her. A few clicks brought her to the McGill site, and from there she found an address.

'*Dear Professor,*' she wrote. '*I'm the student you spoke with at the bar before your scheduled lecture . . .*' She paused. Could the scholar really think Dulcie had stalked her? Could it have been her response, or something in her manners? Dulcie backspaced over the letters. Better to be safe than sorry. Staring at the blinking cursor, she wondered just how to do that.

'*Dear Professor Showalter,*' she finally typed. '*I am one of the doctoral candidates with whom you met . . .*' It was formal, but it was decidedly proper, and with only a minor shiver of trepidation, she finished her brief missive and hit send.

'Safe!' Chris yelled from the sofa and pumped his fist. Esmé seemed unconcerned by the violence of his reaction, and soon the two had settled in again: silent watchers of a faraway green.

'Where are they playing?' Dulcie asked.

'Oh, this is a repeat.' Chris didn't even look up. 'September, in Anaheim. There's no baseball in November, Dulcie.'

Dulcie only shook her head. And Thorpe thought her passion was hopeless.

Staring at her own screen, however, felt just as futile, and Dulcie pondered what to do next. She should go back to writing. She had accepted that, almost. But tomorrow would be soon enough. If only she could access the Mildon online. The idea of all those boxes, with their acid-free, non-reactive folders being scanned was laughable, and would be, she suspected, nearly heretical to Griddlehaus. Well, maybe tomorrow she'd allow herself another hour. Maybe two. And in the meantime, there must be documents she could look at. Her university account gave her access to a half dozen other archives, as well as webmail. And until the professor got back to her, she could . . .

Emily. The thought was so simple she couldn't believe it hadn't

occurred to her until now. Emily might have something for her –
something new. The junior had been planning on attending Professor
Showalter's lecture. And when she had realized that she wasn't going
to make it, she had spoken to the professor. Showalter hadn't known
that Emily was collecting info to be used against her, and she'd
agreed to meet the girl. Showalter had left before that could happen,
but still, maybe the scholar had told Emily something, or even given
her a hint about what her lecture was going to contain. Emily had
been gathering material to share with Mina, but surely her room-mate
wouldn't begrudge her sharing it with a grad student, would she?

'*Emily*,' she typed. The undergrad's email had popped up on the
first search. '*I wanted to talk with you about Professor Showalter's
work. I know it's not what Mina is in to . . .*' She erased that. Why
bring up a painful topic? '*. . . about her research*,' she typed instead.
'*It's important. Please call or email at your earliest convenience.*'
It was a stretch. Odds were, Showalter hadn't said anything to the
undergrad. But the idea of reaching out – of asking – had seemed
a good one, maybe even feline inspired. And now that the possibility
of new material presented itself, Dulcie just couldn't wait.

She didn't check, therefore, when her phone rang less than thirty
seconds after. And when she picked up to hear her mother's voice,
she tried to disguise her disappointment.

'Lucy.' It was the best she could do. 'What's up?'

'That's for you to tell me, dear. After all, it was your summons
in the ether that prompted me to reach for more terrestrial means
of communication.' Dulcie closed her eyes. Nine o'clock on the
East Coast. That meant six in Oregon. Was her mother drinking?
'Well, Dulcinea, what is happening with you?'

'Nothing much, Mom.' It was easier, somehow, to talk to her
mother with her eyes closed. 'I'm working. Chris is watching a
re-run of a baseball game. Esmé is—'

'Esmé is an old spirit. The heir in spirit if not in body of your
great guide – what was his name?'

'Mr Grey.' Something her mother said almost spurred a thought,
but it was drowned out as Lucy kept talking.

'That's right, Mr Grey. You could do a lot worse than to listen
to your animal guides, Dulcie. Because if I am getting summoned,
I assume you haven't been. I worried, you know, when you went
east that you would lose the connection to your family. To your
heritage.'

'Lucy, we talk a lot.' She leaned back, wishing suddenly that she were on the sofa and could recline. Her mother often affected her that way. 'And we don't have any family. I mean, not besides Dad.'

'Oh, you're wrong, Dulcie. You are wrong or you are willfully forgetting your lineage.' Dulcie knew what was coming next, and almost managed to tune her mother out. 'A long line of women. Powerful women. Fiery souls. In fact, I was just laying out your cards.'

This brought Dulcie back a bit. She enjoyed the tarot, partly, she admitted, because her card – the Sun – was reliably featured. 'So my card came up?' she asked. 'The "fiery" Sun?'

'Yes, yes, it did.' There was something in her mother's tone that suggested this wasn't for the best. Dulcie paid it no mind. Her mother enjoyed regular crises, managing to create them as necessary. 'Not in your house, though. In the house of your ancestors. Your heritage.'

'Lucy, I don't know if we'll be able to come home during the semester break.' She paused. Her mother really did love her. 'Even for Saturnalia.'

'Well, that is the Great Goddess's holiday, and you, the Sun Child and all.' Her mother sounded disappointed, but not mollified. Dulcie predicted another month of such calls. 'But that's not why I was calling.'

It never was, although Dulcie resisted the urge to say so aloud.

'What I was calling about was your direction. Your path through this current darkness.' Dulcie sat up, mildly curious. 'The cards were quite clear on that. You are to keep on, Dulcie. Through the dark forest. A life – a woman's life – depends on it.'

'Okay.' Dulcie knew she hadn't told her mother about the attacks. She'd seen no reason to worry her. Then again, maybe the commune had gotten cable since she'd last been home. Would street crime in Cambridge make the national news? That wasn't the question to ask her mother, though. 'A woman,' she asked instead. 'But not me?'

'She is connected to you. Part of you. Family even, but not of you.' Dulcie tried to phrase the next question – how could someone be 'of' her, when they had no known relatives. But Lucy was done. 'And now I must run, my dear. Samhain got rained out last week, and we crones decided that tonight was auspicious.'

'Enjoy,' said Dulcie as she translated silently: the rain had finally stopped, and they could party. 'Love you.'

'Love you too, dear.' Her mother already sounded far away. 'Blessed be.'

Holding the silent phone, Dulcie mused over her mother's words. Lucy wasn't psychic, at least not in the direct way she so craved. But she did tend to connect at times to her only child's mental state. Had Lucy picked up on Dulcie's frustration with the fragmentary manuscript? Had she sensed that Dulcie was longing to learn the heroine's fate – to find out whether the fleeing woman was a murderer or worse? That would make sense: someone who was connected to her – 'of' her – and yet not a relative.

She turned to tell Chris, when something happened on screen. 'He's out!' Chris called, sitting up. Even Esmé seemed engaged, running to the foot of the sofa to be closer to the screen.

Shaking her head, Dulcie turned back to her computer. It was hopeless. Or, no, it was the goddess's way of telling her she had a little while left to work. Lucy would like that, she thought, touching her computer to wake it. And as she did, she saw the blinking light of a message. Not, as she'd hoped, from Renée Showalter. But from Emily Trainor.

'The professor isn't who you think she is,' the email read. 'Can't wait to tell Mina. It was all faked.'

THIRTY-NINE

D ire Deeds awaited along one path. If she could flee, if this carriage could carry her beyond His reach, she would be safe. She would be freed of the Burden. Those nefarious Acts which she feared she must do, she most dreaded. And yet, still she hoped, for she could no longer pray. She leaned back in the carriage, hoping to lose herself in the Shadowed dark as had the Stranger opposite. And yet she sensed his eyes, those green and piercing orbs, following her. Could he indeed grasp that which she most feared, that Evil Act which drew her on – the final resort of a desperate Soul? Could he conceive a choice – a Risk – such as hers? Indeed, those Eyes which bored so deep, seemed to plumb

her soul. Perhaps, e'en, she dared to hope, such emerald Orbs could
perceive another option, another route—

Dulcie woke, the question so fresh in her mind, she almost woke
Chris to ask if she did indeed dare. 'Wait, no,' she stopped herself.
'That wasn't me – that was . . .' Who? Esmé stirred as Dulcie sat
up, and the cat's green eyes brought back the dream.

'Good morning, stranger,' Dulcie murmured as she rose and
headed toward the kitchen. Esmé followed, tail high.

'Breakfast?' Esmé sat up, obligingly, and waited while Dulcie
opened a can. She was a darling cat, especially after a night when
she'd received sufficient attention from both her humans, but too
familiar to be the mysterious stranger. No, Dulcie thought, as she
placed the food dish on Esmé's mat, her dreams were becoming
obvious. Clearly, she wanted to find out more about this woman,
the protagonist of the manuscript. Pursuing that – her – in the face
of Thorpe's disapproval was one risk. Just as clearly, she now had
doubts about Professor Showalter, too, doubts that were growing.
It wasn't just Emily's email; in retrospect, the red-haired professor
had promised much more than she'd delivered. After all, not only had
the scholar not singled her out for a private meeting, as Dulcie
had originally thought, she hadn't even remembered their appointment.
And if Emily was right, the material the scholar had hinted at wasn't
to be trusted either.

The dream had an emotional component, too. It showed Dulcie
how confused she was – how lost. Clearly, she was hoping Mr Grey
would come to her aid. The reality, however, was that she needed
to do what she could, by herself and – she thought of her feline
guardian's veiled message – with her friends. She might never know
what was going on with this book, and she really should get back
to more solidly researched ground.

Dulcie set the coffee up to brew and retrieved her laptop from
the living room. If Professor Showalter had responded, she might
know what she and Emily had been talking about. There was nothing,
though, and although Dulcie told herself that it was still early, she
couldn't help but read it as a sign of something worse. The professor
had forgotten her. Or, worse, remembered her as some kind of
stalker. The professor had nothing to share. It was all, in Emily's
words, faked.

As the coffee dripped, Dulcie let her cursor move down to the junior's enigmatic email. She'd put off responding last night, uncertain even what to ask and not wanting to hound the poor girl. This morning, though, she wished she had. She looked at the clock. Not yet nine, too early to call an undergrad. Maybe she'd give her till ten, and then try her.

In the meantime, she reread the short missive, trying to make sense of what it said. What had been faked? Could such a respected scholar have gotten away with a full-fledged forgery?

Unless Emily was referring to something else. Could she mean the professor had faked the attack? Dulcie thought back to the day before. Emily had seemed all eagerness as they had entered the hotel. By the time Dulcie had met her, the junior had been in an entirely different mood. Dulcie had attributed the change to fatigue and disappointment. However, it was possible that the junior had discovered something. Had, maybe, wanted to think it through before sharing it.

But would Showalter have falsified the assault? It was possible. Maybe she had arrived in Cambridge and had second thoughts. Maybe she'd had stage fright – or even too much to drink at the pre-talk gathering – and decided that she wanted out. Canceling, once she was already here, would be awkward, especially as the university had probably footed the bill. And besides, word would get out, sinking her chances of other invites – and other offers.

Had Showalter heard about the earlier attacks? It was possible. At the very least, when she checked into the hotel, she had probably been given an introduction to the area – where to get a taxi or the T. And where not to walk after dark.

She had seemed like a sensible woman. That didn't mean she was immune to nerves. Or, if she had faked the attack, was it because of something else going on? That scrap of conversation came back – the idea of a stalker. Showalter had referred to a woman, hadn't she? Maybe Dulcie had misheard. And if followed up on the idea of something else going on, something threatening, she had to once again consider her adviser's strange behavior.

Maybe she was being unfair. Dulcie poured herself a cup and thought about what she'd learned recently. For all she and her friends tended to consider grad students to be the bottom of the pile, it didn't seem like the pressure let up, even as one ascended. Martin Thorpe, at least in Nancy's opinion, had been nearly undone by the pressure of the competition. Dulcie still had some doubts about

what was really bothering her adviser, but surely, knowing that
international candidates were being flown in for a job he had
considered his own couldn't help. Especially since . . .

No, Dulcie got up to get the milk. It wasn't her fault, and Thorpe
couldn't blame her. If anything, she told herself as she stirred in a
good-sized dollop, what she had done as Thorpe's charge should
reflect well on him.

'Mrup!' Esmé was pawing gently at her leg.

'No, Esmé, it's not good for you, now that you're grown.'

Dulcie returned the milk to the fridge and hoisted the little cat
up on her lap. Somehow, a warm cat always helped her concentrate.
But as Esmé kneaded, Dulcie found herself wishing she could bounce
ideas off the feline, too.

'You could weigh in you know. Any time.' Esmé ignored her,
and Dulcie, glancing at the clock, thought of her boyfriend. Quarter
to nine. She should wake Chris, but she didn't want to. Because
of her boyfriend's strange schedule, he was permanently exhausted.
She'd shower first; that would still leave him plenty of time to
get ready for his first section. Then, after her own first class, she'd
call Emily. At the very least, she would find out what the girl
had meant.

Maybe Lucy wasn't the psychic one. By the time Dulcie emerged
from the shower, Chris was awake, and she refilled her mug to join
him at the breakfast table.

'This is nice, huh?' He got the cereal bowls.

'Definitely.' She smiled. 'No offense to Esmé, but I'm really glad
to have someone to talk things over with.' With that, she filled him
in on the strange email from the night before.

'Did you try asking her?' Chris looked at her under his long
bangs. It was a cute look, but Dulcie wasn't swayed.

'No, I guess I was afraid.' She made a face. 'It seemed like the
kind of thing that I'd want to talk to her about, and I didn't know
if it was too early. Though maybe she'll have explained herself
more.' She tapped her laptop to wake it but the only new message
was something from the Coop. Logo sweatshirts were on sale.

'Maybe this is good news for Thorpe.' Chris wisely decided to
change the topic, or at least veer it in a different direction. 'I mean,
if one of the stronger candidates is disqualified, maybe they'll start
to appreciate the solid job he's been doing.'

'Not necessarily.' Dulcie thought through the factors that might influence the search committee. 'For starters, he doesn't have a big coterie of grad students. As far as I know, I'm his only doctoral candidate, and I'm nowhere near finishing my thesis.' She didn't have to explain. As incomprehensible as they might be to outsiders, in the rarefied world of academia, both of these facts would reflect badly on Thorpe, no matter how unfair that was.

'You did publish that article, though.' Chris, after a good night's sleep, was determinedly optimistic. 'And, who knows? You really might be on the verge of a momentous discovery.'

'Except that I have no plans to publish about it.' She softened the blow with a smile. 'Not yet, anyway.' Publishing, they both knew, was the only marker of success in academia. 'Besides . . .' She stopped herself. The idea of publishing had made her think of her last paper. 'There was all the brouhaha in September, and I was at the center of that,' she said finally. Chris would know what she was talking about.

He did. 'They couldn't still be blaming Thorpe – or you – for that, could they?'

Dulcie shook her head, as if she were uncertain. He was in a good mood. They'd had a lovely evening, and she didn't want to mar it. But when she looked down at the cat, those green eyes held a harder truth. Yes, she acknowledged silently to Esmé. It wasn't fair, but they could.

'What do you think, kitty? Do you think old Thorpe has a chance?' It wasn't exactly what Chris had asked, but it was a question she dared voice aloud. Esmé blinked, once, but didn't otherwise respond, leaving her humans to finish their coffee in silence.

FORTY

Dulcie and Chris had gone on to cheerier conversation before heading off for the day. Chris had hopes of making his schedule change permanent, he had said. Three nights a week, he hoped to be able to come home by a reasonable hour. Dulcie had been happy – for him. But also a little concerned. The overnights were the best-paying shifts, which is why he'd held them for so long. If Chris, as Dulcie suspected, was changing his schedule around simply because he was worried that she couldn't – or wouldn't – take care of herself, then he was doing them both a disservice.

He'd sounded so happy that she hadn't wanted to bring it up, but she made a mental note. If she – or, okay, Rogovoy – didn't get to the bottom of these attacks soon, she would find a way to convince Chris that she was a responsible urban dweller.

At quarter to ten in the morning, though, the streets of Cambridge were anything but threatening, and it was hard to picture them as dark or scary. She'd meant to email Emily again, or even call, but it had been so nice lingering over coffee with Chris that time had gotten away from her. She'd left him setting up for an online help session, still in his pajamas, and greeted a day as crisp and fresh as a local apple.

On a day like this, even the idea of returning to her thesis was brighter. Dulcie pulled out her phone as she strode down the sidewalk. She had a section – Early Romantic Poetry – right in the Yard. It would be the most natural thing in the world to hop from there over to Widener. She still had a ton of notes on *The Ravages* that she hadn't written up yet. If she applied herself, she could have another chapter ready before Thorpe's new deadline. In fact, she promised herself, if she could get through those notes by lunch, she'd reward herself not with another three-bean burger, but with an hour in the Mildon. This wasn't taking the place of her work on her dissertation. It was a side project. And if she were lucky, well, she and Martin Thorpe would deal with it then.

In the meantime, she dialed the number for Emily and Mina's dorm room.

'Hello?' The voice on the other end sounded so tentative, Dulcie worried that she had called too early.

'Hi, Emily? It's Dulcie.' She bit her lip. The junior seemed so frail at times; she undoubtedly needed her rest. 'Am I calling too early?'

'Huh? No, I just – I had a bad night. I was at the health services.'

'Is it Mina?' Dulcie couldn't forget that this girl's room-mate still lay in a coma. 'Emily, if I can do anything . . .'

'Oh, no. She's, well, her condition hasn't changed. I had to have some tests.' Dulcie could hear the thud of the cane as the other girl walked. So that was why she had sent such a terse note last night.

'I'm sorry.' It wasn't really the right response, but she didn't want to pry. She also didn't want to rush the other girl, even as the sight of the Yard's red-brick wall reminded her of why she had called. 'But Emily? I wanted to follow up on that email you sent last night. About the professor?'

'Oh, yeah.' More thudding. And a beep – Dulcie had another call.

'Would you hang on a moment?' Dulcie regretted the words as soon as they were out of her mouth. She couldn't afford to lose this girl. Emily grunted something that sounded like assent, though, and so Dulcie clicked over.

'Dulcie? It's Raleigh.' Dulcie was about to make an excuse to call her back when Raleigh continued. 'It's about that kitten. Can we talk?'

'Uh, yeah.' Dulcie thought fast. 'Hang on one minute?'

Dulcie clicked back. Emily was still there, barely.

'I'm sorry,' she was saying. 'I've got to go. I'm trying to get off to class.'

Dulcie scrambled. 'I understand. How about lunch?' It wasn't time at the Mildon, but perhaps it was more important.

'Uh, okay.' Emily sounded uncertain, so Dulcie tried to make it sound as social as she could.

'How about Lala's? I love that place, don't you?' Maybe she'd have something besides the burger. 'How's twelve thirty?' That would give her a little library time, at least.

'Sure, sure.' More thudding. 'See you there.' Emily hung up, leaving Dulcie with the impression that her hard sell hadn't worked and that more than fatigue was weighing on the junior.

Meanwhile, she was outside Longfellow Hall. Her section would start in two minutes, and Raleigh was on the other line.

'Hi, Raleigh. Sorry about that. What's up?' Dulcie looked up at the big clock. One minute. This had better be important.

It was. 'It's that kitten, Dulcie. He's a real sweetheart, a real cuddler. But that just makes it worse. Lloyd's using his inhaler constantly. I mean, he doesn't want to say anything. He certainly doesn't want me to take the kitten to a shelter, but . . .'

'No, no.' Dulcie responded with a sinking feeling. 'I understand.' She had left Raleigh and Lloyd in the lurch. This was her fault; she had to do something. 'Look, Raleigh? I haven't checked with Chris.' Or with Esmé, she wanted to say. The tuxedo cat had been so possessive of her lately, she couldn't see her taking a newcomer lightly. 'But maybe I could take the kitten. Just for a while, as a foster.'

'You don't have to do that, Dulcie.' Raleigh sounded very calm for a woman with an asthmatic boyfriend.

'No, really. I'm sure it will be fine.' She could keep the kitten in the bathroom, maybe. That would serve as a kind of quarantine, until she could have a vet check the little marmalade out – and until she could convince Esmé that the tiny creature was a friendly visitor, rather than an intruder or prey, and a temporary one at that. 'I can pick him up, let me see . . . I've got a section, and then a lunch, but—'

'Dulcie, you don't have to do this,' Raleigh interrupted, 'because I've already found a new home for the kitten.'

'What?' Dulcie felt like she'd missed something.

'I just wanted to let you know, because, well, I know how you feel.' Raleigh was talking slowly, as if explaining something to a child. 'I've heard you, and I know what your fears are. But, honestly, I don't think in this case your worries are based on anything real. And I do think that little orange furball may do some good. He may even have come into our lives for this very purpose.'

'No—' Dulcie tried to interrupt, but Raleigh kept talking. She knew what was coming though. 'We can't be sure,' she tried to say. 'It's not safe—'

'I've talked to Lloyd and to Nancy, too, and we really think that this is a mutually beneficial solution, Dulcie.' Raleigh steam-rolled over Dulcie's objections. 'Better for everyone, really. You don't need another cat. I know that. But we all know someone who does. Someone who really could benefit from the comforting, the *calming* presence of a pet. Dulcie, I've given the kitten to Martin Thorpe.'

FORTY-ONE

Dulcie tried every objection she could think of. The kitten could already have an owner, someone who had lost it. But Raleigh had already called the local shelter to inquire about lost pets. The kitten could need veterinary care; Raleigh had already set up a visit for the usual swipes and shots. By the time Raleigh had announced that she was going to hang up, more than five minutes had passed. Dulcie was late. More than that, she was scared.

'Are you okay, Ms Schwartz?' Rita, a sophomore, looked concerned.

'Yes, thanks.' Dulcie tried to calm herself and gave up. 'I'm sorry,' she announced to the eight students facing her. 'I've just got some bad news about a friend.' That was stretching the truth, but not by much. 'That's why I was late.'

The soft sound of sympathy floated up to her, comforting her and reminding Dulcie of why she was there.

'But enough about me,' she said, with a forced jollity. 'Who wants to talk about this week's reading?'

Nobody did, at least not at that moment. When Nina finally raised her hand again, it wasn't with the question Dulcie had expected. 'Yes?'

'Did your friend get attacked in the Square?'

Dulcie was taken aback for a moment before it hit her. The undergrads would have all received a university police text alert, a warning she would do well to drive home. 'No, it wasn't that. However, you have probably heard that something – someone, I mean – has been targeting women in the Square at night.'

Nods all around, and she heard Laurie, in the back, whisper something. 'Laurie? Do you have a question?'

'Not exactly, Ms Schwartz.' The girl looked down at her notebook as if embarrassed. Dulcie waited, and sure enough, she looked back up. 'Only, can you tell us if there's any truth to the rumor? We've heard that the attacks had something to do with the moon. They're calling him "the slasher".'

For a moment, Dulcie lost her place. This was too close to what she had just been thinking. Only, she hadn't heard that the attacker had a name. And she did have some facts. 'I think that's all speculation at this point.' She was trying for calm. She was, after all, the adult here. 'There is evidence that the attacks – the initial one, anyway – were domestic in nature. Someone the victims knew.'

More murmurs and nods greeted that news, and Dulcie realized she should wrap this up. 'But still, this is a city. Please don't forget that, and use good common sense – especially at night.'

Even as she said it, she realized who she was sounding like. And, it hit her, then, that she knew what she had to do next. Emily might not like it, and Dulcie had to accept the possibility that this would sour their relationship – and close off that source of information. But this wasn't a game, and Dulcie had a responsibility to the community. As soon as she had met with the junior, Dulcie was going to gather everything she knew. Then she would go talk to Rogovoy.

'Ms Schwartz.' Thomas Griddlehaus greeted her at the Mildon entrance. She might not have much time before her lunch, but she'd make use of every minute.

'Mr Griddlehaus.' Dulcie smiled as she returned the greeting. 'I trust you were able to put everything right after yesterday's . . . event?'

'Of course.' The librarian sounded a bit taken aback, as if Dulcie had questioned his competence. 'But, thank you for removing . . . him.'

Dulcie breathed easier as Griddlehaus signed her in and led her to her usual seat. When he deposited the box of papers in front of her and left them for her to sort through, she knew she was back in his good graces.

Of course, it could also have been that he was distracted. 'So, you seemed to know that . . . person.' He was hovering, and not, she was pretty sure, to watch how she removed the first of the five stacked pages.

'Yes.' She paused after laying out the second page. In part, she was wondering if he would object. She had a good reason: the story had seemed to jump and she was wondering if looking at the text in sequence would help her decipher any of the missing parts. However, what she had done stretched the protocol slightly.

His mind, however, was elsewhere. 'How curious,' the little clerk continued. 'Because, if you don't mind me saying so, Ms Schwartz, he doesn't seem like the type whom you would normally befriend.'

Dulcie ducked her head over the first document. It was intended as a compliment; she knew that. What surprised her was the urge to defend the hapless Josh, even though he had broken the library's most basic rules.

'He's not that bad,' she said, after a brief pause. 'Really.' Just then, the library air-filtration system must have kicked in, because she felt a breeze, like a soft brush of fur, by her face. 'He means well.'

With a shrug and a non-committal noise that sounded like something a small animal would make, Griddlehaus seemed to accept her non-explanation, and when he returned to his desk, she went to work.

'Be Wary of whom you gift your Trust.' Thunder rocked the coach, yet still the Stranger's voice gained her ear. Beyond their near confines, the howls had faded, their Demonic voices taken by the Wind. 'Fate may afk—' Afk? Ask, of course. Forty-five minutes in, and all she'd gotten were these few lines. Dulcie put her pencil down and closed her eyes.

Concentrating was difficult, however. Partly, Dulcie knew, that was because she had less than an hour before she was due to meet Emily, and thoughts of that lunch were preoccupying her. What had the email meant? Was Professor Showalter really faking her injury or – worse – had she been making up whatever research she had promised to share? Dulcie's laptop was locked in the cabinet by Griddlehaus's desk – house rules for the Mildon – and she itched to retrieve it and to check whether the scholar had replied to her email. Only the thought that her time here in the Mildon might be limited kept her going, working away at the tantalizing manuscript.

Partly, she realized, she was distracted by her own reaction. Why had she defended Josh when he had so clearly been in the wrong?

As she sat there, eyes closed, the draft seemed to brush her face once more. It was a pleasant feeling, soft and a little warm. Welcome on a November day. Friendly. That was it: Dulcie felt friendly toward Josh. Despite her suspicions – and those of Rogovoy and, apparently, Emily – she had warm feelings toward him.

That was dangerous, as she well knew. *'Be wary of whom you gift your Trust.'* The stranger, that mysterious green-eyed fellow traveler, might as well be speaking to her. Besides, Dulcie knew, the worst psychopaths were the ones who seemed unassuming, even downright nice. But somehow she didn't see Josh as an abuser. He was so open, and really seemed to care about Mina. Could she really have been misled? Or was Josh being set up somehow, the perfect fall guy for someone else who wanted Mina out of the way? And if so, what was her responsibility here – to trust her instincts, or to listen to the concerns of others? If she listened to all the portents around her – the text, even that stray draft of air – maybe she would know. Then again, maybe she'd end up just like Lucy, looking for signs and symbols in a world that really wasn't that into her.

No, she was a scholar, not a psychic. No matter what kind of adventures her favorite fiction might describe she had to rely on what she could prove to be true. Shaking her head free of such fancies, she got back to work.

'*Fate may ask the impossible of you, and Friends, as well as Foes will decide upon your future – as you will decide upon theirs.*'

Well, that was enigmatic enough. And as Dulcie copied this last bit out, her soft pencil worn down to a stub, she noticed the hour. It was time for fate to play its part, or, at least, to serve up lunch.

FORTY-TWO

E mily didn't look good. She did, however, look like she would benefit from a solid meal, and Dulcie realized how happy she was that they had decided to meet here, at Lala's. As she waved to the wan young woman, Dulcie was already ordering in her mind. Unless Lala herself came over to dictate their lunch, Dulcie would get lentil soup for them both, and then a burger. Maybe they could even split an order of fries.

'Emily! Hi!' Dulcie stood so Emily would see her, and watched in dismay as the younger woman hobbled over, leaning heavily on her cane. 'How are you? Your leg . . . it's worse?'

Emily seemed to shrug as she sat, but that could have been the awkwardness of negotiating herself into the seat. Dulcie kicked herself for not thinking about access when she had grabbed the quiet table away from the counter.

'It's about the same.' Emily said as Dulcie handed her a menu.

When she didn't open it, Dulcie took the lead. 'Why don't we start with soup? Then we can have the house special. It's a vegetarian burger with this great, spicy sauce.'

Emily was shaking her head. 'That's too much.'

'My treat.' Dulcie couldn't afford to take all her students out, but this girl needed some pampering.

'I'll have the soup.' Emily looked up at the server, handing him her menu. Turning to Dulcie with a strained smile, she explained. 'I just don't have any appetite these days.'

'I'm sorry.' Dulcie didn't know how to ask. 'Is it your leg? Or . . . Mina?'

The nod could have covered both. 'I can't believe everything has gotten so screwed up,' she said. 'Mina, that professor.'

This was Dulcie's opening. The lead in to what she really wanted to ask. It seemed selfish to rush right in, though. 'Any word on Mina?'

'They've told me I shouldn't even try to visit any more.' Her voice was soft, but the tone was harsh. 'I mean, I'm only her best friend.'

'Why?' Dulcie asked, fearing the worst.

'I don't know.' Emily shook her head. 'I guess I was in the way.'

Dulcie bit her lip. She'd seen how awkward the younger woman was, navigating between the tables. Still, it seemed harsh, if not discriminatory, to bar her.

'Are they letting in other visitors?'

'I thought I saw her ex there.' Emily leaned in. 'Josh.'

'Josh? I didn't know they'd broken up?'

Emily tossed her hair. 'They were going to. That's what happened. He took advantage of her.'

'You still think he did it?' Josh had mentioned a disability, a vulnerability of some sort. Some men could sense them, would seek out weak women like, well, like a wolf hunted its prey. Dulcie hadn't seen this trait in Josh. Then again, she had never seen him with Mina.

'Don't you?' Luckily, Emily didn't wait for an answer. 'He was just trouble from the start, trying to split us up.'

'It's funny.' Dulcie didn't know why she wanted to defend Josh, but she did. 'He doesn't seem like the type.'

'They never do.' The waiter came with their soups. Dulcie dug in

– and stopped as she saw Emily listlessly drag her spoon through the olive-green potage. 'Mina was fooled at first, but then she realized the truth. He wanted to separate her from everyone. To have her for himself.'

'But he said she was very social.' Dulcie motioned with her spoon, urging Emily to eat. 'That she was in all these political groups.'

'Support groups.' Emily sipped the soup. 'Because of him.' She put her spoon down and sat back. 'I'm sorry. I can't talk about this. I really miss her.'

Dulcie was afraid she was going to leave – and not only because the junior hadn't answered her questions. 'Please, I'm sorry. We won't talk about it any more.' She watched the girl. 'Please eat. We won't talk about him,' she added.

Emily nodded, as if she'd reached a decision. 'Thanks, it's hard for people to understand.'

Dulcie wanted to commiserate. To jump in and tell this young girl about her friendship with Suze. They'd both moved in with their boyfriends over the past year, and their friendship had changed. But Suze was still her closest friend. Though, come to think of it, Dulcie couldn't remember the last time the two of them had spent any real time together. Maybe it was just as well not to mention Suze.

At any rate, Emily was eating, if a bit slowly. And Dulcie had other questions for her.

'Emily, I wanted to follow up on your email.' Emily looked up as she took another spoon. 'About Professor Showalter? You said she had faked it – did you mean, she faked being attacked?'

'What?' Emily dropped her spoon. 'Oh, no. I didn't – I'm sorry.'

'Oh, that's a relief.' Dulcie heard herself. 'I mean, not a *relief* relief, but, well, I'm glad to know she's not a liar.'

'But she is.' Emily looked down at her bowl.

'What?' Dulcie had almost forgotten her own lunch. 'Emily, what do you mean?'

'Her research.' The junior took another sip. 'So-called. The paper she's working on?'

'No, I don't know about it.' Dulcie shook her head. 'She didn't get to give her talk, and then—'

'I know.' Emily cut in. 'But I thought she spoke to *you*.'

'She didn't have time,' Dulcie said sadly. 'We were going to talk. It turns out, we're both doing research on the same author, and I've

found something in the Mildon.' Her regret gave way to a warm
glow of pride, and she leaned in. 'Something really amazing, actually. A primary source.'

Emily shrugged. 'Sounds impressive.'

'It is – to me anyway.' Dulcie remembered the girl's prejudice
and decided to backtrack a bit. 'I don't know what Professor
Showalter had, if she had anything. But, Emily, I'm pretty sure I
have the real deal.'

'Huh.' Emily looked up, a grudging respect in her eyes. 'And
you found this – these papers – at the Mildon?'

Dulcie nodded. 'I've been transcribing them into my laptop, trying
to piece everything together. But what I've found is incomplete, at
least, so far. That's why I was hoping . . . Emily, what do you think
Professor Showalter faked?'

'Well, maybe "faked" is too strong a word.' Emily put her spoon
down, leaving half the bowl. 'And, as I've said, this isn't really my
area of expertise. But from what Mina has taught me, well, I just
think she's wrong about some things.'

'Wrong about what?' The lack of specifics was making Dulcie
dizzy.

Emily waved the question away. 'You see, this is where I get in
trouble. Like I said, I really don't know this stuff. Just something
she said, something about some imagery – no, it was about a creature. Like, a werewolf or something, in one of those novels? Only,
I know that Mina reads those like anything – and this lady was
saying that there's no connection between werewolves and the moon.
Or something. It just sounded totally wrong.'

It was the longest speech Dulcie had heard Emily give, and she
stared at her, waiting for her to continue.

'I guess "fake" was the wrong word.' She chuckled a little. 'I
haven't been sleeping well, and this whole thing with Mina, with
Josh.' She looked around as if the answer was on one of the other
tables. 'I'm just angry with the world, I guess.'

She finished that with a big smile. 'So, this is really your treat?'

'Definitely.' Emily's answer hadn't made much sense, but Dulcie
had to give her some slack: she'd been through the mill. Besides,
now that the girl had eaten a little, Dulcie knew she had to break
her own news – to tell Emily that she was going to talk to the
cops. But just as Dulcie opened her mouth to speak, she felt it.
Sharp and quick – the slap of claws. It was a warning. About what,

she couldn't be sure, and she opened her mouth again – only to feel it once more, a strike of claws so real she reached up to her cheek. There was no blood, none she could see, but she'd gotten the message. Mr Grey was telling her to be quiet, to leave well enough alone. 'I'll get the check,' she said, instead of any of the other comments whirling around her head. At least Emily seemed rejuvenated. The food – half a bowl of Lala's lentil – had done her some good.

Much more quickly than she'd come in, Emily was gone, a testimony to the healing power of Dulcie's favorite chef. Dulcie took a little longer to leave. First, she finished her soup, although she couldn't be said to have tasted it. Then, as she flagged down the waiter, she tried to make sense of what the junior had told her.

Emily didn't like Josh; that was for sure. She still saw Josh as the probable culprit in the attack on her room-mate. But if that was the case, why didn't she want to talk about her own assault?

The waiter came with the check just as the answer came to Dulcie. Emily must have confronted him. She had called Josh out, and he had lashed out at her. She probably felt stupid – and she was smart enough to know that if she tried to press charges herself, it would have an effect on Mina's case. Dulcie could easily imagine Suze's take on that, and knew it would be import-ant. Whether it would have helped or been ruled prejudicial, Dulcie didn't know, but she could see why the girl wouldn't want to muddy the waters.

Emily's gripes against the professor made even less sense, but maybe that was good. As Dulcie got up and made her own way to the door, she acknowledged that she was clutching at straws, hoping for something new that would help her in her search for the missing manuscript. Emily's vagueness had renewed that hope. Maybe Showalter did have something, some new information or a document to share, and Emily was simply being a loyal – and misguided – friend.

As it was, Dulcie knew she'd made too much of Emily's message. That was the problem with email. There was no effect and no sense of the mindset of the person on the other end. Sometimes, she decided, pushing open the door, the other person was just fatigued.

That was a feeling Dulcie could relate to, and the idea of walking up to the university police headquarters only compounded it. Surely, the day hadn't been this cold and blustery before. A gust of wind roared down Mass. Ave., causing Dulcie and her fellow pedestrians to shrug into their coats and collars. Maybe she should go home. Put a hat on, if not a warmer coat, before trotting all the way past the Common.

But, no. Dulcie didn't need the claw-like sting of flying grit to remind her that there was no time like the present. If anything, Emily's erratic behavior underscored her initial instinct: it was time to tell everything to Rogovoy. The junior might get angry, but she wasn't thinking clearly these days. She'd said as much herself, and Dulcie had an obligation to the community.

As she began to walk, however, she wondered just what she would say. She'd tell Rogovoy about the attack on Emily, that was for sure. But maybe she should also tell him about her chats with Josh. He'd seemed so friendly, so guileless, that she couldn't see him as a bad guy.

She could, however, imagine the burly detective's response to that. He'd shake his big head in what she imagined would be a fatherly fashion. He might even reach out and pet her hand with one of those big paws. And then he'd pick up the chubby undergrad for more questioning, if not to charge him.

Was it the right thing to do? Was she misreading her heart – if not the signs from Mr Grey? The blinking red walk sign gave her an excuse to pause. And while she was pondering, she felt the vibration in her bag. For a moment, it didn't register. Then she realized, it was her phone. Maybe it was Professor Showalter, calling to discuss her work rather than emailing.

She scrambled through her bag and answered before checking to see who was on the line. 'Hello?'

'Dulcie! In the nick of time.' It was Lucy, but Dulcie satisfied herself with rolling her eyes as the light changed and she crossed the street. 'It's not dark there, yet. Is it?'

'Hi, Lucy. How are you? And, no, it's not even one thirty.' Dulcie tried to keep the exasperation out of her voice. Lucy would never master the three-hour time difference.

'Good, because if there's moonlight, watch out.' Another gust of wind had Dulcie ducking her head, and she missed her mother's next words.

'What was that, Lucy?' Dulcie considered pleading work, but

she had a good ten-minute walk ahead of her. It was as good a time
as ever to humor her mother.

'Wolves, Dulcie. Beware of the wolves.' Clearly, Dulcie had
missed a reference to a dream or some kind of vision.

'We don't have wolves in Cambridge.' Dulcie said. It wouldn't
do to tell her mother about the eerie howl she had heard the other
night. Lucy didn't need any encouragement.

'That's funny.' Lucy sounded confused, and for a moment,
Dulcie's heart went out to her. Lucy was her mother, even if she
had a wild case of empty-nest syndrome. 'I was sure I saw you,
out in the dark. Maybe on a road somewhere, with wolves.'

'I must have told you about what I'm working on.' Dulcie didn't
remember doing so, but she must have. The alternative – that her
mother truly was psychic – was not worth considering. 'I'm piecing
together a bit of an old manuscript. It looks like another Gothic,
a horror story. There's a woman fleeing some kind of danger, and a
coach picks her up. There are wolves howling outside, and I think
there's something strange about them. Maybe they're werewolves.
I don't think there are any references to the moon, however.' She
paused. 'Maybe those got lost.'

'Maybe it was only peeking through the clouds.' Lucy sounded
back on solid footing now, and Dulcie regretted encouraging her.

'C'mon, Mom. Everyone knows you need a full moon for a
werewolf to come out, and that was last night.'

'Dulcinea Schwartz, do you believe everything you read?' For a
moment, her mother was the formidable woman she must have once
been: a Philadelphia Main Line matron with all the force of society
behind her.

Dulcie laughed, a short, startled laugh. 'Lucy, I think I know the
conventions of the Gothic novel.'

'You may understand fiction, young lady. But you know next to
nothing about supernatural fact.' Dulcie tried to think of a response.
Before she could, Lucy was talking again. 'Full moon, indeed. What
balderdash,' she was saying. 'What kind of animal only needs to
feed once a month? Granted, alpha predators don't need to feed that
often. That's why they sleep so much.'

Dulcie thought of Esmé and let her mother ramble. It could do
no harm.

'But when they wake, they feed. They hunt and feed. It's in their
nature, whether they are in the alpha predator form willingly, or

not. And it's moonlight that wakes them, Dulcie. Any hint of moonlight, full or crescent. That's why I asked you about moonrise,
Dulcie. The month after the harvest moon is always a dangerous
time, and that vision, Dulcie? It wasn't some random heroine I saw.
It was you.'

FORTY-THREE

'**M**y mother is nuts.' Dulcie said more or less to the air
around her – and only a little to the grey squirrel that had
paused halfway down a tree trunk to stare at her. 'She is
just not a rational human being.'

The squirrel didn't comment, only scampered up the tree, and
Dulcie was forced to confront the absurdity of her position. Yes,
her mother had lectured her on werewolves. But here she was, a
doctoral candidate, seeking a second opinion from a rodent.

'I was hoping to hear from you, Mr Grey,' she added. To consult
with a feline specter, after all, was a different story entirely. 'I mean,
what was that warning about? Were you telling me to leave the
restaurant so I could take Lucy's call?' She paused. It was conceiv-
able. Still, it wasn't the consult she'd have wanted.

Nor was it strictly necessary. Dulcie knew Lucy's quirks. For
starters, she could probably discount anything that her mother cred-
ited to a dream or, as she'd put it, a vision. Lucy didn't take quite
as many psychoactive substances these days as she had in her – or
Dulcie's – youth. But Dulcie had spent enough time talking her
mother down to know that sometimes the Great Earth Spider was
really just a daddy long-legs on the outhouse wall. Likewise,
although Dulcie appreciated the sentiment behind the warning, she
knew that her mother's premonitions were just that – a manifesta-
tion of a maternal instinct, frustrated by a daughter's independence
and the width of the continent that separated them.

As for the rest? Well, Dulcie knew that her mother was a reader.
She'd gotten her own love of books from her, along with a slightly
battered copy of the Riverside Shakespeare. It was just that Lucy
tended to read everything, indiscriminately. Especially if it dealt
with mysticism or the occult.

Therefore, Dulcie told herself as she crossed a side street, Lucy's knowledge of anything in particular was suspect. Good intentions aside, she wasn't to be trusted. It wasn't as if—

The squeal of car brakes, and Dulcie jumped back. The car – a beat-up Honda – hadn't been bearing down on her, however. In the middle of the street, Dulcie saw a squirrel, surely a different animal, frozen, staring at the monstrous machine that had paused only centimeters away.

'Squirrel!' Dulcie called. It was better than yelling, 'Mr Grey.' And after all, this was only a dumb rodent, probably a little crazed by the blustery weather. The small creature turned toward her, its black eyes unblinking, before darting off down that side street.

No, Dulcie turned back toward the police station, it wasn't the same. Just as her mother's preoccupation with psychic phenomena was nothing at all like her own preoccupation with a certain author, or an unfinished book. Not to mention a mysterious manuscript . . .

The wind was really picking up. She pulled her sweater tighter around her as grey clouds whipped overhead. No wonder that squirrel was in a frenzy. This was going to be a night to stay in, for sure. It would be cozy to be home with Esmé, even if Chris couldn't spare another night off work. Besides, the little cat clearly had been feeling neglected, and they'd both benefit from the time together. She probably should be happy for Thorpe that he might have that same kind of homey warmth. If only she could shed those last few fears.

It was the weather, as much as anything. A leaf came flying by, scratching at her face with its dry edge. This wind was whipping everything up. It would be a pleasure to stay in and work. And soon she wouldn't have to worry any more about anything but her work. Even as her curls blew across her face, she could see the blue light up ahead. The emergency call box on the corner meant she'd reached police headquarters. She'd tell Rogovoy everything – everything about Emily, that is. She'd already tried to explain the Thorpe situation and that had gone nowhere. Besides, no matter what Lucy had said, it seemed unlikely that even if her worst fears were true . . .

Thinking of that squirrel, Dulcie looked both ways before crossing. Everybody was on edge today. Maybe they'd even get snow. It was early in the season, but a wind like this could herald a few flurries or the kind of icy rain that made her long for the more moderate West Coast mists. If only Lucy weren't quite so nutty. She couldn't be right about werewolves, could she? Everyone knew that they needed the full moon to transform.

Except that two of the attacks had happened before the full moon. If that had been Thorpe, that is. If he had indeed become one of – how had her author put it? – *'Those fiendish things, the Beasts of the Night.'*

No, it wasn't possible. Besides, she was almost there. Half a block – she stepped from the curb. And came up coughing. Something about this wind and the cross streets combined to toss more grit in the air. Another sharp-edged leaf, oak, dry and brittle, whipped by, clawing at her face and tangling in her hair. Dulcie batted at it, squinting into the wind. It had gotten tangled in her curls, more brown than her own reddish highlights, and she looked up to pull it free. Funny how sharp the leaf's points could be, once it had dried. At least the wind had cleared the clouds; the sky, with that wild irregularity for which New England weather was known, suddenly shone a bright and vivid blue. The clouds that seemed so threatening only moments before were stretched out, horse tails streaming toward the horizon. And there, white against the endless blue, was the moon. Slightly worn, not quite symmetrical, but clear and glowing in the bright afternoon sky.

Dulcie rubbed her cheek where the leaf had scratched in. Blinked away the last of the grit. She was maybe fifty feet from the entrance to the police station. Rogovoy would probably want her to fill out forms. She could be in there for an hour, maybe more, especially if he brought in other detectives to hear her story. The moon was clear above the trees, bright as a new nickel as the last of the clouds dispersed. What if Lucy were right?

Thorpe had the kitten. An innocent little marmalade kitten. Those round eyes, as blue as the sky, had looked at her with such trust. Such faith . . .

Dulcie turned on her heel and started running back to the Square.

FORTY-FOUR

'**R**aleigh, are you there?' Dulcie was panicking. If Raleigh had been available to answer, her phone would not have gone to voicemail. 'Call me? Please?'

Dulcie was heading to the departmental office. If Martin Thorpe were still there, she could talk to him. Stop him. Force him to surrender the kitten. Unless Raleigh had brought it over to wherever her adviser lived.

'Lloyd, pick up. Pick up!' Another voicemail, and Dulcie left a second message, asking simply for a call back as soon as possible.

'Hey, Suze.' Dulcie's voice was broken by her gasps as she trotted down the brick sidewalk. 'We keep missing.' As expected, Dulcie had gotten her former room-mate's voice mail. At least by now, she had a more coherent message planned. 'I'm afraid this isn't just social. You see, I'm in an awkward situation. I may have some information about a crime. Only, well, there may be a really strange twist in the whole thing. Call me?'

Dulcie went over whom else she could call: Trista? Chris? It was useless. She was on her own. They would care, but she doubted they'd understand this particular dilemma. She'd been dithering too long anyway. It was time to act.

The walk signal changed and she came to a halt, breathing heavily. The pause made her take stock. What exactly was she going to do?

Confront Thorpe. That had been her original idea. Confront the acting head of the department and – what? – demand that he turn over his new kitten? As she waited for the light to change, Dulcie realized the absurdity of her situation. How could she separate Thorpe from the kitten? Surely there had to be a way.

Just then, her phone rang and Dulcie fumbled for it, grateful that one of her friends was checking in.

'Hello?' She waited to hear Raleigh's voice. Or Lloyd's or Suze's. Instead, she heard a deeper and more lyrical voice, one she only vaguely recognized, asking for 'Ms Dulcie Schwartz.'

'You've reached her. Me, I mean, I.' The light changed and Dulcie started walking. She'd reached the Common, and it hit her. 'Professor Showalter?'

'Yes, you had emailed me?'

'Yes, I did.' That email – her thesis – seemed like a concern of a thousand years ago. Still, Dulcie tried to rally. 'I am sorry to have disturbed you.' Dulcie couldn't shake the memory of what she had overheard at the infirmary. 'I don't mean to be a pest.'

'Nonsense.' The voice on the other end sounded warm and encouraging. 'I'm only sorry it has taken me this long to respond. What's on your mind?'

'Well, I don't know if you remember. When you were first here, at the bar . . .' There was nothing to do but ask. 'You said that you had some information for me. Something that might be of interest? And then we never got to talk.'

'Of course. You're writing on the author of *The Ravages*.' Dulcie nodded before realizing that the professor couldn't see her. But no response was necessary, it seemed, as the professor kept talking. 'I don't know if it exactly relates. In fact, it may be a wild goose chase, but recently I've come into possession of some papers. A colleague of mine who works at a private collection in Philadelphia came across the most interesting material.'

'Pages from a manuscript?' Dulcie couldn't help interrupting. If Showalter had the rest of the manuscript. If she were willing to share . . . She stopped short, remembering her earlier fears. Well, if the senior scholar had made a discovery, Dulcie would be willing to help her. 'If you're looking for a grad student to assist you . . .'

'No, you've misunderstood me.' Dulcie's heart sank. The scholar was simply notifying her. 'That's not what I meant. These papers are only tangential to my area of interest.' The professor kept talking. 'But when I read your article, I thought they could be useful to you.'

Dulcie stopped short, unable to believe what she was hearing. 'You mean I can have them?'

'Well, yes, if you're interested.' The professor was saying. 'I believe you may already have seen some of them. My friend, the curator in Philly, says part of this grouping may have already been given to the Mildon, and it sounds like it could be related to the work you've been doing. She sent them to me to appraise, as the collection is looking to deaccession more of their uncatalogued papers, and I know she would appreciate them going to a working scholar.'

'Wow, could you mail them?' Dulcie bit her lip. These papers were valuable. 'I mean, or have them shipped? I'm sure I could cover—'

'No, I don't think so.' Of course, these papers were valuable. 'You see, there are some complications.'

She knew it. Nothing could be that simple. Even so, these papers could be worth whatever condition the professor put on them.

'There has been some other interest, you see. I had brought some notes with me. They were lost, I'm afraid, when my bag was grabbed. But I still have the pages themselves.' She paused, as if making a decision, and Dulcie held her breath. 'You should have a chance to see them. I'll bring them when I come for the rescheduled Newman,' Showalter was saying. 'Oh, and Ms Schwartz? They appear to contain some genealogical material. I think you'll be intrigued.'

Well, that was interesting. Dulcie started walking again as soon as she and the professor had signed off. Other interest? Could that have been what Dulcie had overheard at the health services? And what about those notes? A tingle went up Dulcie's spine, like the brush of soft fur. The professor's bag had been taken on her way to the lecture. Maybe it hadn't been a mugging, but a desperate attempt to get her research material. If those pages had been the reason for the attack, then Showalter could be in danger. Dulcie should call her back. Warn her to take extra care.

Only she did want those papers. Genealogical information wasn't manuscript pages, but in a way, it could be better. For so long Dulcie had been trying to put a name to the anonymous author, to give her her rightful place in history. Dulcie crossed into the Common, trying to picture what those pages could be. A birth certificate? Not likely. Wherever her author had ended up, odds were that she was born in London. And how common were birth certificates anyway? Odds were it wasn't something less official. A church registry, perhaps. A notice of a birth or a marriage.

Except that her author didn't believe in marriage. Dulcie stopped short. No, she didn't know that. What she did know was that in her writings – especially the writing Dulcie had found from her later years, in the New World – her author had spoken disparagingly of marriage. She walked on, through the leafless trees. Maybe she had been married to someone she hated. Maybe she'd been happily widowed. Maybe she'd fled—

Josh. There, ahead of her. Dulcie had been so caught up in her own thoughts that she'd nearly walked into him, and now there he was, waving.

'Dulcie! I was hoping to run into you.'

'Josh?' Dulcie swallowed, her mouth suddenly dry. Was he stalking her? It couldn't simply be coincidence, running into him here, in the Common, where Professor Showalter had been attacked. Could he think she had those papers – whatever they were? 'What – what brings you here?'

'I was up at the Quad.' He said. It was believable; the Common was on the way. 'I've been doing some reading on this author that Mina's into. I didn't realize you were writing your thesis on her.'

Dulcie blanched. He was stalking her. 'You know?'

'I read that article. I made a copy, too. It's not exactly Mina's area of expertise, but the timing is right. I told you about this woman she's trying to trace? So I thought it might interest her.'

It might indeed, especially if the subject of Mina's study was . . . No, that was too much of a reach. Besides, the woman she'd been hearing about wouldn't be interested in the author of *The Ravages*. Dulcie felt herself relaxing. 'It's probably not theoretical enough for Mina,' she said. He looked at her blankly. 'Nothing about the semiotics of the assumed gender roles,' she explained.

'What? No.' Josh responded, shaking his head. 'That's not – Mina's into connections and relativity when it comes to books and authors. Not that abstract stuff.'

Dulcie opened her mouth – then shut it. Clearly he saw his girlfriend – ex-girlfriend? – in a different light than her best friend did. At any rate, he had moved on.

'But that's not the big news. I'm going to visit Mina.' He was saying. His cheeks were glowing, though with the cold or the excitement, Dulcie couldn't say. 'She's – well, she seems to be waking up.'

'She's conscious?' That would solve quite a few problems.

But Josh was shaking his head. 'No, she's sort of talking though. Moving around. It's like she's in a dream. The doctors say . . .' Now he seemed to have trouble talking. She watched him swallow, twice. 'The doctors say that maybe this is the best she'll be. But I know her, and, well, I think she's trying, Dulcie. I think she's trying very hard to wake up.'

'And you're going back to see her?' Dulcie didn't know if that was a good idea. 'They're allowing visitors?'

He shook his head. 'Well, no, not yet. But I'm going to, Dulcie. They can't keep me away from her. They have no right.'

Maybe it was love – or maybe that's what he told himself. Something about his words, however, chilled Dulcie even more than the wind.

FORTY-FIVE

Dulcie wasn't even sure what she said. Something about 'good news' and 'good luck.' All she knew was that she had to get away from the red-cheeked junior as quickly as possible. The only saving grace was what Raleigh had told her: no visitors were being allowed in. The further from the Common Dulcie got, the more she relaxed. Josh couldn't get to the girl. The health services knew she'd been attacked; they'd protect her. And once she had seen Thorpe – and secured the kitten – then she would go back to Rogovoy. She'd call him after hours, if she had to. And then warn Showalter as well. Those papers could be some kind of a time bomb.

First, however, she had a mission. Turning onto Broadway, she lengthened her stride. If Thorpe wasn't there, she could ask Nancy for his home address. Nancy would understand that Dulcie needed to talk to her adviser; she wouldn't have to explain. Although maybe she would tell the kindly secretary about Showalter's news, about how she had a possible breakthrough for Dulcie. Nancy would understand how excited she was to work with a scholar who understood her enthusiasm for this author.

Dulcie slowed as she thought it through. No, she couldn't tell Nancy, not about all of it, anyway. Certainly not about her hunch that Showalter's notes might have been the real motive of the attack. Nancy might not like Martin Thorpe; Dulcie knew that the acting head was an extremely difficult boss. She was loyal, however. Especially since she now saw Martin Thorpe as needing support.

It wasn't like Dulcie was intentionally undermining Thorpe. There would be benefits to her if he kept his job, and for better or worse she had managed to get along with him. Just because she wanted to work with a visiting scholar and had a wild theory as to why that scholar had been attacked. Just because she wanted to take her adviser's new pet away on the possibility that he was some kind of horrible monster. Like she had thought Josh might be, only moments before.

Her walk had slowed almost to a stop. She was being as bad as Lucy. Superstitious and illogical. If Josh had attacked Mina and, thus probably, Emily, then Thorpe was innocent. If Josh hadn't attacked Mina and Emily, and the notes were the reason Showalter had been jumped, then Thorpe was certainly suspect – but then how had the other two young women been involved? What evidence did she even have linking them?

None. She started walking again. If it wasn't Josh, then there was really very little she could do. But if she could get the kitten from Thorpe, just for safe keeping, and talk to Rogovoy, well, then maybe everything would sort itself out. At the very least, Dulcie would know that she had tried.

If Josh, then Thorpe . . . the possibilities started playing themselves out like one of Chris's equations. But if Thorpe, then . . . No, there were too many variables, including Professor Showalter. If only Mina would wake up and put an end to all the speculation. Dulcie heard herself and laughed: so now she was only hoping for the junior's recovery in order to put her own mind at ease? Maybe Nancy was right, and she was becoming more selfish. Did Nancy know more than she was letting on? Did Josh?

So deep in thought was she that when her phone rang again, Dulcie almost didn't hear it.

'Emily!' The junior had barely said hello when Dulcie jumped in. 'I've heard the news. That's so great.'

'Wait, what?' The voice on the other end was so surprised, Dulcie could have laughed. It was nice to be able to share good news for a change.

'Mina's responding! That's what . . .' She stopped herself. Whatever Josh's involvement was, his girlfriend's room-mate certainly blamed him. 'That's what I heard, anyway. She's not awake, but she's beginning to respond to stimuli and the doctors are hoping she'll wake up soon.'

'Oh, that's great.' Emily gushed, then got quieter. 'I wonder why they didn't tell me that?'

Dulcie felt for her. 'Maybe it happened after you left?'

'Maybe.' The silence felt awkward. Emily must have thought so, too. 'That is great, though. Thanks for telling me.'

'So how can I help you?' Dulcie couldn't stop smiling. 'I mean, besides giving you some good news for a change.'

'Oh, I was going to ask about the papers. But, well, if Mina's waking up, maybe it doesn't matter.'

That didn't make much sense to Dulcie. Then again, the term was winding up – and her news had probably been overwhelming.

'Are you sure? 'Cause I have—' But Emily had hung up.

Poor girl. She'd been through so much, she really needn't worry about her class work. Dulcie knew she should call back, reassure Emily that she could make up any missed assignments – and she would. But Dulcie had arrived at the departmental office and other priorities were pressing. Get the kitten, get out. Especially if Mina was on the verge of waking up, Dulcie didn't need to accuse anyone of anything. She only needed to ensure one small creature's safety. That was all.

'Hi, Nancy.' Dulcie stuck her head into the side room to see the secretary at her desk.

'Hello, Dulcie. Mr Thorpe is in his office. With his new charge.' Nancy was smiling, her voice soft. She must think that I had something to do with bringing the kitten over, Dulcie thought. And here I am, planning on taking him away.

Nothing for it. Dulcie climbed the stairs. 'Mr Thorpe?' The door was ajar, but she knocked anyway.

'Come in.' She entered to face an empty desk. And yet, his voice . . .

'Over here.' Her adviser was in the corner, squatting beside a cardboard box. With a sinking feeling, Dulcie joined him. Inside the box, sat the marmalade kitten, unharmed. In the sun that now streamed through the window, she could see the pale stripes in his orange fur and his round blue eyes as he stared up at Thorpe.

'Isn't he a cute little fellow?' Her adviser extended a finger, and the little cat batted at it. 'Feisty, too. I was going to take him straight home but then I thought maybe he'd be lonely. In a new place and all that.'

Dulcie watched her adviser with a sinking feeling. Seeing him like this, wiggling his finger to entice the kitten, he looked almost human. She looked up. The moon wasn't visible from the office window.

That didn't mean, in a few hours, when he left, that he wouldn't feel its effects.

'About that kitten, Mr Thorpe.' Her mouth was dry, and she paused.

'Oh, yes.' He looked up at her. 'I meant to thank you. Raleigh told me that you rescued him from an alley.' He turned back to the little creature. 'That must have been horrible for this little fellow. When I think of what could have happened to him . . .'

That was it. She had to think of what could happen to the kitten. Swallowing the lump in her throat, Dulcie broke in.

'That's just it, Mr Thorpe. He was lost, and we found him. But – ah – we may have been over hasty in bringing him to you. He may have people. People who love him and have been looking for him.'

The face that turned up toward her was bereft. 'But . . . Raleigh said he needed a home.'

Dulcie nodded, feeling worse with each passing second. 'I know. She called the area shelters. But, well, I've heard of someone who is looking for a lost kitten.' This was awful. 'If you lost a kitten like this, you would want to know he was all right, wouldn't you? And you'd want to get him back?'

It didn't help that Thorpe had turned from her. She saw him nodding and knew she had won her case. But still she stood there, frozen, as he reached down and stroked the little orange head. In response, the kitten reared up to attack, wrapping his front paws around Thorpe's fingers. Dulcie didn't think it was the kitten's tiny teeth that caused Thorpe's sharp intake of breath.

'Of course.' He said, with a little sniff. 'Of course, someone would want this little fellow back. He must be so relieved. Or she, of course.' Still crouching, he carefully disengaged himself from the tiny claws and started to close up the box. Dulcie saw where ventilation holes had been knocked in the side. A minuscule paw poked out, feeling for his new friend, and Thorpe gently touched it with his own finger before handing the box to Dulcie.

'I was going to call him Tigger,' he said.

FORTY-SIX

She was a heel. A witch. A cruel, cruel person. With each step Dulcie took, she came up with another name. It didn't matter that she had done what she could to mitigate the situation – promising to bring the little orange kitten back if he did not happen to have an owner (which really meant if she could prove that Thorpe wasn't a werewolf). It didn't matter that she had even consoled herself with the thought that her adviser could probably find another pet, thanks to the desperate – and non-supernatural-suspecting auspices of the local shelters. What she had done was mean and hurtful, and it had been all she could do to go through with it, taking the box from Thorpe and averting her own tear-filled eyes in her efforts not to see his. Thorpe had bonded with the kitten. With Tigger. If Dulcie's fears were accurate, her adviser had bigger problems then the loss of a kitten. But this one was on her, and she felt awful about it.

'I'm sorry, little fellow.' She spoke to the box as she walked, trying to placate the annoyed mews that emanated from the ventilation holes. 'I really am. I just had to make sure you were safe. And if you are . . .'

She'd bring him back. Of course she would. She'd make up some story and trust that Raleigh and Lloyd wouldn't expose her. If only she could find out sooner rather than later. But how?

Dulcie had toyed with the idea of luring Thorpe out into the moonlight. The autumn afternoon was already fading, and the sky had remained clear. Surely, that rising moon would be enough, shining down on her adviser's balding pate. If he changed, so be it. She'd deal somehow – it would still be daylight. And if he didn't? No, Dulcie kept walking. She would take Lucy's warning in order to protect the kitten. But she couldn't trust it beyond that. Lucy could be wrong, and a full or nearly full moon be necessary for the transformation. Maybe night's darkness was the essential ingredient. If only she could be sure.

If only someone could tell her.

Dulcie stopped, box in hand. Mina. If the girl had been stirring a few hours ago, maybe she'd be awake now. And while neither Emily nor Renée Showalter had seen their attackers, Mina had had a much more prolonged struggle. Even if Mina couldn't identify who – or what – had jumped her, her description might help Dulcie. A few words from the girl could clear or condemn Thorpe, at least as far as Dulcie and the kitten she was carrying were concerned.

Forgetting all thoughts of home, Dulcie started hurrying toward the university health services. Her jogging pace clearly annoyed the kitten, who was now mewing regularly inside his box. What she'd do with the kitten once she got to the infirmary was a problem, but Dulcie didn't care. She looked up at the Memorial Church clock – it was a little after three. Too late to bring the kitten home and then come back, but maybe she wouldn't have to. As far as she remembered, visiting hours ran until five, and she wouldn't need long.

The kitten had quieted down by the time Dulcie reached the infirmary. So quiet, in fact, that Dulcie had panicked briefly. 'Kitty! Tigger, are you all right?' She ducked by the side of the building and pried the interwoven flaps open. The blue eyes looking up at her blinked once, and she realized she was breathing again. 'Thank you, kitten,' she said, closing the box back up.

As she approached the health services' door, her other problem resolved itself. She'd gotten warm jogging up here and begun to unbutton her sweater. Approaching the front door, it seemed natural to shrug off the bulky knit and casually drape it over the box in her arms. If the kitten started mewing again, she'd be outed, but for now, they were good.

'Miss?' She had been walking past the front desk when the receptionist called her. It was the kitten, she was sure. 'May I see your ID?'

'Oh, of course.' With a sigh of relief, Dulcie put the box down, out of sight of the clerk behind the desk, and fished out her wallet. 'I'm here to visit a friend up on the third floor.'

'Here you go.' The receptionist handed back her wallet. 'Visiting hours end at five today.'

'Thanks.' Trying to look as casual as she could, Dulcie hoisted the box under one arm and strolled over to the elevator. When nobody called after her, she figured she'd made it, but not until the doors opened did she truly start to breath easily.

The first room she peeked into was empty, as was the next. At the door of the third, she heard muted conversation. A doctor or a nurse, probably, and she stepped back until a short man came out, carrying folded bed sheets.

'Hello?' The door was ajar, but she knocked on it softly.

'Miss?' The sight of a university police officer was a little disconcerting. The fact that he had stepped in front of her was even more so. 'I'm afraid I can't let you in.'

Of course. Mina's protection. At least now she knew why Emily had been barred from her room-mate's bedside. But hadn't Josh said that he was going to visit?

'I thought Mina could have visitors?' Dulcie tried her best to look like a clueless friend. At the very least, the clueless feeling was real. 'Can't she?'

'One at a time,' the officer said. 'Supervised.' As if to confirm, he turned and looked into the room behind him. The door was open far enough for Dulcie to make out the white curtain that separated the beds, and a pair of white uniform shoes.

'I don't see anyone in there.' Dulcie peeked by him. 'Just the nurse.'

'Please wait here.' The officer ducked into the room, and Dulcie could hear him consulting with someone who spoke softly. In a moment, he'd come back out. 'I guess you're okay to go in. Her last guest must have left without my noticing.'

Dulcie felt her eyebrows shoot up. Had the guard considered that orderly a guest? Surely, this wasn't the kind of surveillance that would keep a young woman safe. Then again, it wasn't the officer's duty to keep track of who *left* Mina's room – and it wasn't Dulcie's place to say anything. Instead, she nodded and thanked the young cop, and, box balanced on her hip, stepped inside.

The room wasn't, she was glad to see, any kind of fancy intensive care unit. Though there was some machinery and a monitor, Dulcie thought it was showing Mina's heart rate and blood pressure, it looked like any other infirmary room. Her condition – or maybe her security needs – had gotten her privacy, but nothing fancy in terms of accommodations. The room was still divided by curtains, sectioned for four beds, two on each side. Although the curtains were drawn on the left, which was dark, the right was open and Dulcie walked by one empty bed on her way in. This side of the room was softly lit. And on the second bed, back by the window, lay a young woman, her throat heavily bandaged. By her feet, an aide sat, reading.

'Hello.' The aide said. 'I'm Anna. You can sit in that chair if you want.'

'Thanks.' Dulcie pulled up the empty seat, setting the box down, and looked at Mina. Josh had been right; the young woman appeared to be asleep rather than comatose. If it weren't for those bandages, Dulcie wouldn't have been able to tell. Except, perhaps, for her extreme pallor, and the presence of an aide who, Dulcie well knew, also acted as a secondary guard. 'She's been having other visitors?'

'Tons.' The aide smiled. 'I think they're helping. People talk to her, you know. About classes she's missing, about political meetings. Even gossip.' Anna's voice was soft. 'You should, too. I can't leave you alone, but pretend I'm not here. She can hear you, I'm pretty sure.'

'Hey, Mina.' Dulcie spoke softly. 'How're you doing?' It was a lame beginning, but Dulcie didn't dare let on that she had not really known this girl – not with an attendant sitting right there. She could, however, test out the prone girl's reaction to some names. 'I hear you've been having lots of visitors. Lots of your friends have come by. Your boyfriend, Josh.' Dulcie paused, looking for any sign of movement. Nothing. 'I know that Martin Thorpe of the English department has meant to visit.' Nothing. 'You might not know his name, but he's a skinny guy. Bald head.' Nothing, and Dulcie realized that if her adviser had indeed transformed, her description might not be apt. 'Well, actually he's really hairy. Big teeth.'

Nothing, and to top it off, Anna the aide was looking at her funny.

'Well, maybe not, then.' It was time to move on. 'But a lot of your friends did.' She looked at Anna, who nodded. 'And I'm glad.'

Dulcie was: Emily had said Josh had cut her off from her friends. Maybe they had just been waiting for their opportunity to reconnect.

'I'm here because we have some people in common. Maybe something else, too.' She paused. It felt odd to be talking to someone so silent. If she could hear her, though, then maybe she would be interested. 'A certain author, maybe.'

The girl's eyelids fluttered, as Dulcie watched. Rogovoy had been right; she and Mina did look alike, she realized. Not exactly: the head that lay on the pillow was pale, and the curls brushed neatly back were more red. Dulcie brought her fingers up to her lips, curious. Were her own quite so full?

As if on cue, Mina's mouth moved ever so slightly, and Dulcie leaned forward. If the girl was saying something . . .

'I'm sorry, you can't touch her.' The aide was standing.

'I understand.' Dulcie settled back into her chair. 'It's just that I have news.' She turned to the girl, almost certain Mina could hear her. 'It's really exciting, Mina. This visiting professor – Renée Showalter – you probably know she was supposed to give a lecture? She has some new documents she's sharing with me. Something about this author we're both studying. I've found some really great stuff on her in the Mildon that's related, and the professor says there's more. When you're better, I can show you. They're primary sources. Original documents, so you might be interested. I mean, it's sort of genealogical, and I know that's one of your interests.'

Was it? Hadn't Josh said otherwise? 'At least, I think it's one of your interests.' Dulcie looked at the silent girl. She didn't know her, but she wished she did. It seemed like they'd have a lot in common, a lot besides curly red hair. 'I know I don't know you, not really. But I've been hearing a lot about you from your room-mate, Emily.'

Dulcie stopped short: Mina had moved her head, just slightly, as if she were trying to turn toward Dulcie. As if she were trying to say something – to wake up.

'Mina, what is it?' Dulcie stood to lean over the bed. Anna got up, too, but hung back, watching. 'Is it Emily? Something about Emily?'

'Her room-mate was here earlier,' the aide said. 'I think she left to get Mina's prosthetic.'

'Her prosthetic?' Dulcie shook her head. She really didn't know anything about the girl on the bed. Though Josh had said something about a disability.

Anna was explaining. 'There was a car accident when she was a child. Surgeons were able to basically rebuild her leg, but her foot was too damaged.'

'I didn't know.' Was that why Mina and her room-mate had first bonded? Did that partly explain Josh's possessiveness? Did he see himself as the caretaker of a poor crippled girl?

'I'm sure most people don't even notice, but I gather she limps at times,' Anna said. 'Maybe it was wishful thinking that she'd be up and about soon, but we've seen stranger things.'

They both turned to the girl on the bed. Mina was still now, though Dulcie sensed a movement behind her eyelids, almost as if she were looking from one woman to another.

'I think the mention of her room-mate almost woke her,' Dulcie said, watching the pale face. 'Did she respond when Emily was here?'

'That's the funny part,' said Anna. 'She didn't. In fact, she seemed to be holding particularly still.'

FORTY-SEVEN

Although Dulcie spent a while longer, strangely drawn to the girl in the bed, she left the infirmary with more questions than answers. Maybe it was foolish to hope that Mina would have awakened, and would have been able to tell Dulcie – and the police – who had attacked her. Still, she had hoped for something.

As soon as she had left Mina's room, she had gone into the ladies' to check on the kitten. As grateful as she was for the small creature's silence, Dulcie couldn't help but worry. Inside a stall, however, she saw there was no reason: the little creature had curled up, tucking his nose under his tail, and gone to sleep. Dulcie folded the box top back up as quietly as she could after that and tried her best to hold it steady as she left the building.

Five o'clock, and it might as well be midnight. The brutal wind that had cleared the clouds had ushered in a cold front, and Dulcie shivered, holding the kitten's box against her body. It would be better for the kitten, she told herself, if she took him home now. She could create a quarantine area. They could both warm up and relax a little. And Esmé? Well, Esmé had been acting out lately, no doubt feeling neglected. She wouldn't like this, Dulcie was sure, but Dulcie would find a way to make it up to her. And the little tuxedo cat would understand. It wasn't like she begrudged Chris her attention.

Dulcie envisioned her cat's green eyes – the same eyes as the stranger in the carriage. *'You have far to go,'* the stranger had said. *'You bear a burden of Debt to others besides yourself, to those who*

will follow after . . .' No, she couldn't go home. Not yet. She had
to go speak to Rogovoy. She'd put it off long enough.

'Come on, kitty.' Wrapping her arms around the box and bowing
into the wind, Dulcie headed back up Mass. Ave. 'You're going to
be the most traveled cat in Cambridge, Tigger.' She caught herself.
That was Thorpe's name for the orange tabby, not hers – or whatever
his eventual person might chose. Still, she thought back to the way
the kitten had gone for Thorpe's finger. Tigger seemed quite apt.

The kitten was getting restless, however, and as Dulcie walked
she could feel him shifting around inside his box.

'I know, little fellow. You've been in there a while. I'll make this
quick, I promise.' A faint mew reached her, and she felt like a pact
had been reached. In, out, and then a litter box, food, and water.
'I'd like to get home, too.'

With that thought in mind, Dulcie was almost relieved not to see
Detective Rogovoy as she stepped into the headquarters' lobby. Still,
she walked up to the long front counter and asked for the detective,
still holding the kitten's box to her chest.

'Detective?' The younger man at the desk picked up the phone.
'Young lady here to see you.' He nodded at Dulcie, who hadn't
even given her name. 'Go on back,' he said. 'Third door on your
right.'

'Oh, it's you.' The big detective sounded more gruff than usual.
Sitting behind a table in one of the small rooms off the main corridor,
he'd barely looked up when Dulcie walked in.

'You were expecting someone else?' Dulcie took the seat opposite
the big man, placing the kitten's box on the floor.

He shrugged, his mountainous shoulders rising and falling, and
responded with a question of his own. 'So, what brings you here,
Ms Schwartz? Not that it isn't always a pleasure.'

Warmed a bit by that last declaration, Dulcie found herself
relaxing. 'There's something I didn't tell you, the last time I saw
you, Detective. I couldn't, because it wasn't my secret. But, well,
I've come to realize that perhaps it isn't her secret, either, but rather
belongs in the pool of general knowledge that . . . that you'll be
using for the public good.'

She'd kind of worked herself into a corner with that. About
halfway through, Rogovoy had sat up, so she knew she had his
attention. But from the way he was rubbing his hand over his face,
she suspected he was also hiding a smile. Well, in for a penny, in

for a pound, she decided, and launched into her depiction of the scene outside the Newman, three nights before.

'At the time, I thought it might have been that visiting professor, Professor Lukos.' Dulcie remembered the scene she had caused and would have left it at that, but the large detective prodded her.

'Oh, really?' He was leaning over the table, his low voice more like a growl. 'And why was that?'

'Well, he was late to the party, so he'd been out on the street. Plus, he'd been seen talking with Emily's room-mate, Mina, the night before . . . the night she was attacked.' The details were coming back to her. Lukos had said Emily was unfriendly – no, it was Mina he'd called unfriendly. Or, no, 'unaffectionate.'

She shook off that memory. It had no relevance, and she needed to get her story out. 'He was hiding his hand,' she told Rogovoy. 'I think it was cut, or something.'

'And was the young woman – the room-mate? – was she cut at all?'

'Well, no. She'd been grabbed and thrown down.' Dulcie couldn't believe he was being so obtuse. 'But she fought back. She clawed at him.'

'Like a cat, huh?' He was doing his best to stifle a grin, she could tell.

'You don't believe me, do you?' Dulcie was glad she hadn't gone on about the wolf.

He shrugged again, those oversized shoulders eloquent in their silence.

'Martin Thorpe was missing that night, too.' Dulcie felt a twinge of guilt, a twinge accentuated by a movement in the box at her feet. 'So you might want to talk to him. I don't know where Josh Blakely was, either.'

'Uh huh.' Rogovoy was no longer looking at her and had instead gone back to reading the paper before him.

'Aren't you going to talk to anybody?' This was exasperating.

'Oh, I am, Ms Schwartz. Don't you worry about that.' He looked up and put down his pen. 'In fact, I'm going to be talking to Ms Trainor this evening. I expected her to be here by now.'

So she'd decided to come forward. But Rogovoy was still talking. 'In fact, I'm wondering where she is.'

'Why didn't you send a car for her?' Dulcie pictured Emily, limping up the cold, dark street. 'It's quite a hike to get up here.'

'You made it.' Rogovoy seemed to have a point, but Dulcie didn't get it. 'Though, come to think of it, maybe you shouldn't walk back. Hang around for a few minutes, and I'll have someone run you home.'

'Thanks a lot.' Dulcie got to her feet. She couldn't actually storm out, not while she was reaching for the kitten's box, but she drenched her voice with as much scorn as she could manage. 'I'm quite capable of taking care of myself.'

As she left, she tossed her head in the air. Her curls were almost long enough to throw back, but the movement disturbed the kitten, who mewed once loudly. 'Well said,' Dulcie muttered in response, and made her way through to the front of the police station.

'He didn't believe me.' Dulcie was having trouble accepting that idea. 'After all he knows I've been through.' She ran over what she'd told him – she didn't like to think of it as 'her story.' Seeing Lukos at the party, arriving late and possibly injured. Finding Emily. Granted, Lukos left the next morning – so he wasn't around when Professor Showalter was attacked. Unless he was also a victim. Maybe there was something that Lukos wasn't telling anyone. Something too fantastic – like maybe he knew what had happened to Mina. Maybe he'd even intervened, defended Emily. And if he'd been hurt – bitten – then he was at risk . . .

Dulcie stopped in her tracks. Of course, Rogovoy wasn't listening to her any more. Dulcie had become the ultimate cliché: the girl who cried 'wolf.'

FORTY-EIGHT

Besides, it was probably Josh. As much as she liked the ruddy-cheeked junior, Dulcie had to admit, a normal, everyday domestic dispute was a lot more likely than anything supernatural, especially of the lycanthropic variety. Unless Josh was the . . .

No, that really didn't make any sense. Josh seemed quite calm and happy, except when he was worried about Mina. Even when he talked about his girlfriend, it was with pride. That didn't mean he wasn't possessive of her, dangerously so. And wrong about her, too, if Emily was to be believed. After all, Mina and Emily had roomed together for years. Josh was the interloper in that relationship.

Poor Emily. Dulcie couldn't believe Rogovoy was being so heartless. Okay, maybe he didn't believe her, but to make Emily come all the way up to his office just to talk? She shook her head. It was not only cold, it was full dark now. Well, dark enough so that the waning moon overhead glowed with a blue light.

Inside his box, the kitten rustled. She could feel his weight shift and grow awkward as he paced from side to side.

'Hang in here, Tigger,' she said, reaching around to brace it. He was such a little thing, but his movement made the box harder to hold. 'We'll be home soon.'

She was talking to herself as much as to the kitten now. The wind that had dispersed the clouds earlier had picked up, blasting cold air that cut right through her sweater. Her hands, clasped in the front of the box, were growing numb. Maybe she should have waited for that ride. But, no, if Rogovoy couldn't extend that courtesy to a disabled undergrad, she wasn't going to accept it, either.

Still, it was so cold. And, she realized, so dark. Now that she was a block away from the police station, she was more aware of the hour. The freezing wind had driven other pedestrians inside, and the illumination of the street lights was broken by the crazy shadows of bare branches, tossing in the wind.

She thought of Chris. She could call him. He'd come and meet her, she was sure, even if he were working. Only she didn't want to put the kitten down. Didn't want to stop walking. Not because of the dark, she told herself. Not because of the night, or the bright moonlight that cast such wild shadows. Simply because of the cold. No wonder the kitten was agitated.

'We'll be home soon, Tigger.' She leaned forward to speak into the box, her breath reflecting off warm in the frigid air. Poor kitten. She should never have taken him away from Thorpe, not if she was going to keep him in a box for so long – in a box in the cold.

A cab drove by, and Dulcie jumped, shifting the box so she could raise her hand. Too late. Already, she could see its tail lights fading, and although she waved, it didn't stop, undoubtedly speeding down the empty avenue toward some suburban caller.

'Mrow!' The jostling had been too much for one small, but very vocal kitty.

'I'm sorry, Tigger. Really.' Pulling the box back in front of her, Dulcie wrapped her arms around it. She was getting tired, the box heavier. She'd never make it home at this rate.

'I'll get us a cab,' she said to the box. 'Another cab.' Damn the expense. She wasn't dressed for this weather, and, besides, she had Tigger to worry about.

Only three more blocks to the Square. And maybe, if they were lucky, another cab would come by. She'd be prepared this time, she promised herself, as she peered down the empty road.

Headlights – there! She saw one. But even as it came closer, she saw its directional blink. Instead of continuing straight up toward her, it was veering to the left, around the edge of the Common.

Of course, the Commodore had a cab stand. And a lobby where she could warm up if there were no taxis waiting. Dulcie looked down the empty avenue. No other cars, cabs or otherwise. She looked across the street at the Common. She'd walked most of its length already, safely on the other side of the road. Only the last corner – a spit of land, really – remained, separating her from the hotel with its warmth, its lights, and its taxis. She could clearly see the front entrance. The doorman was opening the door for someone – a woman – who had just bustled out of that cab. The cabbie, she could see, was still there, by the curb. Just waiting for another fare.

She checked the road one more time – nothing – and crossed. With no leaves on the trees, the path was clear. The street lights and that moon cast everything in a blue light, making even the trees look like statuary, their shadows etchings on the ground. Inside his box, the kitten began scratching, clawing at the corners. Dulcie clasped the top closed and saw how blue her hands looked – the moonlight was bright, almost as bright as if it were full, but she felt it as cold.

'Soon, kitty,' she said. 'Almost there.'

'Mrow!' The sound was amplified, loud in the dark. Ahead and to her right, a big beech stood silver and strangely foreboding. Dulcie moved to her left, to avoid it. Something about the shadows.

'MROW!' The kitten yelled, impossibly loud. And then suddenly she was down.

'What? No!' Dulcie found herself on her knees, her hands on the gravel. The kitten's box, overturned, lay open a few feet away. 'Tigger!'

Thud! That time she felt it, a blow like a log falling. The moonlight seemed to dim, the pain in her hands, in her head, so very far away. The kitten . . .

Something warm dripped on her face. She was warm. Tired. She closed her eyes . . .

And woke with a start as the world exploded with a fearsome noise. A roar – like a freight train racing by. Like a tornado. Like a maddened tiger. And then what sounded very like a woman's scream.

'My head.' She'd been hurt. She was hearing things. She started to sit up, reaching behind her. She'd been hit by . . . by something. The pavement before her swam with the motion, and she closed her eyes again. Her hand felt the back of her head; it was wet, and her touch hurt. She gasped and fought down a wave of nausea. Maybe she should just stay here for a moment, collect her thoughts.

The night no longer felt cold, and Dulcie so wanted to rest. She put her head back down on the cool gravel of the path and began to close her eyes. Only just then, something brushed against her. Something like fur, insistent and soft. A paw, a head butt. The faintest of purrs.

'Mr Grey?' Dulcie sat up, slowly this time, and blinked until the world came back into focus. She thought of the sound she had heard, like a tiger enraged. 'Is that – *was* that you?'

Her feline friend was nowhere in sight. Despite a throbbing that was becoming more pronounced as Dulcie's mind cleared, she pulled herself up to her knees and looked around. No Mr Grey, not even a squirrel. But seated a few feet away, beside the opened cardboard box, sat the little orange kitten, calmly washing the tiger stripes that were fading back into his fur.

FORTY-NINE

'Tigger? Come here, boy.' Dulcie was crawling, too weak to move much faster – and too afraid to startle the kitten. 'Come on, here we go.'

With a sigh of relief, she got her hands around the kitten, whose fur seemed particularly warm to her frozen, scraped hands. 'Good boy. Good.'

With the little marmalade held against her body, she reached
for the box. It was intact, but when she dropped it – when she'd
been attacked, she corrected herself – the top flaps must have
sprung open somehow. Surely, this little guy couldn't have been
the source of . . .

'Mew?' As she placed him in the box, he looked up at her, his
round blue eyes the picture of innocence.

'Dulcie! Are you all right?' She jumped to her feet and stumbled
back down, clasping the box to her chest.

'You!' It was Josh. She pushed herself back, away from him.
'Leave me alone!'

'What? No, Dulcie.' He dropped into a squat, hands raised before
him. 'I'm not . . . I saw you, and I came to help. Honest.'

She looked at him. Took in his stricken face and the fact that his
hands were empty. That he was, in fact, now kneeling in the gravel,
about five feet away from her.

'I'm going to call 911.' He reached inside his coat, and she shrunk
back.

'No, I'm okay,' she said. He stopped and looked at her for further
direction. 'Just – just help me up.'

He stood and held out both hands to her. She took them and
scrambled to her feet, a little unsteadily.

'Here, lean on me.' He offered his arm, but he was looking at
the box on the ground by her side. 'What's this?' He picked it up.
From inside they both heard a small 'mew.' Strangely, that made
Dulcie more confident, and she took his arm.

'It's a kitten,' she said, perhaps unnecessarily.

'Oh.' He was nodding. 'I thought I saw . . .'

He broke off, prompting her to ask. 'What? What did you think
you saw?'

He shook his head. 'There were a lot of shadows. I heard you
yell, and I saw you fall. Someone was behind you, holding a stick
or something. Then – I don't know . . . whoever did it must have
run off.'

Or was chased off. But by what? The question was on the edge
of Dulcie's tongue, but she held back. She'd been hit on the head.
She hadn't seen – or heard – anything clearly.

'Do you want to go to the police? To the health services?' Josh
was asking.

Images were crowding Dulcie's mind. The health services, where

Mina lay prone. The university police . . . 'I was just at the police
station,' she said. She took a few steps back toward the street,
leaning on Josh's arm. Inside his box, the kitten had grown quiet
once again. 'This detective I know was waiting for someone to
come by.'

She reached back to the back of her head. It was tender, and she
could tell there'd be swelling, but the wetness was sticky now. What
had she been hit with, a stick? A baseball bat? Something else?

'Josh, tell me something.' None of this was making sense.
'You said something about Mina getting strength, about her being
strong.'

'She is.' He was nodding. 'She's one of the strongest people I
know.'

'You didn't tell me she has a prosthetic foot.'

He shrugged. 'Sometimes I forget. When you know her, it's not
relevant.'

'But it must affect her walking, right?' Dulcie didn't wait for an
answer. 'Did she use a cane?'

'Sometimes, yeah.' He was looking at her strangely. 'When she
was tired. Why?'

Dulcie wasn't sure she understood, either. 'And her room-mate,
Emily?'

'What about her?' They were moving, albeit slowly, to the street.
Dulcie's head was ringing, but she needed to talk to Rogovoy again.
What she would say exactly wasn't clear.

'Does Emily use a cane?' It made no sense. Maybe it was because
her head was hurting, but Dulcie felt like she was talking about
different people: Mina, Emily, Josh . . . which versions were the
real ones?

'I don't think so.' Josh was looking at her, concern in his round
face. 'Dulcie, are you sure you're all right?'

'No.' She shook her head slowly. Anything more hurt. 'I'm not.
But I've got to talk to Detective Rogovoy right away.'

'Okay.' Inside his box, the kitten mewed. 'If you say so.'

Another mew. That little orange fellow was as demonstrative as
. . . Esmé! Dulcie stopped and turned toward her companion. 'Josh,
you didn't attack Mina did you?'

He shook his head. 'I don't know why everyone thinks that.'

'You didn't try to isolate her?' She examined his face. His broad
and open face. 'To take her away from her friends, did you?'

Another shake of his head.

'And Mina wasn't about to break up with you, was she?'

'What? No.' Josh looked so crestfallen, Dulcie wondered for a moment if she was going to have to hold him up. 'We had just decided to move in together. Get a place off campus. We were going to start looking, only she had some personal stuff she said she had to deal with first. She didn't even want my help, she said. I would never . . .'

'No, I know you wouldn't.' Dulcie still felt shaky, and her head was throbbing. About this, however, she was sure.

They had reached the street, and at Dulcie's urging turned left, back toward the police station.

'What's the deal with the cat?' Inside his box, Tigger had begun to mew again.

'We found him in an alley. He . . .' Dulcie stopped. Something had chased her attacker off. Had someone – or something – also jumped Emily in the alley? Was that what she didn't want to talk about? 'No, it's not making any sense.'

A wave of dizziness hit her, and she lurched across the sidewalk to slump against a street light. At least here, in the artificial glow, the moonlight wasn't shining down on them.

'Dulcie, I don't think this is a good idea.' Josh put the box down and knelt beside her. 'Please, let me call an ambulance.' She shook her head. There was too much she needed to sort through. 'Is there anyone I can call for you then?'

Chris. She started to explain, when it hit her. 'You said you and Mina were going to move in together, right?'

'Yeah.' He nodded. 'Still are, I hope. I wanted to start looking at apartments, you know, for the spring. But she said she had to clear something up first.'

'I bet.' Dulcie felt the pieces falling into place. 'So, Mina hadn't found out that you were related, like distant cousins or something?'

'What? No.' He was definite about the negative now. 'That's crazy. I don't even know much of my family history.'

'You're not from some old Colonial family? Blakely?'

He was shaking his head again. 'No, all my grandparents came over from Poland. On my dad's side, they changed it from Plakowicz. Thought it sounded more, I don't know. More American.'

'Which Mina would know, if she were into genealogy and all.' Dulcie struggled to get to her feet.

'I told you.' Josh stood and gave her his hand. 'That was Emily's thing. Not Mina's. I mean, Emily was trying to help Mina out – she might even have found some evidence that Mina is related to the woman she's studying. But Mina doesn't care about that stuff. Emily's the one who's descended from some big-deal British family. Coat of arms and everything.'

'Coat of arms, huh?' Dulcie felt more like herself now, if not necessarily better, and when Josh lifted Tigger's box, she reached for it. Somehow hugging the kitten's carrier to her chest steadied her. She looked down through the ventilation holes. Two blue eyes stared back. 'I must have been distracted.'

It wasn't until they were in the lobby of the police headquarters once again that Dulcie realized how she must look. The young man behind the counter did a double take and ran out to greet her.

'Miss, please, sit down.' He tried to take the box from her, as he ushered her into a chair, but she held on. 'I'm calling an ambulance.'

'No, not yet,' said Dulcie. She'd made it this far. 'But Detective Rogovoy – is he busy?'

'Hang on.' The receptionist and Josh exchanged a glance, and then he ran back around his desk to his phone. 'He'll be right out.'

'I guess his interview never showed,' Dulcie said. Josh looked confused, and she realized she hadn't explained. Well, she was tired. Her head hurt. They could all hear it together.

Dulcie didn't know what the receptionist had said on the phone, but the way Rogovoy came lumbering out of the back offices made her worry for his heart.

'I'm fine. Really,' she said. 'I mean, I'll go get checked out after.'

'After?' He was leaning over her, close enough that her eyes were starting to cross.

'I figured it out,' she said. Inside his box, the kitten was pacing. Dulcie could feel his weight shift as he moved. 'It was Emily. Emily Trainor all along.'

Rogovoy looked from her to Josh, who shrugged. Then they both turned back to her.

'It was all in her approach. I tried to explain, Detective. I did. The clues were all there. You see, Emily kept trying to cast Mina as this strict post-structuralist, viewing everything in absolutes. But

Mina had moved beyond that. I mean, she took all these political classes. Gone into history and lit. She was seeing everything in context. Almost new-historical, really. Emily thought she was losing her. I mean, she wasn't – not really.'

Dulcie paused, thinking of herself and Suze, friends forever. Her head was throbbing, though, and she needed to get this out. 'Emily tried to win her back,' she said. 'She was into genealogy and she'd dug up some wild history, tracking down one of Mina's ancestors and tying her into this woman Mina was studying. What she didn't expect to uncover was that her own family had crossed paths with Mina's a few hundred years ago, with unpleasant consequences. Mina didn't care – but Emily did.

'What happened next was probably just really bad timing. Mina and Josh were planning on moving in together. Mina knew that Emily was fragile. She told Josh she had to clear something up before they started looking for a place. That 'something' was breaking the news to Emily.

'I think she told Emily, and Emily freaked. I think she attacked her. Wildly – like an animal. Like her great-great-great-whatever had done. And from that point on, Emily started to spiral out of control. She blamed Josh, of course. Tried to make out that he was the bad apple from a bad tree, and that she was the victim. That she was the one who had been attacked. That she was the one with the limp, even.' Dulcie shook her head. The dizziness was back, and she fought it off. She had more to say.

'I don't understand it all, but I think it's got to do with guilt. Friendships can be difficult, and Emily – Emily was an absolutist. But there's a conflict – a conflict between the experience and the abstract. It's all in the theory, if you just look at it.' She closed her eyes, felt the kitten moving. There was more she had to say. 'Oh, and Thorpe isn't a werewolf. At least, I don't think he is.'

'We're taking you to the hospital,' said Rogovoy. It was the last thing she heard.

FIFTY

White. The world was white, and too bright to bear. Dulcie flinched away from the painful light of the moon.

'She's awake.' It was Chris, and she blinked open her eyes to see his sweet face, pale and worried, hovering above her. 'Dulcie, you're awake.'

'Of course I am.' Her head hurt and she was annoyed. And then, suddenly, concerned. 'Where's the kitten?'

'In the nurse's lounge.' A stranger appeared, with a small flashlight. 'With some water and the insides of a tuna sandwich.' The light was small, but very bright. 'Follow the light with your eyes, please.'

'Do you have to shine it right in my eyes?' Dulcie protested, but let her eyes move back and forth anyway. The doctor clucked with what sounded like approval and withdrew. 'Is Detective Rogovoy here?'

'Of course.' The gruff voice announced the detective's presence, just outside her line of sight. 'You weren't out long.'

'I was out?' Dulcie tried to shake her head, but Chris's hand came up to her cheek. That was nicer.

'You gave us all a scare.' He was smiling now. 'I gather you kept refusing to go to health services.'

'I had to talk to Rogovoy. I had to tell him about Emily.'

'And give me a lecture on literary theory along the way.' The big face appeared over Chris's shoulder. 'Don't worry. We sent a car for her. Didn't want you to be angry with me.'

'I was. But not because . . .' It was all too confusing.

'We had our suspicions,' he kept talking. 'I was going to ask her about some coincidences. There were some reports that should have been red flags. A women's group had had its bulletin board vandalized. The other room-mate – the one who had been assigned to live with Mina and Emily freshman year? She had reported some threats. It was all coming together.'

Dulcie nodded, gingerly. 'She faked her own attack, didn't she?' It was a pity. That first sound she'd heard, almost like a roar. Dulcie had wanted to believe that the kitten hadn't been abandoned in that alley, but had gone there to apprehend, to warn . . . No, it didn't bear thinking about.

'We think so,' Rogovoy said. 'The bruises on her neck could have been self-inflicted. Probably were, from what one of the shrinks here has been telling me. Also, that area was fairly heavily trafficked that night, and nobody saw anything. Maybe more to the point, nobody *heard* anything until after you'd found the kitten.'

'So she wasn't hurt, she was hiding.' Dulcie paused. 'Or waiting for someone.' If it weren't for the kitten . . . Maybe he had played a more benign role, keeping watch on Emily – and on Dulcie.

'But why Professor Showalter? Or was that a random mugging.'

Rogovoy shook his head. 'We've interviewed her. She described meeting a student who was a little too interested in some biographical papers she'd written about in some journal. That's what was in her bag when she was attacked. Copies of some old letters. Papers that I gather she was going to pass along to you.'

Of course. Dulcie had been telling the semi-conscious Mina about them. Emily had just been there. Dulcie thought of the dark curtains. Emily must have been lurking – and listening. Emily had thought Dulcie had the documents already. That was why she'd attacked her. Because even though Dulcie hadn't responded, Emily must have thought the professor had left a package for her at the hotel. And if Dulcie shared an interest with the professor – and with Mina – then she was another threat. Another interloper planning on coming between the two room-mates.

'Mina knew.' Dulcie murmured. She was suddenly very sleepy. 'She tried to say something when I said Emily's name. She tried to warn me.'

'We know.' It was Josh again, leaning over her, a big grin splitting his wide, innocent face. 'She's woken up, Dulcie. She's still groggy, but she's awake. She's going to be fine.'

'It'll be a while before we piece it all together,' Rogovoy cut in. 'There are still a lot of questions.'

'Which can all wait till morning.' The doctor, again. 'You've seen her, and now she needs her rest.' Chris started to protest, but the doctor cut in. 'Head injuries are tricky, so we're going to keep her under observation for twenty-four hours. If all goes well, she can go home in the morning.'

'Tell Esmé I'm okay.' Dulcie looked up at her boyfriend as he bent to kiss her. 'She's been . . . I understand now.'

'I'll do better than that, Dulcie.' His hand cupped her cheek and he blinked back tears. 'Now you go to sleep.'

'The kitten . . .' She was slipping under, she could feel it.

'I'll take him home,' Chris was saying, as he leaned forward to kiss the unbandaged part of her forehead. 'I'm sure he and Esmé will have a lot to catch up on.'

FIFTY-ONE

'*T* *was not love, but Madness. A bewitching of the Senses, much as the moonlight o'er those mountains do bedevil those poor foul Beasts, driving them to such a State.' She spoke these words unwilling, her face turned still to the coach's leathern side. Before her, still, the Stranger sat, the warmth of those strange green eyes holding her, though she would not meet their gaze. ''Twas madness that lured me in, beyond the point of Reason or recompense. Beyond – nay, I will not name Remorse – for am I not so bless'd now that I would suffer all again. Suffer gladly, if only . . .'*

Her voice declined, carried off by the wind that howl'd still through the barred door. Still, the Stranger watched, waiting for a moment or a Sign. His emerald eyes, glowing, beheld the young woman, her raven hair loose. His eyes lit upon her gloved hands, cradling her belly as if to protect that of which she dare not speak.

Dulcie woke with a gasp. Pregnant! The heroine of the unnamed manuscript was pregnant? Could that mean . . .?

She reached for the glass of water on the nightstand, taking a moment to acclimate herself. Yes, she was in the infirmary. Yes, she had been hit on the head, which doubtless contributed to the odd three-dimensional quality of her dream. Still, despite its extraordinary vividness – Dulcie had seen the characters and heard their voices, speaking the lines of what sounded like the book. And the dream was in character with so many she had had before that she trusted it. She had to: it explained so many things.

She tried to sit up and, with a groan, sank back into her pillow. The sudden movement had started her head throbbing. It had also woken her critical instincts. What was she thinking? Just because the storyline suggested something . . . Just because an undergrad's research was following a certain woman who was best described as a survivor, a woman who had been brutalized and fled, along with her child. That didn't mean this woman was a certain author, an English émigré in Philadelphia who may have born a child as a result of rape . . .

The biggest fallacy in literary theory was mistaking your author for her characters. Dulcie had had this argument with Thorpe many times. And while he was enough of a postmodernist to let her get away with her particular mix of content and context, this would be taking it too far.

If her dream was accurate, and the heroine of the fragmentary manuscript was dealing with an unintended and possibly unwanted pregnancy, that was interesting in and of itself. Her author, as Dulcie well knew, had basically been an early feminist. What better way to discuss the standards of her time than to take on the saga of a single mother who seemed to be fleeing the father of her child. That did not mean that such a pregnancy, such a relationship were behind the author's own flight from London to Philadelphia. It did not account for those years of silence, for the hint that she'd hidden her name and written under a pseudonym.

Or did it? Dulcie closed her eyes. So many years as a scholar, so much literary theory, and it came down to this. She had to admit the truth. She, Dulcie Schwartz, identified so strongly with this writer's characters – with Hermetria in *The Ravages of Umbria*, with this unnamed woman – that she believed she was reading about the author.

It didn't have to be. The book was still compelling as a narrative, its language and imagery striking. Plus, it worked so well as metaphor: the woman in the coach was every woman, for wasn't every woman – possibly every person – ultimately alone in the world, fleeing the past for a future that was dark and unknown. And the wolves? Well, they could easily be the author's way of dramatizing the societal forces that would come howling after such a woman. And the green-eyed stranger could be the inner voice that calmed one, kind of like . . .

'There we go.' The curtain around her bed slid back, revealing a smiling aide with a breakfast tray. 'Would you like to sit up?'

She managed it this time, slowly and with a little help, and found that her appetite had returned with a vengeance, even for what appeared to be powdered scrambled eggs and toast that had gone cold. The food left her feeling stronger and more clear-headed.

'Excuse me, do you think I'll be able to leave soon?' The aide was opening the blinds, his back toward her, which was good. The bright sun streaming in had made Dulcie wince, waking a new and piercing pain behind her eyes. She looked away and was managing a smile by the time he turned around.

'I would imagine the doctor wants to see you first,' he said. 'But it looks like you're doing well to me.'

With that, he was off, leaving Dulcie to scrape up the last of those soggy eggs. If she could get out today, she'd head straight for the Mildon. Surely, after all that had happened, she could take another day or two to seek out more of that manuscript. It might even be called therapeutic. If she could find some pages . . .

Gingerly, aware that any motion seemed to make that headache worse, she swung her legs over the side of the bed. A cabinet, off to the side, would at least have her phone. She could call Chris or – she checked the clock – email him. She was in luck: her bag had been tucked in, behind her sneakers. In a minute, she had the break-fast tray on the windowsill and was back in bed, the laptop purring and assembling itself on the tray in front of her.

Good morning, sweetie! She fired off an email to Chris. *I'm awake and feeling great. Hope to be home soon.*

As soon as that was sent off, she flipped over to her own new mail. There was a flood of messages. Of course, she figured, Chris had probably told all their friends what had happened. There was even something from Rogovoy, she saw. Well, he probably had loose ends to tie up – or maybe he wanted to thank her. She'd deal with that in a minute. What caught her eye was another address: RSHOWALTER.

Greetings, the short note began. *I've been thinking about our brief talk and have decided to scan one of the pages I had mentioned. As you are no doubt aware, it is difficult to copy such delicate documents but I wanted to give you an idea of what I had. These were found in a private collection in Philadelphia, but they seem to belong to the author we were discussing. This is not the biographical material I had mentioned, but a text that may be more directly related to the material previously gifted to the Mildon. I've received some queries about these papers from an undergrad at your college who is not, I believe, aware of their full literary implications. You*

may want to contact her at some point, but we should speak first.
The curator who came across this mentioned a package of letters
that may contain additional corroborative biographical material.
Maybe you can locate? Hope to be back in Cambridge next month,
but am accessible online. – Renée.

Another student? An undergrad? A stab of jealousy aggravated
Dulcie's headache, and she fought the urge to shake it off. She had
already told Mina about her discovery. Clearly, Professor Showalter
had decided Dulcie was the more deserving candidate, but she could
share – she *would* share. First, however, she had to see what there
was. She clicked on the attachment. The professor had not only
copied what looked like a scrap of paper, she had provided her own
translation of the elegant, but faded writing below. After a quick scan
of the familiar writing, Dulcie skimmed down to the professor's
translation and started to read:

'*There may be solace found,' said the Stranger, his green eyes*
warm as coals. It was the same book. '*Though the hazard be*
great, Love is worth such risk, and in generation, we find our
fortunes . . .'

'Well, I don't know if you should be working on a laptop just
yet.' Dulcie looked up to see grey hair and a white coat. 'Why don't
I put that aside while we check you out?'

'Hang on.' Dulcie made sure she'd saved the file before letting
the doctor take her computer away. Then she submitted to a series
of questions, and that probing light, all the while trying to downplay
the throbbing behind her eyes.

'I don't know . . .' The doctor seemed to be considering, wrinkles
of concern framing her own grey-green eyes.

'Please, Dr . . . Kranish,' Dulcie squinted at the name tag as the
doctor removed the dressing. 'I promise I won't overdo it. But I'd
like to get home. See my cat.' As she said it, she realized how true
it was.

It also seemed to be the right answer. Dr Kranish lit up, those
wrinkles compressing to reveal a smile. 'Well, the wound is small,
and you seem to be alert and well oriented. I guess we can let you
go. Though I'm going to want you to come in for a follow-up.'

Dulcie agreed with all the proscriptions – no drinking, no contact
sports – only half listening. Yes, she did want to see Esmé. And
Chris. But it was close to nine. Griddlehaus would be opening the
Mildon soon. Three minutes after the doctor left, she was dressed.

'You're leaving us?' The aide came in as she was lacing up her sneakers. 'That's funny. I thought there was someone you would want to see.'

'There is,' said Dulcie, flashing him a smile as she headed for the door. 'Just not here.'

FIFTY-TWO

Jogging made her head hurt, so Dulcie held herself to a fast walk. She'd probably take a sick day today, anyway. Chris would insist. She'd have all day – but after so long, she didn't want to wait any longer.

'Ah, Ms Schwartz.' Mr Griddlehaus looked up from his ledger. It was two minutes past nine by the time she arrived, and the punctual clerk had the security gate already up. 'Good to see you so bright and early this morning,' he said. 'We are popular today.'

'Excuse me?' She handed him her bag and tried not to fidget as he locked it up and signed her in. 'Has someone been asking for me?'

'Not for you, Ms Schwartz. You're simply not our first visitor today.' He leaned over with what could only be described as a conspiratorial grin. 'I believe the university community is finally beginning to recognize what a treasure we have here.'

'Another visitor?' Dulcie tried not to feel disappointed. It wasn't as if the Mildon were her private playground, after all. She and Mina just might be approaching the same woman from different angles, but right now Dulcie was too excited to feel threatened. She – they – were on the brink of something. Something nobody else – with the exception of Renée Showalter – even had a clue about.

'Yes, indeed.' Griddlehaus was almost purring. 'She's new, but she has clearly read the rules.' He put the ledger away. 'And she's quite respectful. Asked me very nicely for the Philadelphia bequest.'

'For the – what?' It couldn't be. It didn't make sense. Could Mina have recovered so completely? Had she talked to Showalter?

'The Philadelphia bequest.' Griddlehaus looked vaguely annoyed.

'A package of letters and family histories that were left to the Mildon several years ago, why—'

'Excuse me.' Dulcie barged past him, ignoring his startled protest. Back to the reading room. There, behind the long table sat not Mina but Emily, looking positively green with fatigue. In front of her was a box; one of its documents, spotted and dark inside its polypropylene folder, lay on the table top before her. Now that she was used to the writing, Dulcie thought she could make out the words: *Worth such risk.* It was that curious question; the one she'd first deciphered four days before.

'Ms Trainor, please excuse Ms Schwartz here.' Griddlehaus was right behind her.

'Emily. What are you doing here? Where have you been?'

She blinked up at Dulcie, her large eyes set deep in her bruised-looking face. With one gloved hand, she brushed the hair back from her face. The other was in her sweatshirt pocket.

'You're wondering why I'm not in custody?' Her voice was soft, but clear over Griddlehaus's protests. 'Why your detective friend hasn't taken me away?'

Dulcie nodded, and Emily shrugged.

'I had something to do first,' she said. 'Something I had to see for myself.'

Dulcie couldn't help herself. She approached the table. 'What is it?'

Emily reacted quickly, reaching around the page to shield it. Her other hand, Dulcie couldn't help noticing, stayed in her pocket. 'I think you know.'

'I think, maybe I do, too.' Dulcie was getting worried. 'But it doesn't mean what you think it means.'

'Because it lies?' Emily blinked up at her, something almost like hope lighting up her incredibly thin face.

'Because it's fiction. A story, that's all.' Dulcie took a step closer. 'Just because a story says that a woman was abused and had a baby, doesn't mean that the author went through anything similar. It doesn't mean that anyone is at fault, or that anyone's family is to blame.'

'It's got to be. It's the only reason.' Emily's face went dark as she scowled. 'And we're not talking about a story here. These are letters, from a woman to her daughter, about a nobleman named Trainor, Esteban Trainor.'

It happened so quickly, Dulcie almost missed it. Emily's other hand came out, holding a lighter. Even before she registered what it was, she heard Griddlehaus gasp. The Mildon had a remarkably advanced fire suppression system, but that one page . . . Emily flicked the thumbwheel.

And Dulcie lunged. Throwing herself over the table, she reached for the page. Shoving the box to the side, she scooped the clear plastic envelope up in her open palms, and let her momentum carry her into Emily, onto Emily's lap. Holding the paper aloft, Dulcie felt herself tumble to the floor as they both fell backward. Heard a grunt as she realized she had landed on Emily.

'Mr Griddlehaus! The lighter!' Dulcie called. She looked up, and the mousy clerk was standing above them, the plastic Bic in his hands and an expression of sheer horror on his face.

FIFTY-THREE

'We may have to start searching patrons.' Griddlehaus was shaking his head. Even after the police had taken Emily away, he had sat there, slumped in his chair, despondent. 'Install detectors of some kind.'

'I don't think that will be necessary.' Dulcie, sitting beside him, used her softest voice. 'Do you?'

'I don't think you can ever really stop the crazies.' Rogovoy had remained to take their statements. His gruff voice wasn't the tonic Dulcie had hoped for though, and she shot him a look across the reading room table. 'There's always some element of risk,' he added, sounding mildly apologetic.

'Thanks a lot.' Dulcie gave him her best glower. 'And for telling me you had her in custody last night.'

'I said we'd sent a car for her.' Rogovoy was a little defensive. 'One girl, how hard was that going to be?' He snorted, in confirmation that Emily had, in fact, evaded his officers overnight. 'I sent you an email alert. You were in the infirmary. I wasn't going to bother you to tell you any more.' He paused. 'Besides, we had eyes on you.' That aide. 'Plus, we knew it was about the room-mate. We'd heard enough from other sources by then. We didn't know how you figured in, except that you'd talked to the boyfriend. Nobody'd said anything about some old letter.'

'Some old letter!' Now it was Dulcie's turn to scoff. She hadn't had a chance to really study the document. It was enough that she'd saved it, but the bit that she'd seen was promising. A letter in a familiar hand, addressing a young woman. Telling her of a troubled family history, of a father left behind in another land. There was no guarantee that the letter was authentic; she'd only glimpsed at the handwriting. Nor was there any guarantee that the letter was being honest. Her author was known for her fantastic fictions, after all. But Dulcie was hopeful.

She was also, she realized, a little dizzy.

'Ms Schwartz, are you okay?' Rogovoy was leaning toward her, and she blinked up at his big face. 'You look a little pale.'

'I'm not feeling great,' she admitted. 'In fact, maybe I should lie down.'

'I'll get an ambulance.' Griddlehaus jumped to his feet.

'No, I'll be fine . . . I just.' Moving fast for a man his size, Detective Rogovoy was suddenly behind her, cradling her as her legs gave out.

'Back to the infirmary,' he said.

'Didn't I say, "no strenuous activity"?' The doctor leaned back, shaking her head. 'You can't heal if you don't give yourself time.'

'I know.' Dulcie resisted the urge to nod. 'I'm sorry.'

'She's a heroine,' protested Griddlehaus. 'You shouldn't talk to her that way.'

Dulcie smiled at the little clerk. He had insisted on accompanying her, even though it was primarily Rogovoy who carried her out to the cruiser – and drove her the roughly five hundred yards to the infirmary.

'It's okay,' she said, closing her eyes. 'The doctor's right.'

'Head injuries are tricky.' The doctor had lowered her voice, but Dulcie could still hear her ushering her guests out. 'And rest is crucial.'

So she was rather surprised to see Chris's smiling face above her. 'Good morning, sweetie.' He was holding flowers. Drugstore carnations, but they still smelled sweet. 'Or should I say, good afternoon?'

'Good afternoon?' Dulcie sat up without thinking, and only then realized that her headache was gone.

'Yeah, I was watching you sleep for a while. I know you said you were ready to leave, but I guess you needed the rest. And I was thinking.' He paused, as if uncertain, and Dulcie nodded, a bit tentatively, to encourage him. 'The whole literary-theory thing that you were trying to explain to me? I didn't realize how much sense it made, before. But now I do, especially that bit with narrative being relative. In fact, this is kind of the perfect example. Emily Trainor was the author of her own narrative. Or at least trying to be, only she kind of got the context wrong.'

'Huh.' Dulcie wasn't sure if she wanted to tackle that one. Not yet, anyway. 'Hey, is the doctor around?'

'Why, are you feeling dizzy?' Worry creased Chris's face.

'No, I'm actually feeling good.' She looked at the cabinet. 'Would you see if my clothes are in there?'

Chris was too law-abiding to spring her, however, and it took another hour for Dulcie to be discharged – with strict warnings against overdoing it.

'Wow, they're tough on you.' Chris wondered aloud. 'I mean, they've had you here overnight.' Dulcie smiled; he'd hear the rest of it soon enough.

'Hey, may we make a detour?' Dulcie didn't really need to lean on Chris's arm, but it felt nice, and so she looked up at him as they approached the elevator.

'Sure,' he said, and let her lead him away from the elevator and toward another patient's room.

'I just want to see if maybe . . .' Dulcie left off. The seat outside Mina's room was empty now. The guard gone, but Dulcie sensed movement inside. 'Do you mind?' She asked her boyfriend.

'Ah, sure.' Chris looked a little confused, but took the seat, leaving Dulcie to walk in on her own. As before, the bed at the far end was the only one occupied, the sun illuminating a pale girl with red-gold curls.

As Dulcie drew close, those curls moved. A pale face turned toward her, and brown eyes opened. 'We have some work to do,' Dulcie said softly. 'Together.'

'We do,' Mina replied. 'Cousin.'

FIFTY-FOUR

'I don't know,' Dulcie was shaking her head. 'There's something special about this kitten.' Now that it was time to relinquish the marmalade kitten, Dulcie found herself reluctant to do so. Thorpe, she knew, had nothing more sinister going on than a bad case of anxiety. And her friends had even agreed to support her white lie – that she had had to investigate the possibility that another owner had been located. And while Esmé hadn't been openly hostile to the little newcomer – her most royal Principessa Esmeralda was much too imperious to deign to such behavior – she had made it clear, through the withdrawal of purrs, that she did not approve of the little one's continued presence. And as soon as the carrier – that same ventilated cardboard box – had come out, she had made herself scarce.

'There's something special about every kitten.' Chris spoke gently, but from the way he was looking at her, Dulcie knew he wasn't going to allow her to argue this one. He knew about what had happened at the Mildon by now. She had even told him about the night on the Common – about the roar and the shadow. She couldn't tell if he believed her, though. Truth was, she wasn't entirely sure what she had seen or what had happened out there, in the dark.

Before Dulcie could agree, or start to explain, the doorbell rang. Chris opened it to let Raleigh and Lloyd in, trailed by Martin Thorpe, looking smaller and more tentative than usual.

'Ms Schwartz, I'm sorry to intrude,' he started to say.

'We thought that since you aren't at your best, we'd save you the walk.' Raleigh finished the thought. The look that accompanied it let Dulcie know that, even if the younger woman was sticking with Dulcie's story, she wasn't going to brook any delay. 'And let Mr Thorpe take the kitten back with him.'

'Of course.' Dulcie bowed to the inevitable. 'We were just going to put him in the carrier.' They'd been standing outside the bathroom, where the kitten had been quarantined. 'One moment, please.'

Without waiting for a response, she let herself in, closing the door behind her. 'Hey, Tigger.' She looked around, spying the kitten under the cabinet. 'Your new person is here. Is that – will that be okay?'

She held out her hand. If she was right, this little animal had extraordinary powers. Would Thorpe appreciate him? Would anyone else?

'We'll be fine.' The voice, deep and a bit rough, startled her, and she smiled as the kitten emerged. She scooped him up and emerged. Raleigh was already holding the box.

'Bye bye, little Tigger,' Dulcie said, her voice soft. Then, on a whim, rather than placing the kitten in the carrier, she handed him to her adviser.

'Take good care of him,' she said.

'Oh, I will,' he said, smiling for the first time that she could remember as he cuddled the small orange tiger to his cheek. 'And I suspect he will take good care of me, as well.'

With that, he reached to place his new pet in the carrier. But before he could, the little kitten turned back toward Dulcie. He opened his pink mouth, exposing tiny fangs, and mewed what Dulcie knew was a nearly soundless mew. Still somewhere, in the back of her mind, she heard a tiger's roar.

'How are you doing?' Chris came into the kitchen, where Dulcie was standing by the window. 'Are you okay?'

'Yeah, I'm fine.' She'd been watching the party walk down the street, Martin Thorpe hugging the box to his chest. 'And you?'

'Now that things are back to normal,' he chuckled. 'Yeah. I've been meaning to tell you: I got a senior tutor position, starting next semester. I'll still do some overnights, but I won't have to do as many. We'll get to spend more time together. Have some adventures, even. But please, Dulcie, let's stay out of trouble for a bit, okay?'

'Oh, that's great.' Dulcie leaned into his arms, even as she realized that she had avoided answering. After all, she still didn't know what had howled that first night, and she had other questions, as well.

'Well, I'll keep doing what I can.' The soft voice surprised them both, as Dulcie felt the velvet fur against her legs. *'Sometimes, a little risk is necessary,'* Esmé continued. *'For the right reason.'*

'A little risk?' Dulcie asked her own pet as she scooped her up. Esmé nuzzled a wet nose against her cheek, and Dulcie closed her eyes. The headaches were almost gone. Soon, she'd be able to get back to work. To explore this new story – and the connections that linked her to Mina and maybe farther back, as well. It would be a gamble – a hazard, as her author might have put it, though she'd have said it a little differently.

'*What prize is worth such risk?*' That was the question, the curious one from the text, and it echoed in her mind as Esmé began to purr. She had never deciphered its meaning. Maybe she never would. Thorpe had reason to pressure her, she knew. He was a conscientious adviser. But she was going ahead into this next phase of exploration – and discovery – anyway, with the support of her friends, of Chris, and maybe of some new-found family as well. Somehow, she was no longer scared.

'*Because you know.*' She felt, rather than heard, the deeper voice. Chris must have, too, because he reached toward Dulcie and Esmé, wrapping his arms around them both. '*You know the answer,*' the voice said, its warmth enveloping them all. '*Love is worth such risk.*'